WHO IS HE TO YOU?

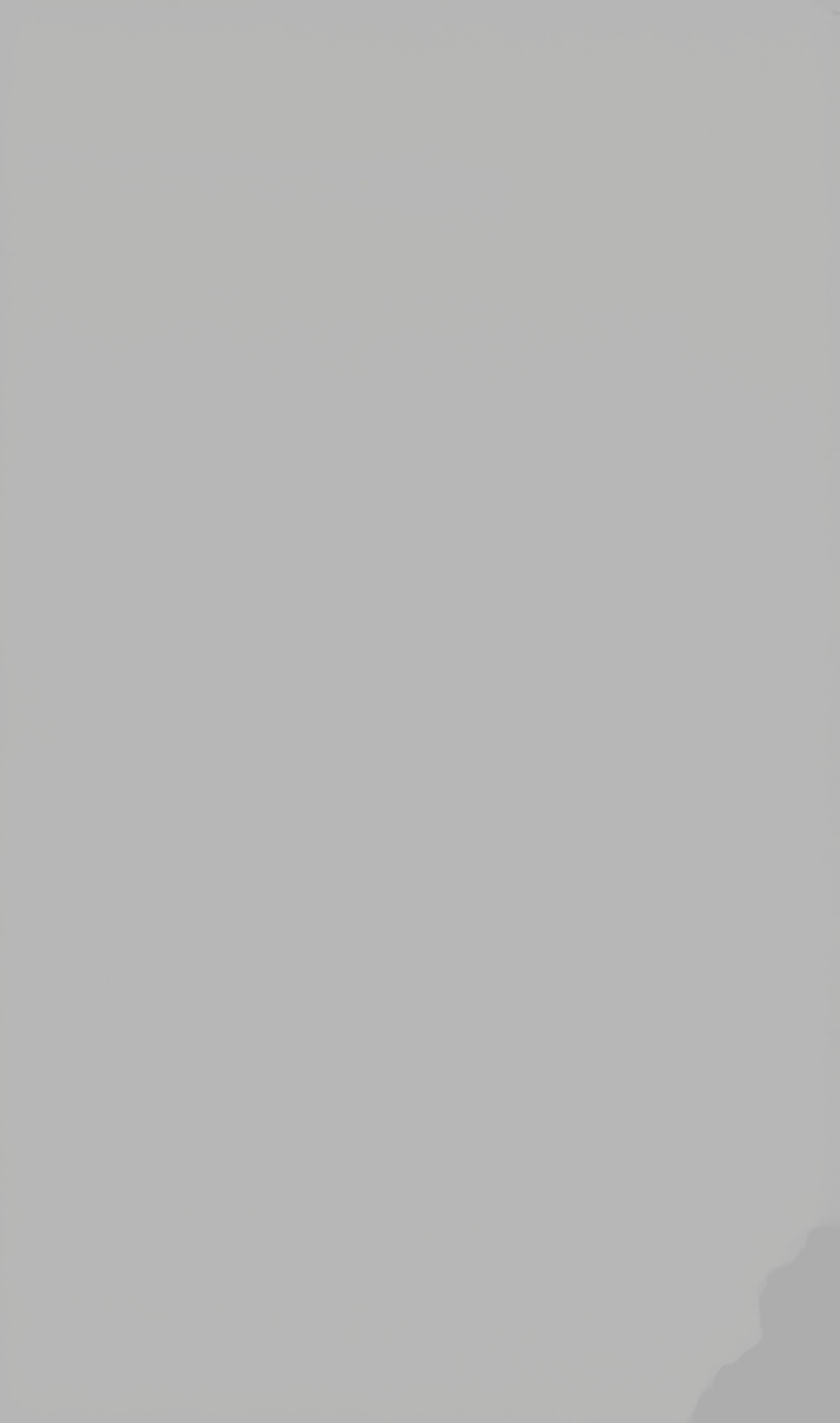

WHO IS HE TO YOU?

MONIQUE D. MENSAH

KISA PUBLISHING
SOUTHFIELD, MI

This book is a work of fiction. Names, characters, places, and incidents are the product of the author's imagination or are used fictitiously. Any resemblance to actual events, locales, or persons, living or dead, is coincidental.

ISBN 13: 978-0-578-02348-9

Published by Kisa Publishing LLC
Southfield, MI 48076

Printed in the United States of America

First Edition June 2009

Cover Design by Marlon E. Hines

Layout by SelfPublishing.com

Acknowledgements

God has blessed me with the gift of writing and story-telling. Because of Him, I have fulfilled my lifelong dream and what I believe to be my purpose. Thank you Lord for giving me the drive and passion to share my gift with the world. You have seen me through innumerable trials, and carried me through the toughest periods in my life. Without you, nothing is possible.

To my mother, Adaku Mensah. You started this whole thing. You were the one who read to me everyday as a child. You are responsible for my love of literature, which sparked my interest in writing. No matter what I said I wanted to do, you've always supported me. You've always made me feel like I can do anything, because I was the smartest, most beautiful girl in the world. When I decided, at eight years old, that I wanted to be an author, you were the first one to stand behind me and cheer me on because you believed I could do it even more than I did. Your love, support, and nurture has been a constant in my life, from the time I attempted my first book at ten years old, until the completion of Who Is He To You. You gave me invaluable advice and critiques to make my debut novel stronger and I thank you for that. Had it not been for you, I would not be who I am and I am eternally grateful. I love you.

To Alana, my daughter, you are my inspiration. You

remind me everyday that I am doing this for me and you. My success is yours too. Thank you for always believing in me and loving me unconditionally despite my faults. I know that I'm not the perfect mother, but you make me feel like the best mom in the world. I love you and I will always do whatever I can to give you the best of everything because you deserve it.

Brooke Williams, I feel as if the title, "best friend" is an extreme understatement and a misconception to anyone reading this. You are so much more than that. Despite our differences over the years, you have proven to be one of the most important people in my life. You push me to be a better person everyday. You know and understand me like no other. You were the one who told me to write this book and you've been an invariable source of encouragement and support throughout this journey. I think you may have been more excited about the book release than I was! Your friendship is indescribable and your loyalty unmatched. Thank you for being the friend, sister, counselor, and voice of reason that I've always needed (even when I didn't want it).

To my editor, Judith Allen of Marketing Solutions, thank you for being the first set of unbiased eyes to lay eyes on my manuscript. You were professional and honest and you inspired me with fresh ideas and new perspectives. When I felt like I couldn't write or re-write another word, you gave me a new sense of energy and restored sense of excitement about my manuscript. Thank you for believing in my story and helping me create a polished work of art.

Sylvia Hubbard and the Motown Writer's Network, you have been a great educational resource for me as well as other writers in the Detroit area. You were the first person I went to when I began the publishing process and you pointed me in the right direction. Thank you for all of the workshops, meetings, and events that assist Detroit authors in making a career out of the passion of writing.

Beverly Jenkins, you were one of the first authors I reached out to when I completed the first draft of my manuscript. Thank you for taking the time out of your busy life to share your wisdom and expertise with me. I still have the emails you've sent me and I appreciate the advice.

To Shayla Stephens, Although we are two very different people, we have grown to be great friends. You read my manuscript, chapter by chapter as I was writing it. Thanks for offering your opinion early on and for just being a good friend throughout the years.

Marlon Hines, one of the best photographers, retouchers, and graphic designers in Metro Detroit. Thank you for everything you've done for me. The business cards, the promo cards, the photos and, most of all, the cover. They are all beautiful. You went above and beyond what I expected from you. You came through when I needed you and, best of all, you became a great friend. I look forward to working with you on future projects. Thank you!

Nakkia Rawlins, I haven't seen you since the ninth or tenth grade (I can't remember), but when we reconnected, you reminded me of why we were best friends during our early years. When I needed some objectivity and an honest opinion of my manuscript, you came through. You told me my novel was a "mouse-clicker" (read electronically) and you believed I had promise. As a fellow read-aholic, I respect your opinion. Thank you!

To the ladies of my book club, R.E.A.L. Women Read, you all are amazing. Tina Stallings, Alysha Massey, Shayla

Stephens, Tosha Willis, Lauren Willis, Jacqueline Harrington, Shari Jordan, Glenda Stallings, Adaku Mensah, Tiara Brock, and Jasmine Barnes, you all are a group of some of the most intelligent, outspoken, well-read, readers in Detroit. Thank you for joining my book club and sharing one of my favorite hobbies. I can't wait to hear what you think of this one! I will see you soon.

To all of my readers and everyone that has offered a kind word of encouragement along the way, thank you, thank you, thank you!

To my mother,
because you saw greatness in me
before I recognized it in myself.
This is for you.

CHAPTER 1

SIMONE

HE was coming! Simone knew he was coming. She could feel it in the air. It was colder, thinner. The atmosphere was pitch black, darker than dark. Everything was always more extreme, more heightened when he was coming. The tree branches scratched at the windows from outside. The wind whistled a chilling tune, and fat raindrops plopped on the windowsill. It was the soundtrack of her trepidation.

She was alone, surrounded by nothing but the dark shadows that engulfed her as she floated in the darkness of the starless, midnight air. But she knew that she would not be alone much longer because he was on his way. She knew it because she could feel the fear breaking through from inside of her. She could feel her heart pounding, fighting relentlessly as if struggling for freedom from the imprisonment of her chest. The pounding was getting louder, so loud that she knew he too would hear it soon. If the lights were on, she was certain she would have been able to see her heart throbbing in and out, back and forth, trying to escape, faster and louder. Her heart was about to explode!

Oh my God, am I dying? Am I having a heart attack? Yeah, that's it I'm dying of a heart attack.

Oh God, please take me before he gets here. He's coming! Lord, please take me now! I want to die.

She wanted to escape that place and become a beautiful angel bearing brilliant, white wings and long, flowing hair. She would have wings so massive, fluffy and white, that she would be God's favorite angel. She would dance in the clouds and slide down the rainbows, laughing and playing with angelic benevolence. It would be just like a fairytale. She was certain the Lord would finally answer her prayer that night. He would not let her down. He couldn't, not again.

She could still feel her heart pounding, but she refused to move or make a sound. She just closed her eyes tightly, squeezing them shut as hard as she could.

I know that in a minute I'll be gone. Any minute now, I'll be up in Heaven, smiling and dancing with the angels. The pounding will stop and he won't be there. He will never come again.

She allowed a flush of serene calm and happiness to overcome her.

Any minute now...

"Hey, baby girl."

He's here! Why is he here? Why am I still here? Lord, I asked you to take me up to Heaven. I asked you to take me from this place. Why won't you save me from him? Why would you leave me here to suffer? Don't you love me? Don't you want me to be happy? I've been good. I do my homework everyday after school. I do everything my mother tells me to do. I make sure my clothes are neat and clean. I get straight A's. I brush my teeth every morning and night before I go to bed. I pray every night and go to Sunday School every Sunday. I do everything I am supposed to do and you just left me here. I've asked you every night to save me, to take me to Heaven. Why won't you answer my prayers?

"Are you sleeping?"

Simone refused to move or open her eyes. But her heart was still pounding. She was certain he could hear it. He knew she was awake, petrified with dread. She could hear his breathing; it was louder than the pounding of her hammering heart. His breathing was heavy, as if derived from exhaustion. With every inhalation, she could imagine him sucking the breath right out of her lungs, leaving her to die a slow death of suffocation. He was staring at her. His eyes were piercing her through the night. He could see her through the darkness, right through her purple fleece blanket. The blanket kept her covered and did the best it could to shield her from his eyes, but she knew it wasn't working. She suddenly flinched as his cold presence snapped her back to a brutal reality. She was no longer floating in the midnight sky. She was at home, in bed, eyes still shut tight, heart still pounding uncontrollably and wishing she were dead. He knew she wasn't sleeping. He knew she had been up all night, fearing that he would come, and praying that he didn't.

He knew that she hated him and he hated himself. He told her the night before last. He hated himself for loving her and craving her the way that he did. He wanted to take her every night and he tried to fight it, but his desire was just too strong to control. The nights that he did not come were the times that he was able to win the battle with himself. Those nights were becoming sparse.

He would often talk to her about when she was a baby. He remembered holding her when she was just a few months old and looking down at her wiggling in his arms. She was so tiny, chubby, and pink, the prettiest baby he had ever seen. He would put his finger out for her to hold and she would grab it with the strong grip of a grown man. He would always laugh about that. He used to talk to her about what she would be when she grew up. He imagined her being a famous actress, singer or model. With a face like hers, she was destined to be on somebody's stage. Simone had an undeniable beauty. With the kind of face that one would only come across once in a lifetime, she was too pretty to be called pretty. She was extraordinary. Her skin was the color of roasted almonds. Her jet-black hair, thick and curly, grazed the small of her back. Her huge, green, emerald-like eyes were hypnotic. She had a perfectly symmetrical face with striking features that hit you with the impact of an explosion if you were lucky enough to catch sight of her. She was phenomenal and he was mesmerized from the day she was born.

He promised her, from the beginning, that he would be the best father possible, and he kept his promise throughout the years. He made sure that he played with her everyday, just the two of them. He bought her anything she wanted, before she would have to ask. She always had the best of everything and he made sure that she attended the best schools. Even on his busiest day, he took the time to help her with her homework. Her hair and clothes were always impeccable. Her poise and grace were flawless. Most of her peers hated her for her beauty and even more so for her perfection. He never let her forget how much he loved her.

He sat on the left side of her bed. Still, she wouldn't open her eyes, but she knew he was still looking at her, longing to touch her. He pulled back the purple blanket and exposed her shivering, petite frame. He tenderly touched her face and wiped the salty tears from her cheeks. She was lying there frozen with her hands glued to her sides as if prepared for burial. She tried her best not to make a sound, but eventually a sniffle crept through against her will.

Come on-- Come on, just do it! What is taking him so long? Why is he making me go through this?

Another sniffle interrupted the silence, but it was not her own. She finally opened her eyes to see her father, his back turned to her, crying. The cry was a soft one at first, then with uncontrollable sobs. His broad shoulders shook as his face rested in his large hands. Simone was confused and did not know how to react. Dumbfounded, she fought the urge to comfort him. This man had ruined her life. This man caused her infinite pain and self-loathing, yet she could not help but to feel sorry for her father.

"I'll pray for you, Daddy." She looked up at him and softly said this just above a whisper.

He turned to face her with tears streaming down his face. He was overwhelmed with love for her – this time the kind of love a father is supposed to have for his daughter. He wanted to hold her, but resisted the urge to act. How could he continue to destroy the one thing that he adored more than life itself? How could he be so monstrous and self-serving? He was killing his beloved baby and he knew it. He despised himself.

"I love you, Simone. You know that don't you? You know that I love you more than I can begin to express to you. Don't you ever forget that I love you, baby. I do this because of *how* I love you. No matter how hard you try, you just can't control who you love. You'll understand that when you get older. I know you think I'm horrible and that I want to cause you pain, but that's not true. You have to believe that. I don't want to hurt you, baby girl. I want to love you and I want you to feel the same way. You are everything to me and I'm just too weak to fight it when I know that I should."

Simone remained silent. Tears ran rapidly from her eyes. She knew that he loved her. She read it in his eyes every time he looked at her. She heard it in his voice and felt it in his touch. There was no doubt that he loved her. He was *in* love with her. She listened as he continued his attempt to justify the sick actions and irrational feelings he had for his 14-year old daughter with the word "love." Love. What was love anyway? She thought she knew at one time, but if this was love, she wanted no part of it. Love was pain. Her father was in love with her because she was the most beautiful creature he had ever laid eyes on. Her body had developed into that of a beautiful young woman, sparking a lust in his eyes. He constantly told her how gorgeous she was and she hated it.

She hated the image that stared back at her while looking in the mirror. She hated it so much, that she tried to avoid her reflection at all times. She kept her head down when passing mirrors. It felt natural to avoid pictures and to hide her face whenever possible. God had cursed her with her looks. He damned her to a life of misery and pain -- at the hands of her own father.

"I know you love me, Daddy. I just wish that you didn't."

He stood slowly, letting the tears fall freely down his face and forced himself to walk out of the room with slow, measured strides. He had won the battle for that night. But the following night he was defeated yet again.

CHAPTER 2

RYAN

HER hands trembled uncontrollably as if powered by AAA batteries. No matter how hard she tried, she couldn't stop the shaking. She tried clasping her hands together then sitting on them and laying them flat on the cocktail table, but nothing could stop the trembling. Her head throbbed with a vise-grip headache. Her stomach twisted and turned into knots. She was crying in jagged spasms that smeared her lipstick and caused black mascara to streak her face.

I'm crackin' up!

Ryan clutched at her head to stop her shaking hands and calm her headache. As she applied more pressure, she could feel her veins pulsing on her temples. The pounding was agonizing, thumping to the tempo of emerging insanity. She quickly started grabbing and pulling at her hair, trying desperately to snatch a handful of freshly permed locks right out of her head. Her loud sobs escalated into screams due to her self-inflicted pain. She continued to screech and bellow until her throat was raw.

Then she began to pace the floor, carving a trail in the carpet between the living and dining room. She stopped in the living room with her back against the wall only when her legs collapsed from exhaustion, forcing her ankles to twist awkwardly and her four-inch stilettos to cave beneath her weight. She slid down the wall onto the floor. With a loud thud, her favorite painting came crashing to the floor. The couple depicted was holding each other in a loving, lusty embrace; they seemed to taunt her in her misery and relish in her pain. They were so in love, happy and dancing without a care in the world.

Why is this happening to me? I'm going crazy.

She cursed the painting and held her throbbing head between her legs as she continued to weep. She was convinced that she was going insane and needed to be committed to a psychiatric hospital.

This isn't natural. This isn't normal. I'm out of control.

She imagined being strapped to a gurney, wearing a white straitjacket as a gang of stiff paramedics hauled her away. They would deposit her into an all-white rubber room and shoot her up with hard to pronounce anti-psychotic drugs to stop her kicking and screaming. The thought of the drug injection almost calmed her as she imagined the numbing relief it would provide. It was as if she was depersonalized -- standing outside of herself, watching a character on a soap opera. She saw herself completely breaking down. She was beginning to become nauseous as everything around her continued to spin out of control.

She was alone. No one could understand what she was going through. No one would be able to relate to her. There was no hope and no help. This was the end. Ryan held herself tightly and began to rock back and forth, humming a tuneless lullaby.

It'll be okay. Everything will be fine.

Then, she raised her head slowly as she heard the soulful voice of her favorite singer, Sierra Nightly, in the distance.

"We've been apart for too long
Baby, I can't do this alone…"

Ryan quickly jumped up from the floor as she realized her cell phone was ringing.

"…So I'll sit right here until you get home."

She couldn't find the phone. She checked both the living and dining room. She kicked off her shoes, and before she could see them hit the floor, she ran into the kitchen. Then she peeked in the bathroom.

"Anyone who's ever been in love with you knows just how this feels…"

She was becoming frantic, "Where is the damn phone?"

She ran upstairs into her bedroom. After tripping over a different pair of shoes, she checked her dresser, nightstand, and then the armoire.

"Now I know there is no life without you…"

Finally, she ripped the covers from her bed and revealed her cell phone's hiding place. With a glimmer of hope, she looked at the caller ID to see her best friend, Lauren's, name glowing on the LCD screen. Her hopeful face turned into an ugly scowl of anger and frustration. In her fury, she threw the phone against the wall with all of the force she could muster and watched as the screen shattered and the small device slammed to the floor. She began to cry all over again.

"Shit, now I have to buy a new phone."

She headed back downstairs into the bathroom, reached into the medicine cabinet and grabbed her prescription bottle of Xanax. She exhaled a huge sigh of relief as she opened the bottle.

An angel must have made this drug up in Heaven's kitchen.

Xanax was the greatest thing created since Ford created the assembly line. It would take her to another place. Soon she would leave this crazy, tortuous world and enter into a realm of calm and serenity. It would effectively extinguish her pain (at least for the next 6-8 hours). Anxious to numb herself, she poured water from the bathroom faucet into her hand and swallowed the small pill with one big gulp. Relieved that the knots in her stomach would soon be untied and the banging in her head would come to a cease, she headed back upstairs to climb into her bed and cry herself to sleep. It would all be over soon.

After two hours of much needed sleep, the music of Sierra Nightly awakened her. Amazed that her cell phone still worked despite her abuse, she lumbered to pick it up with the grace and enthusiasm of a zombie.

"Hey, baby. I know you're mad."

She quickly snapped out of her Xanax-induced haze.

"Mad? Mad! Where the fuck have you been, Anthony? You were supposed to come get me at seven! That was eight hours ago! You had me waiting here like a damn fool!"

"Baby, calm down."

"Don't you dare tell me to calm down! I rushed home from work to make sure I had time to wash my hair and get dressed before you came. I put on my makeup and even my damn shoes! I just bought these shoes today on my lunch break. Five hundred fucking dollars, Anthony! I sat here on my couch waiting for you like a damn fool. I called you at least a hundred times. You saw me calling you, but I guess you were too damn busy to pick up the phone. You tell me right now, what in the hell were you doing?"

Nothing this bastard could say would serve as a justifiable explanation. He did it again. Again! After they had just talked about this very thing that morning, he had the audacity to stand her up again! It was becoming a habit now. This was the third time in a month. What in the hell was going on? Was there another woman? Had he fallen out of love with her? She was losing him. He was slipping right through her fingers. What was wrong with her?

"Okay, just give me a minute to explain."

"Your minute starts now."

"Okay. I had to work a little later than expected, so I didn't leave the office until about seven thirty. I still had to go home, shower and change clothes, so I knew I was going to be late. I would've called as soon as I left work, but I left my cell at the office, and you know I don't have a landline. So by the time I got home and changed, it was like eight thirty. I didn't want to keep you waiting too long, so I was speeding on the freeway trying to get to you. I was going at least ninety miles an hour!"

Ryan listened impatiently, waiting for him to get to the point. Drumming her fingers on the nightstand, she prodded, "And then what?"

"Listen, I'm telling you now. Anyway, then I got pulled over by the state trooper. You know when you get pulled over it takes forever for them to run your plates and check your license. Of course, I wasn't pulled over by a black cop. It had to be some racist, cracker-ass white boy with a damn Napoleon complex. I'm telling you the dude was like 4'11" at the most!"

"Speed it up! I'm about five seconds away from hanging up on your ass."

"Okay, okay! So, instead of just writing me a ticket and letting me be on my way, this racist asshole tells me he smells liquor on my breath and tells me to step out of the car."

"Wait, I thought you said you were coming from home after getting off of work. Where did the liquor come in?"

"Well, I took a shot of Chivas with the rest of the partners in the office because it was Bob's birthday. It was just one or two shots, not nearly enough to get arrested for a DWI."

"What? You were arrested?" She sat straight up in her bed.

"Yeah. Can you believe it?"

"No, actually, I can't."

"I swear! I wouldn't lie about something like that."

"So what happened? You bailed yourself out?"

"Yeah. I had to pay like eight hundred dollars. I just got out. They wouldn't let me go until they said I sobered up. That's why I'm calling you from a payphone. I'll get everything cleared up by Monday for sure."

She couldn't tell where he was calling from since she'd broken her cell phone's LCD screen. She was beginning to calm down. She could hear it in his voice. He was telling the truth. Who would take the time to make up a story like that? Plus, she couldn't prove it didn't happen. So if she couldn't verify his story, she had to trust him.

She just could not understand why he was so inconsiderate as not to call. They hadn't spent any time together recently and she was so looking forward to their special date. He was taking her to Morton's, their favorite restaurant. The food was excellent and the service was superb. The upscale restaurant was the site of their first date and Ryan had cherished the place ever since then. She could taste the decadent five-pound, steamed lobster, dripping in butter along with an insanely tender filet mignon, topped off with a couple of bubbly glasses of Dom Perignon. It was sure to be pure Heaven. She was certain that he was going to come through that time. He had promised. He begged her not to leave him and swore that he would treat her right from then on. She thinks he even cried a little. He loved her. He never intended to hurt her. He was just absentminded and careless at times.

What more can I ask of him?

Still, she had to play the hard-bitch role.

"Now, why in the hell would I believe that?"

"Come on, baby. You know I would never try to hurt you. I'm so sorry for not stopping at a payphone and calling you sooner. You know I do dumb things sometimes. Give me another chance to make it up to you. I promise I'll make it right. You're everything to me, Ryan. You have to believe that. You just have to calm down sometimes. I really do get tired of you bitching me out all the time because you always assume the worst. Think about all the good things between us instead of focusing on the negatives."

Ryan did her best to suppress the smile that was creeping up at the corners of her mouth. She had a good man. She just had to learn to control that temper of hers. He was right; she did always assume the worse.

If you weren't always so negative maybe he'd want to spend more time with you. No man wants a woman that bitches all the damn time.

She was the problem and it was up to her to fix it. She didn't want to drive him away. She knew he loved her. He had proved it many times on so many different levels. And she loved him more than she could say. She loved him more than she loved herself.

"Breakfast tomorrow morning before work, baby?"

"Okay, but I'm telling you, you better not stand me up or it's over. I mean it."

"Trust me; I wouldn't miss this for the world. Goodnight, baby. I love you."

"I love you too." As she hung up the phone, she fully released that creeping smile. She laid back down and fell asleep peacefully.

I have a good man who loves me. I'm so lucky.

CHAPTER 3

JESSICA

THE lavender scented candles gave off a romantic glow. The fireplace wrapped her in a soft and cozy warmth. Lorraine Dubois' sexy, bluesy vocals wafted through the air, tenderly caressing her ears. Her head rocked from side to side in a slow and lazy sway. She was riding her own personal wave of relaxation and comfort. A half-empty bottle of Riesling sat lonely on the cocktail table, begging for more attention. She gave it a promising look of return as she finished the last swallow in her glass.

Jessica lay across the sofa with her legs dangling over the armrest and her head propped up by pillows. She closed her eyes and only opened them occasionally to watch the reflection of the fireplace's flames dance on the wall. The wine was beginning to take its toll, engulfing her in a feeling of languid sexiness.

"This is crazy love; it's crazy love…." She sang along to Lorraine's seductive ballad, feeling as if the song was made just for her ears.

She was completely naked except for the silkiness of her robe. Her feet were bare and her hair damp from the shower.

Her finger and toenails were freshly lacquered, and her body was exfoliated and smooth from her papaya sugar scrub.

"When I cry for you, a piece of me dies for you. There's nothing like what we have, suga."

She swayed to the rhythm and snapped her fingers with the, now empty, wine glass in her free hand. She lifted her head slowly and tried to reach the bottle but failed. She sat up and planted her feet on the floor, careful not to smudge the polish. She started to pour another glass, but quickly decided against it. She had an even better idea. Instead, she reached inside the right pocket of her robe and pulled out her "feel good."

Never interrupting her steady sway to the beat of "Crazy Love," she opened the dime-sized package and let the aroma of the brownish-green herb float to her nose. She licked her lips in anticipation. From her left pocket, she removed a small package of rolling papers and began to roll a beautiful, fat joint, perfectly round and incredibly inviting. She seemed to be rolling her body along with the joint to the mellow, provocative melody floating from the sound system.

Perfection.

She smiled down at her carefully crafted work of art. She licked the paper to make it stick and then lit the joint. The first toke was always the sweetest one, lifting her up and carrying her to a harmonious world of slow motion and tranquility. She let her head hang back as the effect of the marijuana traveled through her system, making love with the half bottle of Riesling already flowing through her body. Now it was time for another glass. She poured carefully, cautious not to spill a drop. She positioned herself back on the sofa, once again laying back with her feet over the armrest. She took another hit of the joint and closed her eyes, holding the smoke in her lungs for several seconds before releasing it through her nose. Lorraine was now crooning "Savor the Day," a special edition written only for Jessica.

She was floating, each hit taking her closer to euphoria. Her left hand held the "feel good" as she let her right hand tenderly massage the nape of her neck. Her head and shoulders swayed back and forth, never missing a beat. She let her hand slip from her neck to her chest, reaching inside the opening in her robe to caress her right breast. She began to squeeze and caress her breast in her hand and then used her thumb and forefinger to pinch her erect nipple. She let a soft moan escape her lips. She took another hit of the joint in her left hand, while using her right hand to untie the belt to her robe. The robe fell open, exposing her naked body. While her right hand was still free, she used it to grab the wine glass and take a generous sip. Almost immediately, she found her hand right back on her body. Her fingers softly grazed her skin, traveling up and down her stomach. Before she knew what she was doing, she let her legs fall open just as the robe had done. She began stroking her inner thigh up and down gently, until her fingers finally rested on the lips of her vagina.

She took another hit of the joint. Everything felt so good: the wine, the weed, the music, and now her fingers slipping inside her vagina. She started with two fingers, then three, then four, mostly moving in a circular motion, then using her forefinger and middle finger to drum inside her walls. There was no conscious thought given to her actions now; she was acting on instinct. She was giving her body exactly what it needed. She removed her index finger, leaving the other three behind to caress her wetness. The lone finger fondled her clitoris in a way that made her soft moans graduate to full-blown wails of pleasure. She had forgotten the joint dangling in her left hand, as she began to work her hips, breathing harder with every round. She had a goal to accomplish and she would not stop until she achieved it. She continued to push her fingers in and out, working her index finger on her clit and thrusting her hips. It was coming. Her moaning and deep breathing became more intense as her climax approached. Finally, it had arrived, her sweet satisfaction. The orgasm was heavy as if it was waiting to be unleashed, bursting through her body, causing shock waves and shivers. Still breathing heavily, her body collapsed. The orgasm drained all of her energy. Jessica laid her head back on the pillows and instantly dozed off into a deep sleep.

"Damnit!"

As quickly as sleep came to Jessica, it was snatched away. The feeling of burning ashes singeing her leg abruptly awakened her. The forgotten joint had fallen from her fingers and dropped to her leg, burning her flesh. She jumped up quickly to brush away the ashes and put the roach in the ashtray. Checking the clock on the wall, struggling to focus on the blurry calligraphic numbers, she realized her time for R&R was over.

Oh Lord!

She had to get moving. Everything had to be immaculate, in its proper place. She started with the Riesling, quickly draining the last few drops in the glass, swallowing it in one gulp and pushing the cork back into the bottle. She placed what was left of the joint in the plastic baggie containing the rest of her stash and slipped the baggie back into her robe pocket. After blowing out the eight lavender candles and turning off the simulated flames of the fireplace, she rushed the ashtray and wine glass to the bar and washed them thoroughly, making sure there were no traces left as evidence of her guilty pleasures. She pushed the wine bottle to the back corner of the cabinet beneath the bar, hiding it behind the empty ice bucket. It vanished behind the dark shadows. She placed the ashtray by its side. She hung the glass above the bar with the other wine glasses, neatly in its place. She ran to the bathroom, grabbed a bottle of fabric refresher and sprayed everything down, from the sofa to the pillows, the carpet and her robe. The refresher successfully masked the incriminating smell of her herbal indulgence. Whoever created that ingenious concoction had succeeded in making the weed smoker's life much easier. Jessica had every scent.

After making sure that everything in the entertainment room was springtime fresh, she fluffed each pillow and set it in its place, double-checking for ashes on the cushions. Perfect. Smiling with pride at a job well done, she removed Lorraine Dubois from the CD player and headed upstairs.

Delores, the housekeeper, was busy cleaning in the kitchen, fixated on the task at hand. The whole house could have been on fire, but Delores was not leaving until that counter was spotless. Jessica easily slipped past her without notice and slid up another flight of stairs to the master bedroom.

Once inside, she stood in front of the full-length mirror to inspect herself. There was much work needed. Her hair had air dried into long, fluffy, bouncing curls. She racked her fingers through her locks and shook her head to allow the chestnut curls to fall seductively over her face. She removed her robe and hung it on the hook inside the closet door. She covered her body in coconut scented body butter cream. It was her favorite and would have any man crawling on his knees begging for a bite of her apple. She slipped on her sexiest lace thong, but decided against the matching bra. She wanted her nipples to poke playfully through her blouse. She slipped on a pair of tailored, winter-white, wool slacks with a matching blouse. The shirt was sexy, hanging off both shoulders and tapered at the bottom, showing just a hint of her midriff. After brushing her teeth, she put on her make-up. She carefully covered her face with a light coat of foundation, and then added a light brown liner to her lids to illuminate her smoky, brown eyes. She added a bit of pinkish nude lip-gloss that gave her lips a sensual, suckable factor. She was looking good and feeling even better. The wine had her feeling a bit tipsy, but she liked the feeling. It gave her a little extra sway in her hips. After a final inspection, she was pleased with the outcome. She gave herself a double "A" for "Absolutely Adorable."

The front door opened and closed downstairs, sending an echo that bounced of the marble floor in the foyer and traveled up the stairs.

He's home! Wait till he gets a load of me.

Jessica eagerly pranced down the stairs to greet Ross, her husband, home from work at his law firm. The sight of him excited her, sending chills down her spine and an erection to her nipples. It was amazing that she still got that feeling after 16 years of marriage. He was the love of her life, and she was ready, willing and able to show him just how much she had been missing him all day long.

"How are you, Counselor?" She leaped off the landing of the staircase, wrapping her arms around his neck and smothering him with kisses before he had the chance to set his brief-case down. He didn't return her ardent embrace.

"Jessica, please! Let me get in the door." He moved his head back to dodge any further kisses and released her grip from around his neck. Her overenthusiastic display of affection visibly annoyed him.

Jessica's cheeks flushed with embarrassment, "Oh, I'm sorry, honey. I'm just happy to see you that's all. I've been missing you all day. Here, let me get your coat and your brief-case. I am going to wine and dine you and just cater to my man. What can I do for you?"

"Well, for starters, you can tell me what exactly is wrong with your hair. Did you forget how to use the comb? I mean honestly, Jessica, you look like you've been in a fight with a cat."

She immediately began to smooth her hair with her hands, slicking it back and pushing it behind her ears.

Where is a damn ponytail holder when you need one?

"Oh, I was just trying something new. If you don't like it, I'll fix it. Really, it's not a big deal."

"Not a big deal? Is that what you think? That your appearance isn't a big deal? Is that why you are dressed like a damn streetwalker? My God, Jessica, you don't even have on a bra! What were you thinking?" He contorted his face with disgust.

Ross' words stabbed her like a dagger to the heart. The air abandoned her lungs and she felt small and weak. She was ashamed and rushed to cover up. Biting down on her bottom lip to keep from crying, she tugged at her shirt and stretched it to hide her exposed stomach. She pulled the loose collar of her blouse to cover her shoulders. Her left arm stretched over her chest to cover her jiggling breasts.

She bowed her head in humiliation. What *was* she thinking? This was stupid. It was absurd. Ross hadn't touched her in months, not the way he used to. He didn't hug her and kiss her like he used to. He didn't caress her and cuddle with her. When they did have sex, it was hardly lovemaking. It was a husband's duty to his wife, something that was done *to* her, not *with* her, not *for* her. He used to be so passionate, taking his pleasure in her wherever, whenever he wanted her. They were inseparable, but she was getting old. Her body wasn't the same as it was ten, or even five years ago. Her breasts weren't as perky, and her ass sagged a little. Her waist was still small, but not nearly as small as it used to be. She had gained five whole pounds in the last month, ballooning up to 125 pounds. She caught sight of a few wrinkles in between her eyebrows and could have sworn she had seen a grey hair the other day. She was letting herself go. No wonder he wasn't impressed. She needed much more than just a new outfit and some makeup. She needed a major overhaul.

"I don't know what I was thinking. I'm sorry. I'll go and change right away." Her head was still down.

"Of course you will, and put on some shoes while you're at it. I'm sure Delores will have dinner ready soon and I don't want you sitting at my dinner table looking like a homeless hooker. Show some respect in my house."

His dinner table? His house? The home they purchased together, the home she spent two years decorating and perfecting to his liking, the home that she loved so dearly, was *his* home. She stood still in a choked silence as Ross casually brushed past her, loosening his tie and heading towards the den.

Jessica remained stationary, still standing in front of the door, head down, holding her shirt and covering her chest. She could no longer hold back the tears and allowed them to fall freely from her eyes and drip onto the floor. She was disgraced and disgusted with herself.

What was I thinking?

CHAPTER 4

SIMONE

SHOWERING was a ritual for Simone. It was not just a way to cleanse her body; it was a temporary solution, a quick, sweet getaway. For those brief ten-minute intervals, she was able to absolve any traces of her father's violation. She washed away his touch, scrubbed away his kisses and rinsed away his moans.

She always started with her feet, scrubbing the bottom surface he would tickle to wake her up in the middle of the night. Then she would move to her legs and thighs where he would grab to force her open right before entering her. Her vagina was next where she reeked of his wretched ejaculation. Then she moved on to her backside; he would always wrap his arms around her and rest his hands on the small of her back. The simple embrace would have normally been a sign of endearment, but to Simone, it was a distasteful burden. Next, were her arms. He always expected a hug when it was over. Although forced, it was a small reassurance that his daughter still loved him and understood that he loved her despite his abominable, repulsive actions. On up to her neck, where he would kiss her softly, as if to comfort her until it was over.

Finally, she came to her face, her beautiful face. It was the source of all her problems, the root of her curse and the origin of her pain. It was the basis for her father's infatuation and the reason he decided to ruin her innocence, her joy in life and her belief in him. Her face was the reason why she wanted God to take her life. It was her damnation, her affliction, her torment--her beautiful, ravishing face.

It was funny how girls in school were jealous of the beauty she so desperately wanted to rid herself of. Kristen Snider, in her fifth period biology class, lived to make her life miserable.

"You think you so cute, don't you? You think you the shit cause all these boys like you? The only reason they like you is cuz they know you a ho! Yeah, that's right she's a certified ho. For the right price she'll let you hit it any way you want it."

Kristen had the attention and admiration of the entire class. She was cute, average height, with caramel skin and light-brown, shoulder-length hair that she wore in a neat bob. Her womanly curves were much more developed than Simone's were and she used every opportunity she had to show them off. She was the most popular girl in the 9th grade. She wouldn't let anyone steal her shine, especially some bourgeois, stuck up, rich girl who thought she was better than everyone else was. As far as Kristen was concerned, Simone might have been pretty, but no one would even notice by the time she was done with her. She was the unofficial Queen of Stonecreeke Academy and she walked around as if she owned the halls of the prestigious private school. The first day she saw Simone and the reaction that she had gotten from the boys, she was determined to sabotage her competition. Jealousy did not begin to describe the type of hatred Kristen had for her. Her feelings were irrational and outrageous. She worked hard to build her reputation at the school, based on a carefully crafted series of lies. The imaginary life she created for herself had Stonecreeke's student body in awe of her. It was better than a Thursday night must-see TV drama. She refused to see her hard work and determination go to waste.

In her time at Stonecreeke, Kristen had replaced her 24-year old crack addicted mother with a 30-year old, "successful prosecution attorney" who died while giving birth to her. In place of her unknown father, there was Dr. William Snider, the "renowned heart surgeon who was currently working overseas providing health care for under privileged children in Doctor's Without Borders." She stayed home with her grandmother, a "homemaker and widow of a retired university professor."

Her grandmother was, in fact, a housekeeper making a very modest living cleaning the homes of the upper class well-to-do's of the suburbs for the last 30 years. To say Kristen came from a humble background would be an extreme under-statement. Unlike her fellow affluent classmates, Stonecreeke admitted her with financial aid and a favor from the Dean, who was a former employer of her grandmother's.

To attend Stonecreeke Academy conferred high status. It was unacceptable for one's parents to be mediocre, middle-class, under achievers. Attending Stonecreeke was a privilege, and only the children of elite, prestigious families attended. To reveal the truth about Kristen's life and upbringing would be complete ruination. Keeping up the ruse was easy. The expectation was that every child at the Academy came from money, so no one doubted her extravagant story. The fabrica-tion was one that she told so many times, that she actually began to believe it herself. Because of this, Kristen walked the halls with her head held high with a false, if fragile, sense of assurance. She was overly confident, flamboyant and outgoing. Every girl wanted to be her and every boy wanted to be *with* her. So it was only logical that she destroyed Simone.

Simone looked on with a blank stare as she listened to her opponent's continuous rants. She said nothing.

This girl is stupid. She has no idea what she's talking about. I haven't said anything to her all semester and all of a sudden I'm her worst enemy. She thinks I like looking like this? She thinks I like everybody looking at me and judging me. Watching everything I do like I'm some type of circus freak? She has no idea what I go through when I go home. No clue, but she hates me. Stupid.

"Yeah, you better not say nothing or I'll come over there and fuck you up. I'll wipe your pretty little face all over the floor."

I wish I could just switch places with her so she could see what it was like to be me. I bet she'd shut up then.

Suddenly, Simone's heart pounded rapidly. She felt a lump that had risen from her stomach up to her chest, then her throat. She felt a radiant heat flush her face as rage overtook her body.

I'm sick of everybody blaming me for everything! I didn't ask to be born! I didn't ask to be put on this earth, to go to this school, to be in this class. I'm sick of everybody crying and complaining like I did something wrong. I didn't do anything to deserve this life. I didn't ask for any of this. But she's mad at me?

Simone slowly stood to her feet and focused on Kristen.

God give me the strength. Give me the strength to walk away.

Her face snarled and her eyes squinted in a glare. Her breathing was slow and heavy. With her hands balled into tight fists by her sides, her nails dug into her palms. She didn't notice the pain as the skin began to break under the pressure. She felt as if a spirit lifted her out of her body. She did find strength, but she did not use it to walk away.

I'm sick of this!

"You fucking bitch! You want me? Come get me. You don't know me! You're just jealous because I look better than you and your man wants me. You wish you were me. I'm a ho? Your dead ass mama was a ho! Come here, I'm gonna beat the shit outta you, bitch!" Simone was on fire. She was almost shocked at the sound of her own voice and the curse words that spewed from her mouth.

The words came out of nowhere. The whole class turned to face her with looks of astonishment. She began to charge at her enemy, pushing desks to the side as she rushed through, but a few of her classmates held her back. They tugged at her, forcing her backward until finally they were able to hold her against the wall. She was unable to move. Her body was plastered against the wall like a poster.

Kristen stared at Simone in disbelief. Eyes wide and mouth open, Kristen couldn't believe this quiet, prissy little girl was actually challenging her. What was wrong with her? No one had ever tried to fight her. Intimidation always scared them off, assuming she had the bite to match her vicious bark. Kristen didn't know how to handle a direct challenge and was immediately frightened as she started to back up as to avoid any wild punches that came her way. This girl was crazy!

"Let me go! Let me go! I'll kill you! Oh, you scared now? You talked all that shit and you scared now?" Simone was screaming at the top of her lungs and crying uncontrollably. She wanted desperately for her classmates to set her free to attack her rival. She wanted to fight. She wanted to punch, kick, and scream. She wanted to scratch and bite. But above all, she wanted to be beaten. She wanted Kristen to do all the horrible things she said she would do to her and to have her physical pain from Kristen's hate replace her mental pain from her father's love. Pain that comes from the outside was much easier to endure. The wounds heal, the scars go away and it is over. She could move on. She would live on and forget her pain. The wounds caused by her father, that festered inside Simone's heart, mind and blood would never heal. She would never be able to just move on and forget the scars. Her plan to obtain relief through displacement failed. She watched in disappointment as Kristen shrank away from her and ran out of the classroom.

Coward

A week later the horrendous episode was still fresh in her mind, as if it happened just hours ago. She was still thinking back on that day as she scrubbed her face with aggressive force. She tried her best to wash away her misery and cleanse her soul. Using the rough side of the loofah, she scrubbed until a small abrasion scarred her left cheek. Feeling the pain from the fresh wound, she dropped to her knees, sobbing furiously. This was her third shower that day and still she felt filthy.

"Simone?" Her mother called to her from downstairs.

It was time to eat dinner. She forced herself up and got out of the shower. Quickly gaining her composure, she walked out of her private bathroom past the fog-covered mirror.

"I'll be right down."

She dried off and dressed. She brushed her thick curly locks into a neat ponytail and flooded her eyes with eye drops. With a fake smile affixed to her face, she proceeded down the staircase to join her parents for dinner. Her parents expected her to be presentable, neat and polite at dinner. Her mother would have it no other way. Her parents always asked about her day and she gave them exactly what they wanted to hear. Smiling from ear to ear, she created a story of a happy, cheerful child living yet another delightful day. It was a perfected performance.

As the maid dressed the table with their meal, Simone started the daily, generic dinner conversation.

"Good evening Mom, Daddy."

"Good evening, Simone. You were almost late. Is everything okay?"

"Everything is great, Mom."

"Simone, you know how important it is to be punctual. It is never acceptable to leave your companions waiting because of your tardiness."

"I know, Mom. I'm sorry. It won't happen again."

"Make sure that it doesn't. Punctuality shows discipline and maturity. Make sure that you represent our family well when meeting with others. You will get the best practice here at home."

Simone said a small prayer to keep herself from rolling her eyes. Seemingly, it worked because she was able to keep a straight face when responding, "I understand, Mom. I will be more conscious of the time in the future." Quickly, she changed the subject, "So, how was your day?"

"Just wonderful. Chelsea and I had a relaxing spa day in downtown Birmingham. What about you, sweetie? How was school? That awful mistake of a child hasn't been harassing you has she? I still can't believe she only received a one-week suspension after all of the protests I made. Her parents should be ashamed with a child acting like that. No home training at all!"

It was funny how her mother was able to switch the subject and the tone of the conversation so suddenly as of she was smoothly changing lanes on the freeway.

Simone's father chimed in, "Exactly. What kind of person thinks it's okay to treat another human being that way? I get upset every time I think about it. I mean what's wrong with her? If she is a representation of the type of students that attend that academy, we might have to think about a transfer. Perhaps another Christian Academy like the one you attended from kindergarten up until last year."

Simone discreetly rolled her eyes at her father's mention of her old school. Although Simone embraced her Christian teachings, she knew the only reason her parents sent her to the school and insisted on her Sunday school attendance, was to keep up the image of a classy, well-respected family. The only reason her parents were members of the church and made sporadic visits was because they had to keep up appearances. Simone considered herself to be a devout Christian, but was disappointed that her parents were not.

She allowed the wave of annoyance to pass through her before addressing her father's last statement, "I'm sure she has problems of her own that we know nothing about. Everyone has a story." Simone said this calmly, avoiding eye contact with her father.

Her father nervously turned his head to avoid Simone's eyes. "That's true, but she doesn't have to take her own shortcomings out on you. It's just senseless. Whatever she has gone through in life has nothing to do with you and you should not have to suffer because of it."

Her mother shook her head angrily. She was so protective of her baby girl, her only child. It was unimaginable that anyone would dislike her. She was so well behaved and such a sweet girl. She saw to that personally. It was her job to raise a model child and she did so with pride. If you didn't like Simone, there was something wrong with you. And, if something was wrong with you, you needed to stay clear of Simone.

The dinner conversation continued, with most words passing over Simone's head. It began to sound like senseless murmurs, like the adults on the *Charlie Brown* cartoons, "Whomp whomp, whomp." She heard her mother say something about a charity event and her father complaining about someone at work, the same boring topics every evening. Simone maintained enough alertness until she recognized parts of the conversation as something that applied to her and answered accordingly. She nodded her head in between bites and smiled on cue.

This was it. This was her life. It was the life of the perfect family, the definition of the American dream. Simone had it all.

CHAPTER 5

RYAN

THE sun spilled into the third story bedroom through the cracks in the Venetian blinds. The chill of the early morning air swept across the room, but it had no affect on Ryan. She was on fire.

She was aflame with desire as her gorgeous man slid his tongue down her body, from her erect nipples to her navel. She quivered with sweet anticipation as he sucked her belly button, biting a little just to make her jump. He let his tongue glide across that sensitive area between her navel and bikini line and it sent a chill up her spine that had nothing to do with the cold air that captivated the room. He kissed her *there* -- *smack on* her sweet spot, making it throb. He quickly pulled back to tease her. She squealed with the excitement of a kid on Christmas morning. He kissed and sucked her inner thigh. Ryan was getting impatient and wanted him right then. No foreplay, no more games; she wanted him to fuck her hard!

She grabbed his head to pull his face back up to her vagina, but he firmly refused. With a force that let her know he was in complete control, he grabbed her wrists and slammed her arms back down on the bed, then started again from the top, kissing her neck and sliding his way back down. He twisted his tongue around her nipples and slipped his fingers inside her. He left his thumb out to caress her clit. His fingers were in perfect sync with his tongue as they both twisted and turned, causing her to purr softly. She wiggled beneath him with a strong yearning. She couldn't stand it anymore; she was about to explode.

He laughed a little, looking down at her, "You want this dick?"

"Oh, God! Anthony, please don't play with me."

"You want this dick?" He persisted

"Yes! Yes, I want you. I need it please!" She gripped the sheets, twisting them so tightly she almost broke a fingernail.

He thrust the best of himself in between her legs, but did not enter her. He let the tip of his penis tickle her clit. He rubbed his hardness up and down against her, dripping wetness. He grabbed it, wriggled it right up against the opening, and watched as her moistness started to drip onto the sheets.

"You're driving me crazy. Please stop teasing me." She grabbed behind him toward the small of his back and tried to force him in.

He decided it was time to end her torture and give her what she needed. He went back down to wrap his tongue around her clit. Grabbing her thighs and throwing her legs over his shoulders, he sucked and drummed rapidly with his tongue. He gripped her ass, just how she liked it, licking and sucking until the arch in her back caved in. Ryan moaned, grunted and then screamed out of control, pumping up and down with mechanical precision, as his tongue vibrated on that sensuous button. She was nearing her climax. She went from pulling her own hair to gripping his head. She was not going to let him ease up 'til her orgasm burst through.

But once again, he showed her who was running the show. He stopped -- right before she came -- and thrust his penis inside her with such force, she almost screeched in pain. But the pain quickly turned into an almost unbearable ecstasy. He was giving her everything he had. Each thrust sent her closer to euphoria. He pushed and pulled in and out, harder and harder. She was dying a sweet, pleasurable death. He started grinding, hard and slow in small circles with their bodies hard pressed against each other. They were in perfect rhythm. Again, Ryan was on her way to ecstasy when Anthony slowly came to a stop and pulled out, commanding her, "Flip yo ass over."

Ryan eagerly complied with his orders and turned over on all fours, arching her back deeply and sticking her ass far up in the air. He grabbed her shoulder length hair and wrapped it around his hand, yanking her head back. Once again, he entered her, riding her like a stallion, using her hair as his reins. He used his other hand to grip her waist while he forcibly moved her back and forth.

The back of the headboard beat against the wall with each stroke in a steady, seductive rhythm, causing small chips of paint to fall to the floor.

This is so good. It's better than good – it's transcendent.

They were lost inside of each other, swimming, intoxicated by each other's sexual sounds. His sweat dripped from his forehead onto her back and rolled down through the crack of her ass.

"You like it?"

She could barely speak; all she could manage to muster was a whisper, combined with a soft moan, "Umm hmm."

She was hypnotized with bliss. Her breasts flapped against her skin with each thrust. She quickly glanced back at him to see a look of intense, almost painful concentration on his face. He was working her with the virtuosity and expertise of a sexual grand master. He knew her body well. He knew what she wanted and how to give it to her.

She could hear him sliding in and out. The mix of wetness, with the sweat and friction made such an appealingly nasty sound -- a gushing, slurping, squish. It drove her insane. Her ass neatly smacked against his stomach as he drove himself inside her. He watched as his pumps caused waves to vibrate through her ass cheeks. Her erotic, passionate moans were thunderous, bouncing off every wall in the room. It turned him on and made him push and pull even harder. Their equally matched passion was intense, almost palpable, and undoubtedly made them even bolder.

"I didn't hear you, bitch. I said 'Do you like it'?"

She was coming now, "Oh shit! Yes, I love it, baby. I love it!" She screamed in between heavy breaths.

Her hard-earned climax came forceful and fast; all her energy drained from the inside out. She felt his throbbing manhood as they both collapsed on the bed. He was still inside her, letting his semen drip between her legs and onto the sheets. They always climaxed together. They were in sync with each other--sexually and psychically. It wasn't sex -- it was magic.

After ten minutes of regaining composure and catching his breath, Anthony gently slipped out of her and rolled onto his side. She turned to face him and he tenderly kissed her forehead as he always did after loving her. She caressed his face and snuggled up to his strong, beautiful body, resting her head on his chest.

"Baby, I love you so much."

"I love you too, Ryan. I can't wait till we're married and we get to wake up to this every morning."

The thought of marriage made her insides sizzle. She wanted nothing more than holy matrimony with her man. Within seconds, he was sleeping with soft snores vibrating his chest. Ryan remained awake; she couldn't sleep. She would rather just watch him and try to guess what he was dreaming.

They never made it to breakfast that morning. He showed up at her house at 6:30 in the morning, more than enough time for both of them to eat and make it to work on time. They had every intention of going to the Downtown Breakfast Grill for the usual: eggs Benedict, New York strip steak with wheat toast and mimosas. But when he stepped into her foyer, looking as good as he did, and smelling even better, all chances for leaving the house were over. They had an undeniable attraction for each other, a passion that burned like an inferno. It was a mutual addiction that held them obsessed and captivated with each other. They couldn't kiss without tearing each other's clothes off. It had been that way since the first time their lips met.

Weeks of relentless courting and dating had passed before their first kiss. It was close to midnight. They were snuggled on her couch, watching TV, a reality show. She was addicted to those shows and made him suffer through them as much as she could. As always, he was only pretending to pay attention. She was fighting to stay awake. The show was good:

young, rich, handsome man was looking for the woman of his dreams. The only catch was he was broke as hell. But her couch was cozy, snug and comfortable, coaxing her deeper into sleep. He had been staring at her sexy, full lips for several minutes and fought with himself to collect the courage to steal a kiss. Finally, he did.

"Can I kiss you?"

She didn't say a word, just grabbed his face and went to work. She'd been waiting on him to make a move since the first date, but he was such a gentleman, making sure he didn't move too fast and assuring they had time to get to know and like each other before any physical advances. But that measured, polite man evaporated as soon as her lips were on his. He wasted no time grabbing and hoisting her onto his lap in a straddle position, gripping her ass to move her slowly up and down, grinding against his rock hard erection. His aggression surprised Ryan, but she was too aroused to let it throw her off her game. She quickly followed his lead, unbuttoning his shirt and tugging at his belt buckle. She was more than ready to release eight months of frustration from involuntary celibacy on this fine man in the worst way. Then--he stopped.

"I should go."

"What?" He had to be joking. She brushed off his ridiculous notion and stayed focused on her goal. She almost had his pants loose. They were a little tricky. She couldn't decide whether to start ripping her clothes off or to let him do it. She wanted to give him the illusion of some control, so she thought that maybe she would let him handle undressing her. His cologne smelled so good. It was intoxicating. This man was sexy! Not to mention, she could tell from his slow grinds, that he possessed quite a nice package downtown.

Ooh, I can't wait!

He gently removed her hands from his belt and pulled back, "It's late and I have to go." He was serious.

She stared at him in disbelief. *Is he gay?*

"I have to get up early tomorrow morning for a meeting before work. I really should go. We'll pick up where we left off tomorrow, okay."

"Okay...I guess." She climbed off his lap, a little embarrassed. He had her nose and vagina wide open -- then just slammed the door right in her face. She felt like a horny, desperate fool. Well, she *was* horny, but *desperate*? Never! After this nonsense, he would have to beg upside down with a red leather ribbon around his neck just to smell her pussy.

She swore, after that, she was going to hold out for at least another month as punishment. That resolution lasted for exactly 22 hours. He hit it the next night, right there on the couch with the same reality TV show on the screen.

The physical connection they shared was incendiary. One kiss, one touch, one look and she would be dripping wet. Everything he did was with such passion. When they made love, it was as if they hadn't seen each other in weeks. She had never had a lover like him. He was perfect in every way: perfect size, perfect fit, perfect technique. He could instruct a damn class to Casanova, Don Juan, Hugh Hefner and R. Kelly! She had it all in one man. He was successful, fine as hell, and could fuck her senseless.

Once again, she thought about how lucky she was to have a man like him -- so well put together -- who was in love with her. He was made for her and fate brought them together a year ago.

• • •

Ryan was a very attractive woman, more sexy than pretty. She was the kind of woman who commanded all of the attention when she sauntered in a room. Her walk was a performance and she exuded sex with every step. It would be a cruel injustice to call it a walk. It was an art, one that ordinary women couldn't perfect with years of practice. Men were drawn to her, and her strides had them following like mice to the Pied Piper. Her body was a black man's paradise: wide hips, nice round ass, generous thighs, small waistline and full breasts. Michelangelo could have carved her right out of marble. Her skin was a creamy, dark chocolate and her hair was silk. Her sensual lips, always poised to kiss, curse or suck, were curvy, plump and full. Her sleepy, almond-shaped, bedroom eyes were the color of onyx.

She was bad, but never seemed to notice or appreciate the impact she had on her audiences. The same reactions, time after time, were rather boring actually. How many times did she have to hear the outrageous, sometimes rude, but never clever come-ons before she had had enough? She was not impressed and didn't hide her distaste in her facial expressions. So it wasn't a surprise when *he* walked up casually behind her and tapped gently on her shoulder.

Just another fan.

She was standing at the counter at Starbucks, waiting on her grande white chocolate mocha with an extra shot of espresso. The sweet, frothy, caffeinated pleasure had become her latest addiction. They never added enough whipped cream, so she always made sure to stand watch in order to provide proper direction. She felt the small tap just as the server placed her order on the table and immediately became irritated. Flinching her shoulder up in disgust as if shooing a fly, she held up her hand without turning around to face the violator.

"I'm not interested." She snatched her flavored caffeine from the counter and turned to walk away.

It was only morning but it had already been a bad day thus far. She woke up late, her hair looked like it was thrown on top of her head, she had put a run in her stocking, and her feet were already hurting from her new pumps. Moreover, to top it all off, it was 40 degrees outside in the middle of what was supposed to be Spring. The last thing she needed was some lame ass spitting his "Yo baby" lines to try to get her number just so he could booty call her for some 3a.m. ass. No thanks!

"Um, well actually, that's my drink." He pointed at her white chocolate mocha with extra whipped cream. He wore a three-piece suit, obviously on his way to the office. His tie was an interesting mix of blues, greens and, grays intertwining into colorful swirls. His shoes were sharp. They looked brand new and buttery soft, probably Prada. He wore his neatly trimmed hair in a low cut, but she could tell it was naturally curly from the waves covering his tapered trim. A closely trimmed beard covered the lower half of his face. His skin was a smooth, caramel complexion, and she even noticed his freshly manicured nails. He was definitely well put together, but irritating all the same.

"Yeah, you must be mistaken. I watched them make this

drink. Now if you'll excuse me, I'm late for work." She had no time for games. She tried to brush past him, but he wouldn't back down.

"I can appreciate that, Miss as I am an extremely busy man myself, but I'm afraid you are the one who's mistaken. You see, we ordered the same drink. However, mine is decaffeinated. Now, I would appreciate it if you would hand it to me so I may be on my way. If you'd take a moment to turn around you'll see they've just placed your drink on the counter."

Ryan slowly turned her head, trying to hide her embarrassment. Indeed, there it was, her grande white chocolate mocha with an extra shot of espresso and not *nearly* enough whipped cream! "Oh."

"Right. I'll take that. Thanks!"

He took his drink from her hand and neatly turned on his heel to walk out the door.

Asshole.

She really *was* running late for work, so she did a half run out the door and got into her car. She put the key in the ignition and threw the gear into reverse. Her jam of the month blared from the radio, immediately putting her in a better mood. She gave herself a quick once over in the rearview mirror, her makeup was flawless. One thing seemed to go right that morning. She smiled a little to herself, began to bounce her head to the beat, and pushed her foot down on the gas. No sooner then she began to move backwards, than she felt a thud at the rear of the car.

Damn, I hit something!

Looking in her review mirror, she saw the same arrogant

bastard from the coffee shop stepping out of his Mercedes to inspect its front bumper.

You have got to be kidding me!

Ryan stepped out of her car as well. "What the hell are you doing?" She was pissed with her hands on her hips and her neck already doing the world famous, black woman's head snap 'n' roll.

"Well, I'm checking for any damages from you ramming into my car." He, on the other hand, was very calm. That annoyed her even more.

"Damages? I barely tapped the thing, and where in the hell did you learn how to parallel park? Common sense tells you if you park too close, someone will hit you." She gave her best mock impression of a complete idiot. "Oh, I guess you don't have common sense, huh?"

"You know what? You're pretty rude."

"Rude? Who are you to judge me? You don't know the first thing about me. And if you ask me, you're the one that has the obvious personality defect, walking around here like you own Detroit. Who do you think you are? Don't look like much to me."

"Wow, more insults. Did your mother teach you to speak that way to people you don't know?"

Oh no this nigga didn't!

Ryan stepped up to the arrogant fool as if she was ready to fight. There was no more than a couple of inches in between them as she stood on her tip toes to look at him face to face, jabbing her index finger in between his eyes. "What did you say about my mama? I know I didn't just hear you say something about my mama."

He smirked, "You heard me."

"I will not hesitate to kick your ass."

He couldn't hold it in any longer. He started to laugh.

She was about ready to snatch his head off, "What is so damn funny?"

"Nothing, I'm sorry. It seems like you're having a bad day and you look like your feet hurt."

His comment caught her off guard and disarmed her fury. She even chuckled herself, looking down at her aching feet wobbling and ready to collapse from under her at any moment. "Yeah, actually they do hurt like hell."

"Well, Miss I'm sorry to have inconvenienced you in any way, but there seems to be no damage to either of our vehicles. You want to call it a truce?"

She wanted to maintain her attitude, but the man was charming and kind of cute. Actually, he was kind of fine as hell. She smiled, "Truce."

"Great. Now if you would be so kind, I would like to have the opportunity to make your day better." He handed her a business card. "Please give me a call if you have the time for dinner later, um--"

"Ryan."

"Ryan. I hope to speak with you soon." He turned to walk back towards his car.

"Wait, what's your name?"

"It's on the card." With a sexy, half smile on his face, he got back into his car and drove away.

She looked down at the business card in her hand and smiled. She was impressed.

• • •

She thanked God for that day, the day that changed her life, the day that she met the man she would spend the rest of her life with. She would no longer chase after the emotionally unavailable assholes that promised the world and delivered nothing. This was it, her happily ever after.

My man.

There was still an hour left before she had to leave for work. Her eyes became heavy and she decided to take advantage of the extra time and fall asleep. Still resting her head on his chest, she joined Anthony in his dreams. Both in deep slumber, neither heard the cell phone ringing inside his pants pocket, thrown across the room, bundled in a corner. There were 12 missed calls.

CHAPTER 6

JESSICA

"I'M here to see Wanda Wolinsky please." Jessica stood at the front desk of Maple Village Retirement Community, finally speaking up after several minutes of impatient waiting. She looked down at the twenty-something receptionist. She was too ignorant to act as if she gave a damn about her job, and too rude to give a damn that Jessica was standing there.

Never looking up from her gossip magazine, "And you are?"

Her tone was dry and uncaring, with a touch of belligerence. It was as if Jessica's presence offended her. Jessica peeked at the article she was reading. It was something about a female rapper sentenced to one year in prison for violation of probation. Obviously, it was far more important than addressing her job duties. Ms. Twenty-something was covered in tattoos and dressed for the club. She wore a hot pink top with spaghetti straps with "Sexy" Stretched across her flabby breasts. A "Miss Bitch" tattoo was featured on her left breast. She had a silver ball tongue ring and a bad hair weave that could have been mistaken for a hat. Her nails were at least three inches long and covered with airbrush painted dollar bills. A small key hung from the nail of her middle finger. She looked ridiculous as if she went to the dollar store and bought everything she could find, and then decided to wear it to work. She had to have been related to (or sleeping with) someone in management in order to get the job. Jessica was not impressed.

"Jessica Pembroke. I'm her daughter. I'm on the list. I come here every other weekend to visit, if you would take the time to look at me, you might recognize my face, or does that require too much thinking for you?" She was challenging the girl; a deep scowl covered her face. Jessica was not about to be disrespected by someone who was not on her level, someone who was beneath her.

"Excuse me?" Now, Ms. Twenty-something was paying attention. She stood up to meet Jessica eye-to-eye, glaring at her through cheap, blue contact lenses.

"You heard me, *Home Girl.* Or is it Shiquanna?"

The receptionist leaned up and brought her face into kissing distance of Jessica's. She pointed a long, airbrushed, acrylic nail between her eyes. "You lucky I'm at work right now, or I would knock the shit out of you. You don't know who you fuckin' wit!"

"Are you threatening me? You have just lost your job "Miss Bitch." I guess the next time I see you you'll be ho'in' for your pimp. On second thought, I probably won't see you at all. I don't go to the *hood* to *kick it.*" Jessica was proud of her witty comeback. With her head held high and her nose in the air, she turned to walk toward her mother's room. "Just be sure to check me in, if that's not too much for you, Sha nay nay. I'll show myself to the room."

She walked off haughtily with a brisk step, leaving the receptionist to scream obscenities behind her. Jessica made a mental note to speak with a manager to make sure they fired Jaguanna. No one talked to her that way.

She stopped at the door of her mother's room and stood still for a moment before knocking. She needed to gain her composure and prepare herself for whatever mood her mother was in that day. Visiting bi-weekly was a job, a due diligence owed to a mother from her only daughter. It was a countdown for her long overdue death, an event that was marked daily on Jessica's mental calendar. She had to step outside of herself, drop her pride and take herself back 30 years to a time when she still actually had genuine love for her mother, the kind of unconditional love a little girl has for her parent regardless of countless disappointments. She closed her eyes, took a deep breath, and then finally, tapped lightly on the door.

"Who is it?" Her mother had a raspy, smoker's voice mixed with a little country twang. She sounded like she would just about keel over with every word.

"It's me, Wanda, Jessica."

"Well, what da hell ya waitin' on? Come on in chile." Her mother was in her usual spot, her bed; An *All in the Family* rerun was on the TV screen, mounted on the opposite wall.

Jessica walked in with a forced smile and sat in a chair next to Wanda's musty bed. She could barely stand to look her mother straight in the face. She looked terrible; she hadn't aged well at all. Dark liver spots covered her skin. Wanda's brown eyes were sunken into her face. Her hair was wiry, stringy, and gray. She was balding, revealing the flaking skin scaling from her scalp. She was overweight, about 10 pounds from being considered clinically obese, and her wrinkled skin hung loosely from her bones. She was dressed in her usual attire, a muumuu covered in years-old stains and a permanent dinginess.

"How're you feeling?" Jessica had missed her last visit and felt the need to catch up on Wanda's latest ailments.

"Could be betta. Dis arfritis is kickin' my ass and jus' yestaday, the docta gone tell me they might hafta do surgery on my knee. Like I need anotha damn surgery, old as I'm is. My hemorrhoids been actin' up too. Oh, and they say I gots chronic diarrhea!"

Jessica was hardly listening to Wanda's charming litany, as she was preoccupied with her own thoughts. "Oh really?" She picked up the remote control to change the channel on the TV. Nothing worth watching was showing, so she turned it off. "The Doctor called me last week and told me you haven't been taking your medication, Wanda. Don't you want to feel better?"

"Hell naw. Shit I wish I could hurry up and jus die."

Jessica shifted in her seat. *You and me both.*

Her mother continued, struggling to sit straight up in her bed with no help from her daughter. She turned her head toward Jessica, looking at her critically. "Where da hell ya been Jessie? I ain't seent cha in damn near a month now. I guess you too busy livin' da high life with dat ole' uppity nigger you den married." She finally gave up the fight to sit up and let her body slide back down to comfort. "Yeah, that's it, you too good now. Den forgot where you came from. Livin' ova there in that big ass house witcha high class lawn jockey." She found her last remark to be especially amusing, laughing a painful, croaking hack. "You come all up in here actin' like you betta dan me, but you da one wasn't good enough fo' no decent white man. Had to settle fo' what you could get -- a goddamn nigger!"

The "goddamn nigger" speech was one Jessica was well accustomed to. It no longer had an effect on her. It no longer made her want to cry or run out screaming. The urge to choke or smack her mother every time she heard her call her husband the "*N*" word had ended long ago. It was amazing how she could enunciate that one word so perfectly, but lost all precision when it came to every other word in the English language. Her mother was an old, uneducated, piece of Polack trash, whose only shred of pride hung on the fact that she felt superior to blacks because she was a "pure-bred white woman." Never mind the fact that she had lived in poverty all her life -- she was white. It didn't matter that both her mother and father were alcoholics and she was fortunate enough to inherit that trait as well -- she was white. Not to mention, she'd been frowned upon and shunned by her peers of the same race -- she was white. And being white was always better than being black, no matter the circumstance. Jessica said nothing. She was too busy checking her phone for text messages to give any attention to her mother's ignorant rants.

"…He ain't shit ya know. None of em are. All dem blackies are the same. He beatin' on ya' yet? Huh Jessie?"

Jessica finished checking her messages, "No Wanda, he does not beat me. He hasn't laid a hand on me in sixteen years and I'm telling you for the last time, it's Jessica. My name is Jessica, not Jessie. You got that?" She was bored with the conversation and couldn't keep from rolling her eyes in aggravation.

"Whateva, Jessie. Yeah, jus you wait. It's a comin'. Dey all da same. And I betcha he cheatin on ya too. Dey like dawgs, humpin' every livin' thang in sight. Shit, dat's prolly where he got all dat money from, pimpin'. How many other womens he got Jessie?"

Wanda finally struck a chord, releasing a fury of resentment from inside Jessica's body. Her blood became hot as she stood to her feet to confront the old bitch. "I'm tired of your shit! You hate niggers so much, is that why you hate me? I'm a nigger too. Did you forget that? Of course you didn't. You could never forget that you weren't good enough to keep the only black man that was dumb enough to marry your ass? You sit up here in your own filth and misery, bitching and complaining about anything and everything you can connect to a black man. Why? I'll tell you why, because a black man was the only man that had sense enough to leave your crazy, drunk ass when he figured out that *you* weren't good enough for *him*. I'm glad my daddy left you before you brought him down. I just wish he took me with him."

"Dat nigger left cuz he was good fo' nuffin.'"

"No, he left because you drove him away. You didn't deserve him. You didn't want him. All you wanted was what was at the bottom of a damn liquor bottle, and that's all you have. So please excuse me for living in a seven thousand square foot mansion in Rochester Hills, instead of a raggedy-ass trailer in Hamtramck, thanks to my *black* husband."

Jessica didn't remember too much about her father. He left when she was a toddler. The only man she remembered, the one Wanda forced her to call "Daddy", was her mother's boyfriend, her father's replacement. Jessica never knew his name. To Wanda, he was "Baby" or "That Mutha Fucker", depending on how many drinks she had at the time. To Jessica he was the sorry son of a bitch that couldn't do anything more for her and her mother than keep the roaches company and the sofa warm. Eventually, he left too. They all did. The good for nothing men came and went like the tenants of a rent-by-the-hour, no-tell motel, until she too checked out. It was a heritage Jessica tried her best to conceal and leave behind, but her acrimonious mother made sure it was impossible.

Looking back on her childhood, she allowed it to fuel her rage as she continued to confront the source of her anger. "You will never understand what it's like to be anything more than poor, white trash. I can't expect you to even comprehend what it means to be anything but the old dirt-bag that I see in front of me. Go to hell!"

Her mother laughed that croaking hack again. "Dat gotcha mad huh? Sound like ta me sumfin' wrong in nigger paradise."

"There is nothing wrong with my marriage. We're happy, something you would know absolutely nothing about. He treats me like a Queen. He doesn't cheat on me!"

"Yeah, I bet." She smiled a crooked, menacing smile. "Ya know, ya need to have some respect fo' yo mama. The way you talk to me, you deserve to get smacked upside yo head. If I was in betta health, I'd show yo uppity ass what I'm talking bout."

"Respect? Don't make me laugh. Respect is a privilege. Something you earn and you lost my respect a long time ago, the first time you put your filthy, fat hands on me."

"Aww here you go wit this shit again. Look, you is my chile and every chile needs to be knocked upside they head every now an' again to show 'em who's in charge. You ain't no different. You ain't special. When you got outta line I had to knock yo ass back into place."

"Out of line? Tell me this, Wanda: Was I out of line when that piece of filth you brought into our house, tried to sleep with me when I was just twelve years old and you whipped my ass outside in front of the house because you believed him over me?"

"You was lyin'. He ain't want nonna you."

"You are unbelievable. He tried to rape me! He tried to rape your daughter and the only reason he didn't was because you came home before you were supposed to. Then you beat me with an extension cord until I bled. Me, your own daughter. I was the victim."

"Victim? Hmph. Yo trifling ass was tryin' to steal my man. You deserved an ass beatin'. I gotcha good too." She laughed again, showing what was left of her brown, rotted teeth.

"You know what? You are disgusting. I'm not going to stand here and listen to this nonsense. I'm leaving." Jessica grabbed her purse and marched towards the door.

"When you comin' back?"

She ignored her mother and kept walking.

"Well, did you at leas' bring my package?"

Jessica stopped about two feet from the door. She had almost forgotten. How could she have let something so important slip her mind? She would have cursed herself, had she been so careless as to walk out without fulfilling her main goal. She reached inside her oversized purse, retrieved a fifth of cheap vodka and threw it on the bed. It landed next to her mother's left hand, well within reach. It was critical that Jessica supplied her with her bi-weekly supply. It was her contribution to the old hag's death. She would continue to visit every other week to confirm that her mother's health was steadily plummeting until they finally put her raggedy ass in the ground.

"Enjoy and drink up." She stormed out of the room, slamming the door behind her with a loud bang.

Once in the hallway, Jessica took another deep breath and shuddered a little as she harbored the thought of her husband sleeping with another woman. The notion was one that had gripped her thoughts for months. Was he cheating on her? Is that why he didn't touch her like he used to? Is that the reason she spent countless nights pleasuring herself while he was "working late" and traveling on business? Of course not. She had a good man, even if he *was* black. He was the exception. He was intelligent, educated, and successful. He came from a good family. He was a successful attorney. He attended black tie events and drove expensive foreign cars. He was the epitome of the perfect man. She didn't deserve him. She just had to make sure she did what was necessary to keep him. She was the one who was thankful to him for taking her away from the horrible life she was living. She wasn't living, she was simply existing, surviving the absence of her father, an abusive mother and an environment destined to damage her being 'til the point of no return.

When he found her, she was nothing. She was desperate for guidance, begging for structure and hungry for refinement and growth. He gave her what she needed. He did for her what years of therapy and a gang of skilled magicians could never do. He reversed 18 years of an abysmal upbringing, rolled it into a tight ball, and tucked it away in the deepest, darkest corner of her past. It remained there, completely suppressed and contained. The only evidence of its existence was her mother. Yes, he rescued her like a knight draped in three-piece

Armani armor. With his proper grammar, remarkable poise, and distinguished credentials, he was her Prince Charming. He was to her what the sun was to the Earth, her only source of light and warmth. She would do anything to keep the sun from setting on her life.

Jessica brushed the notion of her husband's infidelity off her shoulder and proceeded down the hall. She stopped by the front desk. An older, white woman had replaced Braquanda.

"Hello. May I see your manager please? I would like to report an incident with one of the employees here."

CHAPTER 7

ROSS

YOUNG Ross watched his mother as she moved swiftly between the kitchen and the adjoining laundry room. She balanced a nearly overflowing laundry basket on her left hip as a greasy spatula dangled from her right hand. The art of washing clothes and cooking dinner simultaneously was one that she had mastered long ago. She was an expert. Not one sock would ever come up missing from the load, not one bleach stain, or white shirt turned pink. The towels and face cloths were free from static cling and everything smelled like fresh rain in the springtime. Dinner was equally flawless. All dishes were well seasoned and prepared just right; she never burned anything. The fried chicken was crispy and the mashed potatoes were always smooth and creamy. Still, she didn't make the work look easy. She was tired and her fatigue expressed itself in the long lines in her face.

Ross would ask her if he could help do something, anything that would make her day a little easier, but he would always get the same reply.

"Baby, you know this here is woman's work. Your daddy would just kill me if he knew I had you in here acting like a little girl, cookin', and cleanin' and carrying on. Go on in the family room and watch the game or somethin' until dinner is ready."

Even though Ross knew what she was going to say, he couldn't help but to allow her primitive words to anger him almost to the point of tears. Her words were not from her own thinking; instead, they reflected the constant mental and emotional beatings of his father, "The Judge."

Ross knew when The Judge came home from work that evening the smooth and creamy potatoes would be "too soupy and lumpy." The chicken would be "too salty" and something just wouldn't be right about the corn. The Judge would then yell at his wife for dirtying up the kitchen and not making time to finish folding the laundry. He would want to know why she didn't think he was important enough to try to fix herself up a little and pronounce how he hated that he had to come home to "Raggedy Ann" every evening. To let him tell it, it was no wonder he left the house as soon as he had the opportunity. He would rather play cards with the guys than to stay in that house and let her drag him down into her own hopeless desolation.

Yes, Ross knew all too well what it meant to have the laundry done and the dinner on the table by the time The Judge got home. It meant absolutely nothing. He was convinced that his mother knew this too. How could she not? After the same old thing everyday, pulling the bags under her eyes further down her drooping face, multiplying the wrinkles in her forehead and the grays in her hair, she had to know that any actions she still carried out in hopes of pleasing this man were in vain. Still she kept on as if there were still some flicker of hope in the bottom of that washing machine propelling her forward to another day of complete submission.

Ross ignored his mother's suggestion to retreat to go watch TV. He grabbed a dishrag and began to wipe down the counter to clean off the flour and cooking oil that had dripped from the pan of frying chicken on the stove. He ran some hot water in the sink and added dish washing liquid to create a sudsy bath for the dirty dishes. He then submerged the stray plates and glasses in the hot water to soak. Although she was hesitant at first, Ross knew that his mother appreciated the help and it showed in the slight smile that she gave her son as she stood next to him, stirring the mashed potatoes in a big silver pot. The circular motion her arm made with the spoon caused her hips to sway slightly. It reminded Ross of music, so he began to hum a tune that was burned into his brain all 18 years of his life. His mother sang the same melody to him when tucking him in at night and making him breakfast in the morning. It was their private time song --"Oooh Child" by the Stairsteps, a song that reminded them that they would always have each other. It was a sweet song. Her smile broadened as she recognized the tune and joined in with a much more powerful and soulful hum than Ross'. For those few moments, they were a happy team. As a grown man looking back on his early years, he would always smile when remembering those few precious moments that temporarily helped to ease the pain of his family life.

Suddenly, Ross felt another presence standing behind them in the kitchen. The person hadn't made a sound. Neither Ross nor his mother heard the front door open and close, nor did they hear the footsteps from the foyer, through the front hall and into the kitchen. His mother was still unaware that anyone, but the two of them, was in the room, and she continued rocking and singing, cooking and cleaning. But

Ross knew The Judge was there, standing and watching in angry silence. He felt the iciness of his father's condemnation circulate through their oversized country-style kitchen, bouncing off every wall, sliding on the floor, and dripping from the ceiling. But he kept right on humming and cleaning next to his mother, soaking up every ounce of their love and goodness that he could gather before The Judge snatched their happiness away. To him, it was a small victory, to be able to show his father that he couldn't control those brief moments when his mother was happy. And brief it was, as his father shattered the rhythm of their contentment with the callous bellow of his baritone.

"What the hell is going on in here?"

Ross' mother swung around to face her husband so fast, the spoon she was using to mix the potatoes dropped to the floor. The thick, white starch smeared across the tiles and the spoon landed near The Judge's feet. He looked down at the spoon and when he looked back up, his eyes held a raging contempt for his wife that issued from his pupils like tongues of fire.

Ross remembered a time, just ten years prior, when his mother was peppy and energized from executing the large responsibilities placed on her shoulders. She worked full time as an executive assistant and part time selling cosmetics. She still somehow managed to maintain a happy home and rear Ross with tender, loving attention. All of Joanna's devotion allowed Lawrence Pembroke the time, space and freedom to complete his law school studies and to begin his career ascent. Unfortunately, instead of gratitude for her outstanding work and sacrifice Joanna's competence and satisfaction bred an irrational resentment in Lawrence.

Joanna stammered and stuttered a bit before managing to get a word out, "Honey, hey! We weren't doing nothing--"

"'Anything'", he corrected her poor grammar with a sharp bark.

"We weren't doing a-n-ything special. I was just cooking dinner and finishing up the laundry."

"And my son? What do you have my son doing?"

"Oh, he was just on his way to the family room. I was just telling him to go watch the game or somethin'--"

"'Ing. I-n-g'."

"Or some-thing, while I finished up down here. Really, honey there was nothing funny going on."

"You're damn right. I don't see anything funny about coming home from work to a half-cooked dinner, a sloppy house with an equally sloppy wife, and my son in the kitchen acting like a woman!"

"He was just--"

"Joanna, don't you dare fix your lips to lie to me. I do all the damn work to provide for this family. You don't have anything more to do than take care of this house and you can't even manage to do that without turning my boy into a faggot!"

"I'm sorry, Lawrence."

"What did you just call me?" The Judge took a threatening step towards his wife. Ross could sense her nerves tightening and issuing spasms thorough her body. She lowered her head, like an obedient dog, before speaking again.

"I mean, Judge. I'm sorry, Judge. I don't know what I was thinking. It was stupid of me to have the boy help in the kitchen."

Ross tightened his grip on a cup he was washing over the

soapy water in the sink. The sound of his mother's weak and trembling voice sent a chill down his spine. Standing there and witnessing her abject humiliation, he realized he was disgusted. He slammed the cup down on the counter with a loud bang, "No! She didn't do anything wrong!"

Joanna jumped, but The Judge didn't flinch. He turned slowly to face his son with a look that half dared him for the challenge and half warned him to back down. Ross, visibly shaking, puffed up his chest and lifted his chin in the air. When he didn't get a response from his first outburst, he took it as a cue to make another.

"She spends all day cooking, cleaning and taking care of this house for you, and all you do is come home and yell at her and make her feel bad. It's not right!"

Joanna, seeing the annoyance in The Judge's eyes turning rapidly to rage, stepped in between father and son. She gently grabbed Ross' arm in an attempt to coax him into shutting his mouth before he got them both into more trouble than they could get themselves out of.

"Baby, stop all that nonsense now. It was wrong for you to try to do woman's work. Your father works hard to raise you to be a strong man and you're in here carrying on like you don't have any good sense. Now hush up right now and go on in the family room." Joanna looked up at her husband with a weak smile, in search of some approval. She never gave up on the possibility that she might say or do something that would please The Judge and regain the love he once lavished on her when they were first married.

Ross searched his mother's face for any trace of recognition of the outspoken and tenacious spirit he knew had once existed inside of her. He felt a tightening in his chest as he acknowledged that it no longer existed.

"Mama, what are you saying? What about all those things you tell me when it's just you and me? You don't like it when The Judge yells at you."

Joanna grabbed both his shoulders with panic in her eyes, "Shut up! You shut up right now!"

"No! If it wasn't for you, he wouldn't even be '*The Judge*'." Ross twisted his lips and spit out the grand title as if it was shit on his tongue. "Tell him, Mama. Tell him that if it weren't for you working seven days a week, paying all the bills and sending him through law school, he wouldn't be anything." The Judge raised both his eyebrows in mock astonishment. Ross continued, "You used to be strong Mama, and I know you still can be! Tell him! Tell him!"

"I said shut up!" She smacked Ross hard across the face. The sting clung to his left cheek and branded his cocoa skin with a red handprint. His mother looked frantically back and forth between her son and The Judge. Unsure of what else to do, she quickly covered her mouth so all that showed was the regret and sorrow in her eyes.

The Judge turned on his heel to walk out of the room. Before he reached the doorway, he called over his shoulder, "I will expect dinner on the table in no more than ten minutes." He left Ross and his mother alone, staring silently at each other.

Her eyes told him she was sorry. The way she slouched her body against the refrigerator, told him that she was defeated. As Ross watched her drowning in her own shame, once again his mind wandered back ten years to when his mother was treated and respected as his father's equal. She came home from work everyday bitching about "The Man", but still had enough energy to pay the bills, order carry-out, and make her husband feel like a king. She was different back then. She walked with her head held high and exuded confidence in every word that she spoke. She was the head of the household while Lawrence attended law school during the day and carried out her orders in the evening. Then, everything changed. The day Lawrence walked into the living room, dropped his briefcase on the floor, and told Joanna she didn't have to work anymore because he landed a job at one of the largest law firms in Michigan, their roles reversed and all of the dynamics between them instantly changed.

Ross stood in the kitchen for as long as he could stand to take in the hopelessness of the shell of a woman before him. A few seconds later, he left too. As he drove to his dorm, his weeping sharply punctuated the silence. While he cried and grieved for the love he had for his mother, he somehow managed to twist it into resentment and loathing for the person she had become.

He hated her as much as he loved her. He hated that she was too weak to stand up for herself and be the woman she used to be, but he could not fight the urge to protect her for those same reasons. She needed him, but he hated that he loved her too much to turn his back.

• • •

Ross carried this mixture of love and resentment into his adult life. When he thought of his mother, he tried to block the images of the weak and submissive woman she had become in order to hold onto the strong woman she used to be. But it rarely ever worked. The aggressive, go-getter he used to know was so far in the past, that he barely recognized her anymore. Therefore, he looked for her former image of strength in the women he dated. It surprised him, how difficult it was to find a strong, confident woman. So many women were ready to honor and obey the whims of a junior partner of the Creswell and Lattimore Law Firm, that they rarely ever showed any self-possession, initiative or assertiveness in their misguided attempts to snag him. It angered and disappointed him as he appointed and then dismissed each one like a member of a jury. He had begun to lose hope in finding a wife, when he met Jessica at a party thrown for one of his colleagues.

She definitely didn't fit his ideal image of the woman he thought he would fall for. The biggest obstacle was that she was white--or so he thought. He told himself for years that he would never mess with a white woman, his wife would be a sister for sure, but Jessica was something fresh, sassy and new that he could not ignore. He watched her the entire night. As she worked the room, all eyes were on her. She possessed a confident knowingness that Ross wanted to know more about. He noticed immediately that there was some tension between her and some of the other women there, but he could tell by the way she addressed them and how they backed down, that she was in control. She knew she had every attendee of that party in awe of her and she was enjoying her power. She was strong. She was a fighter and she knew how to get what she wanted. Ross knew it was completely out of character for him, but he couldn't stop himself from approaching her.

During their brief conversation, he was able to discern her background of poverty and desperation. Jessie was a woman surviving on her own, trying to make it out of the slums.

She was there at the party playing dress up, pretending to be someone she was not. But that didn't deter him. She was ripe for molding. All she needed was a little training and refinement and he could domesticate the fierce and powerful tiger that stood before him into "Mrs. Pembroke." He mentioned his professional credentials to her and watched in amusement as an eager light flickered in her eyes. She tried to act as if she was unimpressed, but Ross knew otherwise. He had her.

In the months of their courtship, she amused him with her survivalist outlook and naïve sense of life beyond Hamtramck. She spoke about her hardships, fighting for and protecting what was hers because no one else was going to do it. He impressed her with his considerate ways, sexiness, extensive wardrobe, education, genteel manners, and general lifestyle. He fell in love with her spirit and her determination and he expressed his love through tips and advice to improve her and prepare her for the life that she deserved.

After a quiet, intimate wedding, he ensured that her etiquette, appearance and grammar were impeccable. He sent her to college and helped her with her studies. He adorned her with beautiful clothes and fine jewelry. He even renamed her. She would no longer answer to Jessie, the name that represented her past. She was no longer that little girl who sought refuge and safety. Ross had transformed her into the distinguished and classy Mrs. Jessica Pembroke. He took great pride in his creation, as did she.

As time continued and the years passed, Ross discovered something in Jessica that he hoped he would never encounter. Whenever they argued, she would give in too early. When it was time to decide on a movie or dinner choice, it was always his decision. When he asked her of her opinion, she would abandon her own and always adopt his. It was whatever or whenever he wanted. Everything she did was for him and never for herself.

She was weak.

He thought that educating her and showing her a better way of life would give her a sense of empowerment and satisfaction. He thought he was nurturing the strong spirit he fell so deeply in love with. He expected her to take her newfound life and persona and run with it, blazing a mark in the world with his help and support. He failed to understand that "Jessie" remained hidden deep inside of all of the designer clothes, makeup and proper behavior. The insecure little girl, who would do anything to leave her old life behind, was too weak to stand on her own. Her self-esteem was too low to believe that she had any part in blossoming into the polished woman she had become. She believed she would be nothing without her husband and felt she had to become subservient in order to please him. It was necessary to keep the life he had been so generous to give her. It was a life, deep down, she felt she didn't deserve. The powerful, confident woman he met at that party was a smokescreen she had picked up from surviving in the tough environment in which she grew up. Yes, she knew how to fight to get what she wanted, but once she got it, she didn't know what to do with it.

Ross' disappointment grew into disrespect and resentment. She had swindled him into buying damaged goods. She was weak and it disgusted him. He treated her accordingly, as the weak are supposed to be treated. He scolded her when she did something wrong. He demeaned her whenever she was out of line. He used her for sex when it was convenient for him, and ignored her when it wasn't.

The two of them fell into roles with which Ross was all too familiar. He was The Judge and Jessica became Joanna. It was her fault, all her doing. She messed up a good thing and he was stuck with the pieces. On their fifth wedding anniversary, he presented his wife with a post-nuptial agreement drafted to outline the rigid guidelines of their marriage--their contractual agreement. He smiled to himself as he watched her sign the paper with gritted teeth and a defeated look in her eye. When he eventually did decide to walk away, she would leave the marriage with the same thing she came with--nothing. Daily, he thought about divorcing her and he wasn't quite sure why he didn't. It could have been complacency. He was comfortable in his life and settled into his role with ease. He would leave when he was ready. Things were just too easy for now. For the remainder of their marriage, he would keep her in line and she would obey, living forever in his shadows.

CHAPTER 8

SIMONE

"YOU know Brandon Stokes in the eleventh grade?"

"Yeah, what about him?"

"I heard he likes you."

"How do you know that?"

"He told his boy Jason, and Jason told his little sister, Adrienne and she told me yesterday in second period. He said he thinks you're cute and he wanna get witchu."

"Me? Why?"

"What do you mean *why*? He wants to *get with you*! And I think you should too. He fine as hell."

Kristen and Simone had become "frienemies" since their confrontation three weeks ago. On Kristen's part, it was more of a surrender. With an "If you can't beat her, join her" mentality she decided it was in her best interest to befriend Simone instead of resenting her. Simone was a great attraction. She got a lot of attention from the boys in school and Kristen was more than happy to lap up the overflow. They were official teenagers now and thought of themselves as being "basically grown" (at least their well-developed bodies would give any man who failed to notice their young faces that impression).

Kristen had already begun to experiment with sex and strongly encouraged Simone to do the same. That's what teenagers did and they needed to get a head start on the competition.

They were standing at Simone's locker in between classes. Kids packed the hall as they rushed to third period before the tardy bell rang. Simone rushed to grab her books and notepad, before slamming the locker door shut.

"Well, I don't want to get with him." Simone was hardly interested in "getting with" a boy. She knew what sex was like, and she knew that she hated it. It was disgusting. It made her feel worthless and dirty. There was no way she would let another man do what her father had done for the past six months. Besides, her mother would have a fit if she found out that she was having sex and she would have to ask God for forgiveness every night for the rest of her life.

"Girl, why not? He's sixteen! He has his license and everything. Sometimes he be drivin' his mom's Mercedes. It's sweet. You just need to get to know him and I *know* you'll change your mind. I'll tell Adrienne to tell Jason to tell him you want to meet him. Aiight?"

"No!" The thought terrified her. She didn't want to meet Brandon or any other boy. She didn't want to let anyone into her life and didn't want anyone to love her. The only man in the world that loved her caused her unimaginable pain. The thought of someone trying to touch her made her skin crawl and her eyes water. She had to get out of this.

"What's wrong witchu? Don't you like boys?"

"Yeah, I like boys. I just don't like *him.*"

"Whatever, you need to stop acting like that before people start thinking you're a lesbo. If you're gonna like *anybody,* it should be him. All the girls want to get with him, but he wants *you*. I'm gonna hook it up. You don't have to do anything with him that you don't want to. Ya'll can just kick it. You can meet him when we go to the Homecoming dance and don't worry, you'll like him. I promise."

"No" was not an option when talking with Kristen. It was going to happen the way she wanted and there was no room for argument. She spoke so forcefully, that Simone began to rationalize her thinking.

I don't want people to think I'm gay. Maybe I'll like him after I meet him. Maybe we don't have to have sex. We can just kiss and stuff like that. There is no way Mom would ever find out about that right? It can't be that bad.

Kristen was her girl and she was looking out for her. She was the one who defended Simone if anyone had anything bad to say. She walked the halls with her almost like a body-guard, threatening anyone who stepped out of line. It made Simone feel good, respected, even if it was manufactured. Without Kristen, it wouldn't be possible. She could trust her. So she did.

"Okay, I guess I can meet him."

"Good. You won't regret it, I promise. Look, I gotta go before I'm late to class. See you at lunch."

"Alright. Later."

Brandon Stokes was the typical big man on campus: tall, cute, affluent and captain of the varsity basketball team. He had every underclassman in Stonecreeke captivated with his charm and humor. He walked the halls with an arrogant stride. The girls fell mercilessly at his feet. He wasn't particularly intelligent though. Anyone who took the time to dig deeper past his surface could easily see that God had hit the boy with the stupid stick. Maybe he had a learning disability. Maybe he was just plain dumb, but you would never know it. He was a straight "A" student. The members of the faculty were even bigger fans of his than the students were. His parents gave a very generous donation to the school athletic fund; the Stokes' name branded the gymnasium walls. Teachers, who had the pleasure of having Brandon in their class, were strongly encouraged to do whatever was necessary to ensure that he passed -- and he did.

Simone knew exactly who he was, everyone did. He very rarely sought after a girl and definitely never chased one. For him to make it known that he wanted Simone was serious, and everyone assumed that he would get what he wanted. It made her stomach turn to think of him trying to kiss her or "get with her." She was nervous about their arranged meeting and wanted out desperately. But she felt trapped. She had to go to the dance. She couldn't let people think something was wrong with her. She had to be normal, happy, and friendly. She had to go. It was a week away. Her mother bought her dress, shoes and matching purse. She would have to just pull herself together and do what she had to do.

She continued to think about her upcoming encounter and coach herself into compliance as she walked to class. Maybe it wouldn't be so bad, meeting this boy. What if she did really like him? What if she became his girlfriend and let him whisk her away into a world where beauty wasn't a curse, but a blessing, a world where her father never touched her and became the perfect father that he once was. They would become close, deep in puppy love, and eventually all of her pain and agony would be a distant memory.

Yes, it could work. It could be the answer to her prayers.

She mentally rehearsed her meeting with Brandon as she approached the classroom door. She pictured the way she would smile at him to show him that she was into him and how she'd flip her hair to let him know that she was "basically grown" and sexy. She would tilt her head to the side when she talked to him and stand bowlegged, as she had seen Kristen do when she talked to other boys. She would be nice, outgoing, and flirtatious, the girl that he dreamed of. They could become the power couple of Stonecreeke Academy, earning everyone's admiration and adoration. It couldn't be too bad. He *was* cute and he *did* have a car too. She said a small prayer while she walked down the halls, considering the pros and cons of hooking up with Brandon Stokes. She finally decided: she was going to get her man.

CHAPTER 9

RYAN

"SO, have you made a decision about your relationship?"

Ryan kept her head down as she responded to her therapist's question, "Yes."

"What are you going to do?"

"I'm going to stay with Anthony."

"But you said that you're not happy. Is that a healthy decision?"

"When we're together, I'm happy. We only fight when we're apart. We can be happy together. We just need to work on it."

"Is he beginning to change?"

"He wants to."

"He wants to, but has he?"

"No."

"I know you've said that you two haven't spent time together lately. Have you talked to him about that and how it makes you feel?"

"Yeah."

"What happened?"

"He promised me that he would make things right. He

begged me not to leave him. He said that he needed me. Then…"

"Then?"

"Then, he stood me up again."

"How did that make you feel?"

"How do you think it made me feel? Like shit."

"Why do you think he keeps doing things that make you feel bad if he wants to change?"

"I don't know. We argue a lot. He says that I nag him and get on his case too much and it makes him not want to be around me."

"Do you believe him?"

"Sometimes."

"What do you nag about?"

"The usual."

"Marriage?"

"We *are* going to get married. We talk about it all the time."

"Ryan, do you ever think he may be stringing you along with the promise of marriage in the future?"

Ryan twisted her face as if she smelled an offensive odor. She shifted in her seat, "Stringing me along? Is that what *you* think?"

"I'm not implying anything; I just want to know what your thoughts are, honestly. Does anything like that ever cross your mind, or do you believe his intentions to marry you are genuine?"

"Of course they're genuine. Why else would he say it?"

"Ryan, you told me that he used to treat you well, that the two of you used to be happy. Tell me more about that."

"Well, it's just like I said before. He was perfect. We had

a relationship straight out of a fairytale. He would call me all day long, sometimes seven or eight times a day and we would talk for hours. We would talk about everything and he would listen too. I mean, he'd really be into what I was talking about, even if we were at work. He sent me flowers every Friday with cute little love notes attached. He took me out at least two to three times a week, and if we didn't go out he would just come over to watch TV or I would go to his house. He did thoughtful little things, like burning CDs with my favorite songs and driving all the way from his job to visit me on my lunch break just because he wanted to see my face. Everyone loved him at first, Lauren, my mother. Everybody at work was so jealous. We even started talking about marriage just a few months into dating. No man has ever treated me like that. No one has ever made me feel like I was more than just a piece of ass or made me believe he would stick around for more than just the sex. He made me feel beautiful, inside and out. I've never experienced anything like it."

"You said that you started to notice a change about four months ago. He began to treat you differently. Standing you up and telling what you believe to be lies and excuses for his strange behavior. Why do you think that is?"

"I really don't know. He says that it's stress from work. I don't have anything else to go on, so I just accept that."

"Deep down, you think it may be more to it than that?"

"Sometimes, but then again, I don't know. I mean, it has only been four months. I don't want to be so quick to jump to conclusions."

"Ryan, do you think you may be settling?"

"What do you mean?"

"You have a lot going for you. You are a young, attractive

woman. You have a great career as an accountant, and you have a lot of potential to take your life wherever you want it to go. Why do you think you are settling for a relationship that you are unhappy with?"

"Who said I was unhappy? I'm just a little stressed. This is temporary. Every couple goes through their fair share of problems before they walk down the aisle. Anthony and I are no different."

"Are you happy?"

Ryan paused to think about the question. At one point, she thought she knew the answer, but now she was unsure.

"Ryan, what are you holding on to?"

Ryan looked nervously around the room as she gained the courage to admit her real fear, "Without him, I'm alone. I'd be thirty-four and alone. If it doesn't happen now, I'll never get married. I'll never have a child. I'll grow old and die by myself. Nobody wants that. Nobody wants that feeling."

"You know Ryan, being single and happy is a realistic possibility. Many people do it. I'm not saying you will be single for the rest of your life, but you must learn to be happy with yourself before you can have a successful relationship with someone else."

Ryan didn't respond.

"How have you been feeling in general? I mean just on a regular, day-to-day basis."

A blanket of silence covered the small office. Ryan's eyes watered as she prepared to answer her therapist's question. She felt like the walking dead, a zombie in the twilight zone. She had been feeling that way for weeks. She could barely make it out of bed in the morning. Her body was heavy and her head pounded with a migraine. She showed up to work two hours late. She hated her job. Once she got there, she cried for no reason until her supervisor sent her home. Her appetite was almost completely gone. She ate only when she reminded herself to do so; most of the time she forgot. She was irritable, lonely, and miserable. She felt like she was dying from a slow death. Her life was falling apart. She was losing her mind.

"I feel like shit. I think you need to recommend that the doctor increase my dosage of Xanax, and I also need a refill."

The daily dosage of Xanax was not doing the trick. Ryan started out popping one pill a day, just as the doctor instructed. It was okay at first. The first three to four weeks it was a wonder drug, calming her nerves with a numbing effect. She wasn't happy, but she wasn't sad; she wasn't crying every ten minutes and then screaming the next. She was cool, relaxed and oblivious to the stress and chaos that was her life. She found herself smiling occasionally and was actually shocked at the sound of her own laughter while having dinner with Lauren. But that was several weeks ago, almost two months to be exact. It was a teaser, a small hint of what it was like to be normal, if one considered normal behavior apathetic and emotionless. If she had to choose between being languid and blah or depressed and miserable -- well, it was not a difficult choice to make.

Depression was something that seized Ryan like a surprise attack, rendering her weak and helpless. She lost herself inside of a dark coldness, imprisoned by the cold restraints of the cruel illness. She could feel herself slipping deeper and faster into a sea of hopeless desolation. She was losing herself and no one could stop it. Lauren saw what was happening to her dearest friend but could do nothing to pull her back to safety.

After several attempts to "cheer her up", with dinners, shopping, and girls' nights, she eventually had no other options but to sit by and watch as the once vibrant spirit of her friend dwindled into barely a flicker. She cried with her as she was suffering as well. It was weighing heavily on their relationship.

The two were closer than identical twins. No one understood Ryan as Lauren did. No one knew her as she did and no one ever would. The same was true of Ryan's knowledge and understanding of Lauren. They were equally intelligent, outspoken, and perceptive, often finishing each other's sentences, saying the same things at the same time, and laughing at their own unspoken jokes. It was highly irksome to anyone that was around both of them at the same time. They had tiffs and even arguments, but only because they were just as much alike as they were different. Each one had to make her opinion known and refused to shut up until she was satisfied that the other understood her point. But at the end of the day their friendship remained strong. That was until now.

The petty arguments became more and more frequent, as Ryan fought desperately to defend her failing relationship with Anthony to Lauren's all-too rational and reasonable insight, that Anthony was the root of Ryan's misery. Lauren didn't understand the relationship that she had with Anthony. They were deeply connected. They were in a place where no one else could go. Lauren couldn't see that he loved her more than anything and would change right now if he could. He just had too much going on right now. There were countless pressures from work, and he had some financial things going on as well. Anyone would crack under such burden.

No matter how hard Ryan tried, she couldn't make her friend see what she saw. She couldn't make her understand. So she just stopped trying. She adopted a sort of take it or leave it mentality. Lauren took it, but she couldn't prepare herself for what she was taking on in its entirety. She would soon find out that Ryan was a junkie fighting an addiction, her drug of choice: love. To addicts nothing matters more than getting that high. They will do whatever it takes to get it, and will take anyone who tries to get in their way head on. All the while, the source of the addiction slowly takes over their lives. It was a tragedy.

Ryan's therapist observed, "You shouldn't be out of Xanax so soon. We just filled the prescription three weeks ago. How many pills have you been taking per day?"

"Well, I *was* doing the recommended dosage: one pill a day. Then, it stopped working. I mean I get stress and anxiety more than just once a day! I have a very hectic life, you know. I go through a lot of shit. I mean with work, and Anthony. It's so hard to deal with. Plus, the doctor told me that I should take it whenever I feel an attack coming on. So that's what I did. Sometimes it was three times in one day! I still feel just as bad as I did in the beginning. I just went from 150 to 300mg of the antidepressant, but it's not good enough alone. I need the Xanax to compliment it."

"Ryan, as we've discussed several times before, your condition can be successfully treated with a combination of medication and therapy. But if you want to be mentally healthy, you have to lead a healthy lifestyle. You have to make some life changes. To be perfectly honest, the relationship that you have with Anthony is not good for you. It is extremely damaging and I am certain that his actions and your inability to cope with what he is doing to you have triggered your depression. Your doctor and I can continue to increase your dosage, but it won't do any good. You will remain in the same emotionally unstable state that you're in until you decide to leave him permanently."

The therapist looked Ryan straight in the eyes with deep concern and empathy covering her face. This was serious. This destructive relationship was something she wanted to get out in the open for the last several sessions. Ryan had been making regular weekly visits for the last four months with very little progress. There were small but distinct improvements in the first couple of months with the anti-depressant accompanied by the Xanax. However, it was only a temporary fix.

"Look, I thought you were supposed to be helping me to be happy!" Ryan snarled.

"I am Ryan, but you can't be happy staying in the same unhealthy relationship. You need --"

"What I need is for you to stop judging me and to up my damn dosage." Ryan was irritated. She didn't come to be lectured. She fidgeted in her seat, crossing and uncrossing her legs in agitation. She was ready to jump up and get in her therapist's face, but she thought better of it.

"I am not judging you. Everyone has something in their life that they can change for the better. Ending this relationship is the change that I think you need to make. Anthony is emotionally abusive and he is driving you deeper into depression. Also, I am genuinely concerned that you may be developing a dependency to the drugs. The last thing I want is for you to become addicted to Xanax. There can be some very dangerous side-effects."

"How could you sit here and lie to my face, telling me

you want to see me happy? How could you possibly want to see me happy if you're telling me to leave the only man that I have ever loved? He's the only one that's done more for me than to just fuck me and leave me. He is the only one who truly loves me for who I am. We're getting married, and you want me to leave him?"

She stood up, bending down to meet her therapist eye to eye. "You don't want to see me happy. You don't give a damn about me. You're not married. Shit, I doubt that you even have a man. As a matter of fact, when was the last time you got some dick? Huh? But you want to tell me what I should do with my relationship? If you really wanted to help me, you'd tell me how I can work this shit out instead of telling me to walk away from him so I can be alone and lonely like your ass. How did you get into this field any damn way? I mean it's obvious that you have issues of your own. You weigh what? Like 250, 300 pounds? What in the hell makes you *eat* so damn much? You're obviously not happy, but you think you can tell *me* how to be happy? Well, fuck you! I don't need this shit! I'm outta here!"

The therapist stood to meet Ryan at eye level. She spoke in a calm voice, trying to regain control of the situation. "You told me that he is not willing to go to counseling. If he is not willing to change, then you have to make a choice. Either it's your health or your demise."

Ryan turned on her heel, whipping her hair into her face. She mumbled to herself,

Everybody claims to know me better than I know myself. Everybody wants to pass judgment on me. Well, they need to take a long hard look at themselves. Nobody's perfect.

She struggled to grab her jacket and purse resting on

the chair she was sitting in. Yanking the jacket hanging on the back of the chair, she caused the chair to tilt on its side, balancing on one leg, threatening to fall. After cursing the chair, she stomped towards the exit. Swinging the door to the office open with an angry force, the doorknob banged against the wall. The thud made her jump a little, but she maintained her grim face, showing the therapist that she wasn't shaken.

"Ryan, please wait. Don't walk out. You're only walking away from your problems." The therapist was starting to sound desperate. "Ryan, please! We can work together and we *will* make it through this."

Ryan swung her head around and glared into the eyes of the woman who was trying to ruin her life, "Are you going to refill my prescription?"

The therapist stood silent. A look of defeat crept across her face as she looked towards the floor and slowly shook her head, "No, Ryan. I will not do that," she said in almost a whisper.

"Then, *we* ain't doin' shit. This was my last visit." Having made her point Ryan stomped out of the room, leaving the door open to reveal her therapist standing motionless and speechless, with her good intentions thwarted.

Ryan rushed past the receptionist's desk, failing to pay her ten-dollar co-pay. She thought she heard the receptionist say something in an attempt to stop her, but she was too consumed with her own indignation to pay attention, let alone take the time to write a check. She would wait for the bill in the mail. Once outside the office building, she rushed to her car and sat silent in the driver's seat for several moments. Her hands were on the steering wheel with her head facedown and her forehead pressed into the BMW emblem. She was deep in thought.

How in the hell am I going to get more pills? Come on Ryan think! What am I going to do? Who can I call? Who has access to these pills? Shit…if this stupid, fat bitch knew how to act I wouldn't have this problem!

Suddenly, she snapped out of her thoughts as she remembered the dinner party she and Anthony attended two weeks ago for her accounting firm. As they mixed and mingled after dinner, laughing and sharing stories with her co-workers, Anthony ran into someone he knew. Dr. Gloria Taylor greeted them with a wide smile and eager conversation. She knew Anthony from college and called him by his last name. The two of them carried on social chitchat for several minutes before she handed both Ryan and Anthony her business cards and sauntered off to mingle with the other guests. Before tucking it inside her small handbag, Ryan glanced at the card. The words, "Dr. Gloria Taylor Certified Professional Psychiatrist. Helping to develop effective communication, stress management, problem solving and coping skills", were printed across the laminated card in calligraphy.

Finally raising her head from the steering wheel, Ryan grabbed her purse from the passenger seat and searched frantically for the card. It was not in the back pocket as she remembered placing it. She turned the bag upside down and scrambled through the credit cards, makeup, pens, receipts and cash. She had just switched purses that morning to match her outfit and threw everything in at once. Finally, she caught sight of the shiny, green card and called the number in bold, black print immediately on her new cell phone.

She was in luck. One of Gloria's patients had just cancelled his appointment for that evening and she was welcome to go in at 6:30 that evening if she was available. Of course she was available. She would be there at 6:20! Relieved to discover a new dealer to feed her jones, Ryan regained her composure and even started feeling good. But she had an immediate craving that she needed to address at that moment. She looked at her purse's emptied contents for her near empty prescription bottle. She didn't see it. After checking on the floor of the car and under the seat, she spotted it stuck in between the passenger seat and the gearshift. She grabbed the small bottle and popped one pill dry with no water. She would make a stop at the nearest gas station for some juice to wash it down.

Now ready to take on the world and to kill some time before her appointment, she started the car and began to pull out of the parking lot. Just as her foot tapped the gas, her cell rang. It was Anthony calling. She put the transmission back into park. Nowadays the police were pulling people over for talking on a cell phone while driving.

She answered (sexily, she hoped), "Hey, baby."

"Hey, what's up?" His voice was flat and emotionless. Almost as if *she* had called *him* and he wasn't happy to hear from her.

"Nothing. I was just thinking about you. What are you doing?" She decided to ignore his tone. He probably just had a long day at work. He would talk to her about it when he felt like it.

"The better question is what are *you* doing?"

"Oh, well, I just got done shopping with Lauren. We went to Somerset. I didn't find anything I liked, but you know Lauren's impulsive ass bought everything she could stand to carry with two hands."

"You were at the mall?"

"Yes." Ryan could sense that he doubted her story. She knew she was about to be in trouble. Something was wrong.

"Where is Lauren?"

"I just dropped her off. I'm on my way home now. Is something wrong? You sound like you're upset."

"Should I be?"

"What?"

"Upset."

"Well, I don't see why you would be. Come on baby, I don't want to argue unless you have some good make up sex for me later." She giggled.

"Tell me this, Ryan. If you were at the mall shopping with Lauren, why didn't you answer my phone calls? I called you five times and I got your voicemail each time. What's up with that?"

He caught Ryan off guard. She wasn't expecting that and was unprepared to answer. Cell phones weren't permitted in the counseling center, so she'd left it in the car. He didn't know about her therapy sessions, and he was not about to find out now.

"My phone was on vibrate in my purse, so I didn't feel it going off. It's no big deal, really. Don't trip, babe."

"Your phone was on vibrate, huh? You expect me to fall for that bullshit? Tell me what the fuck you were doing!"

"Wait, calm down okay? I told you, the phone was in my purse. You don't believe me, call Lauren and ask her. We were shopping! What is with you jumping down my throat?"

"Okay, I see you want to play some silly ass games with me today. Well, I'm not falling for the bullshit. You were with another man weren't you?"

"What!" Ryan's eyes almost popped out of her head. He knew without any doubt that she had never and would never cheat on him. He knew that.

Why is he doing this?

"You heard me. You think I'm stupid don't you?" he never raised his voice and kept the lack of emotion.

"Baby, you're really trippin'. You know I would never be with another man. You know I would never even think about being with someone else. What is your problem?"

"Oh, I don't have a problem, but *you* will if you don't tell me where you were, who you were with, and what you were doing. If you think I'll have a wife that can't be trusted, you need to think again."

"What are you saying?"

"I'm saying, maybe you aren't marriage material."

This bizarre episode was starting to piss her off. He was accusing her of something she didn't do, something he *knew* she didn't do. And now she wasn't marriage material? It was ridiculous. Where was the trust that she had done nothing to foil? Her feelings of irritation quickly changed to anger and offense. "Where in the hell do you get off accusing me of cheating? You are the one who is missing in action at certain times of the day. You are the one who stands me up all the damn time. But *I'm* the one who's cheating? I wish you were standing right here so I could slap the shit out of you! You come to me with these accusations and you have absolutely no reason to believe that I would do such a thing. You are really starting to piss me off."

After taking a deep breath, Ryan decided to change her approach, despite his fault, she still had hope for resolution. "I hope you don't think that we will be going to dinner tonight with you thinking that I've been with somebody else. If you apologize right now, perhaps we can forget the whole thing."

"Dinner?" he snickered, "Tell that nigga you were with to take your ass to dinner. You must think I'm a fool. I've made other plans."

This was unbelievable. Was he doing this on purpose? They had dinner reservations at Morton's at 8 o'clock. Was he trying to get out of it? Ryan was genuinely confused and equally frustrated. "What? You can't cancel on me! And how is it that you already have other plans?"

"I decided to go out to the bar with some of my boys on about the fourth unanswered phone call. Look Ryan, I have to go. I'm about to go to the mall myself and buy something new to wear. Later."

"You fucking asshole! You're not going anywhere! Do you hear me? You can't do this shit to me. We have dinner plans and we're keeping them. You know I wasn't with anybody. You know that! Why are you doing this?" She cried and screamed into the phone, but there was silence on the other end. He had already hung up. After dialing and redialing his number several times with no answer, she threw the phone down on the passenger seat and picked up the bottle of Xanax. She dumped the last pill into her mouth to calm her shaking hands and her steadily increasing heart rate. Swallowing it with ease and laying her head back on the headrest, she closed her eyes as she waited for the high to kick in.

After about ten minutes, she felt her world become lighter, friendlier. Things seemed a little slower and mellow. She had taken two pills within the last 30 minutes so her feeling of euphoria was expedited and increased.

Yes, yes, yes. This is what I'm talking about. I could sit here like this all day.

She had forgotten the disturbing conversation with Anthony. There was nothing else on the planet but her and her high. She was floating through the sky on a cloud of peace and serenity. After several moments of blissful tranquility, it was time to go. She was getting hungry and decided to grab a bite to eat before heading to Gloria's office. Once again, she put the gear into reverse and began to back out of the parking space. A dark grey SUV backed out of the parking spot about five or six spaces away from hers. Continuing out of the lot and onto the busy street, Ryan crossed over into the far left lane in order to get onto the freeway entrance ramp. She did not notice as the SUV also exited the parking lot to cross into the far left lane. Ryan was followed onto I-96.

CHAPTER 10

JESSICA

"YOUR skin is so beautiful, baby. Not one wrinkle. You look just the same as you did sixteen years ago when I married you."

Jessica giggled and blushed with embarrassment.

"No, don't look away. I want to see those beautiful, bright eyes." Ross caressed her face with the loving touch of a man in absolute awe of his wife. "Stand up, baby. I want to see that sexy body of yours."

She stood at the edge of the bed in between her husband's open legs. She untied her robe, revealing her breasts and erect nipples. She took his right hand and guided it from her neck and down to her navel. His left hand followed to travel slowly up her thighs until it reached its final destination, her ass. He massaged and squeezed gently, but with enough pressure to send a chill up her spine.

"I love you, Jessica. Do you know that? Do you know how much I love you?"

Jessica did not answer. A passionate kiss was her reply, a kiss she had been holding in for weeks in anticipation of that moment. This was the moment when her husband took her into his arms and adored her as he once did long ago, when her husband treated her like the loyal, caring wife that she was. She had been waiting for this for months and she was more than ready to show her appreciation.

He pulled back slowly from their kiss, "Just look at you. I couldn't ask for anyone more perfect than you. Take off your robe."

Jessica removed the robe from her shoulders and let it fall slowly to the floor. Its satin fabric slipped seductively over her soft, freshly showered skin. She stood naked before him, staring at him with bedroom eyes and a sexy half smile.

"What did I ever do to deserve you?"

"You've been a perfect man. I'm the one who doesn't deserve you."

He stood up and turned her around, grabbing her by her waist, "Come over here and look. Look at yourself in the mirror. I want you to see what I see. You have the body that women half your age would kill for." He guided her to the full-length mirror mounted on the back of the wardrobe. She smiled at the sight of her naked image. She *was* beautiful. Her body was a work of art.

From behind, her husband grabbed her full, ripe breasts and buried his face in her neck, kissing and sucking until she let out a soft sound of excitement.

He looked up, "Do you love me, Jessica?" He was speaking to her reflection in the mirror. He was so romantic, intense, and dramatic. He could have played the lead role in the next hot romance drama on the big screen. He spoke with a low, almost groggy, breathy tone that tickled her ears with each syllable. She was falling in love repeatedly in a matter of minutes.

"Of course, I love you, baby. I love you more than anything in this world. You know that."

"Good. Then you won't mind if I make love to you right here on the floor, in front of this mirror. I want you to see how your beautiful body looks when I'm inside of you."

Jessica was dripping wet with arousal. She could hardly contain herself. She envisioned the sexy image of their bodies intertwined and the contrast of her smooth, creamy skin against his milk chocolate flesh.

"Of course, baby. You can do whatever you want with me." She turned around to face him and began to unbutton his shirt. He ran his fingers through her long curly locks. He had grown to love the unruly, tousled look he had criticized a few days before. After removing his shirt, she moved down to his pants, quickly unfastened his belt and unzipped his fly. She moved both hands around to his backside and made his pants drop to the floor with a quick push. He stood, fully erect, before her. His 9-inch penis pointed toward her, inviting her to partake. She reached for it through the small opening in the crotch of his boxer briefs and playfully, almost reverently, fondled him.

He laughed, "Damn, you know that's my spot. Be careful with that thing."

She replied with a giggle as well. His "spot" was so obvious. While some men will give general places on their bodies, such as the ears or the neck, the coveted designation of his "spot", her husband was much more direct and to the point. You want to turn him on? Grab his dick and he's yours. Case closed.

"I know this is what you like," she purred as she pumped her hand back and forth across the smooth skin of his shaft.

She whispered her indecent proposals into his neck between kisses, "I know how to do all of the things you like. Just tell me what you want and I'll do anything. I'm all yours."

"Anything?"

"Anything, baby. Just say the word."

"Well, let's see what you can do. I want you to lie down and get --"

Tap tap tap tap tap.

A soft knock on the door interrupted Ross' erotic demands. Jessica tried her best to stay focused, ignoring the rapid knocking. She didn't want to stop, she couldn't stop, not when they were about to make the sweetest love that has ever been made. There was no stopping when he was about to taste her succulent sweetness and she was about to feel his prodigious passion.

She had waited for so long. She was a patient, understanding and diligent wife. She had remained obedient and submissive, letting her man take control just as he had demanded. She was attentive, affectionate, and eager to please. She was willing, waiting, and gave her husband the respect that he deserved. But most of all, she was down right horny! Nothing and no one was going to stop that moment. She was ready to do some things that would make porn stars blush and giggle. Jessica ignored the tapping and kept her eyes on the prize. She concentrated on stroking him with the precision and expertise of a professional.

"What, baby? What do you want me to do? Tell me!"

His breathing was heavy, giving in to her salacious strokes, "I want you to lie down and get --"

Tap tap tap tap tap tap tap.

"Get--"

Tap tap

"Damnit!" Jessica grabbed her robe from the floor and rushed to cover herself. Keeping the robe closed with her hand, she stomped over to the door and opened it just beyond a crack. Delores stood on the other side, holding a laundry basket on her hip.

"Ma'am?" Concern and suspicion pervaded Delores' heavy Southern accent.

Visibly irritated, Jessica snapped, "Yes, Delores?"

"Are you okay, Ma'am?" She tried her best to look past her into the room, but failed as Jessica's array of wild hair blocked her view. .

"I'm fine, Delores. I'm a little busy right now. What can I do for you?" Jessica was quickly loosing her patience and her cool.

Is she stupid or something? They didn't teach her how to catch a hint in Alabama?

Delores stood on her toes to look over Jessica's head, "Are you sure? I heard voices. Is someone here with you? I don't want to intrude." Delores could indeed catch a hint. She sensed that something was wrong. Cynicism and distrust fueled her initial concern. Jessica could hear it in her voice. Something was going on that she wasn't supposed to know about.

"That's ridiculous. No one is here with me. It's the middle of the day. Who could possibly be here?" Ross wouldn't be home from work for at least four hours. Delores knew that, and it increased her wariness. She was loyal to Ross. Being a black woman from the South, surviving Jim Crowe, attack dogs and water hoses, Delores instinctively favored Ross and distrusted his white-looking wife. All white people were the devil and she only tolerated Jessica out of respect and love for Ross. She knew one day the cracker would show her true colors and the cold and deceitful devil would reveal herself. Delores was out to protect the best interest of her employer. If something was going on in his home that he should know about, she was going to find out.

Delores allowed several seconds of awkward silence to pass before she spoke, "I don't know, I'm just checking. I thought I heard a man's voice, someone talking to you." She focused carefully on Jessica's expressions. Her eyes glared as if she was trying to look right through her and into the bedroom.

Jessica kept her composure, "Well, you were mistaken. It must have been the television. Again, is there something I can do for you?" She was getting nervous.

"Actually Ma'am, I am doing the laundry now. I will need to collect your dirty clothes." She pushed the door all the way open with the laundry basket and pushed her way past the mistress of the house with a forceful thrust, inspecting the scene as she entered the empty bedroom. She glanced at the 50-inch flat screen TV mounted on the opposite wall. The power was off. She stole a suspicious glance at Jessica. "I will only be a moment."

Jessica was obviously uneasy, and her embarrassment crept through her voice with each word that she spoke. "Yes, please hurry. I have some things I need to take care of in private."

She watched as the housekeeper entered the wardrobe and filled her empty basket with her and her husband's soiled clothes, lingering a little longer than necessary near the closet door. She was checking the premises for trespassers. After several moments, her curiosity seemed to have been satisfied and she turned to leave.

"Thank you, Delores."

"My pleasure. If there is anything else that you need, be sure to call me."

"I won't need anything else. Why don't you take the rest of the day off? You've been working hard all day. You deserve a break."

"Thank you, but I'd rather stay. The Mister will be home soon and I have to make sure dinner is prepared to his liking. You know how he is. Everything has to be perfect. Nothing out of place, nothing that doesn't-- *belong*."

The overprotective housekeeper, kept a slow, steady pace as she walked out of the door, giving Jessica a quick once over before finally leaving.

Jessica quickly closed and locked the door behind her. Her face was flushed red with embarrassment. She walked back to the bed and plopped her head facedown on the pillows. She was definitely no longer in the mood to finish out her fantasy love scene. She reached under the pillow to retrieve the dildo she had covered before answering the door.

"Mr. Johnson" had become a close companion over the years and was upgraded to her best friend in the last six months. He was always there for her, always waiting in anticipation to feel her thighs wrapped around his chocolate-colored body. He would hum her a soft, seductive lullaby while stroking her to ecstasy. He knew exactly what to do to make her feel like the young, sexy goddess she once was. Shit, who needed a man when all of your sexual satisfaction came ready made in a light pink box with batteries included. Who needed a husband when you could rock yourself to sleep with electrifying vibrations and mind-blowing orgasms? She had all that she needed right in front of her. Mr. Johnson…

Shit! Who in the hell was she kidding? That overpriced, silicone piece of trash didn't begin to come close to her husband's soft, sexy whispers tickling her ear, his big hands squeezing her ass, his rock hard body pressing up against hers, and their sweat intertwined, soaking their bodies. Mr. Johnson was nothing but a quick fix, a substitute (and a poor one at that). It was only temporary though. Jessica knew it would only be a matter of time before she was able to win her husband back. He deserved an amazing woman, one who brought all of his fantasies to life. He needed a woman who made him swoon every time he caught sight of her and made him drop to his knees with a love-induced illness that only more love could cure. He needed a woman to heighten his senses and leave his head spinning with a love hangover. He needed a superwoman and that is exactly what she was going to give him. But first she had to look the part.

She put the dildo back in his proper place, the bottom drawer inside of the wardrobe, under her neglected lingerie. She walked back to the full-length mirror, leaning in to inspect her face. She massaged her forehead with her index and forefinger, the area between her eyebrows. It was so smooth, youthful and, most importantly, wrinkle free. She smiled at her reflection. The Botox injection had done its trick. It had only been four days, and already she could see a difference. She was nervous for the first appointment, not knowing exactly what to expect. However, not long after being there, she realized that she needed it more than ever, before she withered into an old unsightly creature. Sitting next to a middle-aged woman in the waiting room, about ten years older than she, Jessica saw her future. The woman had a drooping face and was in desperate need of a face-lift. Crow's feet invaded her eyes. Laugh lines infringed upon the outline of her mouth. Wrinkles ravaged her brow line. It was horrible. It was down right terrifying and Jessica had to do something about her flaws then before it was too late. She could barely stand to look at the woman. Instead, she kept her eyes glued to the *Good Housekeeping* magazine in front of her. Looking at the ravaged woman for too long was certain to turn her face into stone.

She had started her journey back through time. She would take herself back 16 years when she and her future husband just met. She was vibrant, beautiful and sexy, strongly desired by the man she loved and she was determined to turn back the hands of time so that they could relive their glory days. He would come around. He would see her for who she really was. She continued to let her fingers explore her face, eventually resting on her lips. Her lips were thin and pale, far from the sexy, lush, pouty lips of the super models. She puckered her lips in a weak attempt to make them look fuller, biting them to make the blood rush and give them a slight rosy hue. Her collagen injection appointment was the following week and she couldn't wait to see Ross' reaction. She would have big, beautiful, flirtatious lips like the real black women she loathed and secretly envied. She was well on her way to perfection.

CHAPTER 11

SIMONE

SIMONE stared down at the tiny, egg-shape pill in her hand. It was amazing that such a small thing could have such a huge impact on her entire body, to prevent something as miraculous as the conception of life. She stood still in her bathroom staring at it, thinking of the power and control it had over her.

She had been on birth control pills for two months. While most girls dreaded their "monthly curse", Simone was relieved at the onset of each period. It was her savior, a monthly exit from her daily nightmare. She knew once she had started her period and was able to get pregnant, there was no way her father would risk the exposure. There would be no rationalizing it. Her mother would never believe that her precious, near-perfect daughter would be so careless as to have sex at such an early age, especially unprotected. There would have to have been some other explanation and Simone would provide her with the true one. Her father knew that. He also knew that what he was doing was an abomination, and to get his daughter pregnant would make it all too real, an in his face reminder that he was a rapist, a pedophile -- a monster. However, he was too selfish to give up his guilty pleasure. He wouldn't risk the pregnancy, but he was too self-serving to give up his indecency. He insisted she start the pill. Simone eavesdropped on the debate between her parents as she stood in the hallway outside the living room. She knew her fate before the conversation even started.

"If we put her on birth control, we will be sending her the wrong message, that it's okay to go out and have sex and not have to worry about the consequences. I do not want my baby out here sleeping with every nasty little boy who says he loves her," her mother protested.

"Come on, you have to give her more credit than that. You have to have some faith in the daughter that *you have* raised. The fact of the matter is she is not that little girl you think she is. Kids are having sex at younger ages these days and neither you nor I will be able to prevent that. If she wants to do it, she'll do it, regardless of if she is on birth control or not. Better to be safe than sorry," her father reasoned smoothly.

"I'm sorry, honey. I just don't know about this one. She's only fourteen! She's probably not even thinking about sex and getting pregnant yet. I don't want to go and put those things in her head."

"That's right, she's fourteen and kids are starting to have sex at ten and eleven! I'm telling you. You have no idea what is going on when we aren't around. I'm not saying that's Simone, but I *am* saying that we don't know when she will decide to take that leap, and as parents we have the responsibility of making sure she is prepared when she does. We are good parents and we have done a great job with raising her. She has a good head on her shoulders and her priorities are intact. She knows right from wrong and she understands the seriousness and consequences of having sex. She will understand this too and we have to show her that we trust her."

Her father's persistence wore her mother down. This was their third conversation on the topic and he was making perfect sense. She continued to listen as her mother started to cave in, "Okay, I guess I can think about it. We will need to sit down and have a talk with her about this, you and I together. But I'm not making any promises. I will *think* about it."

"That's all I ask, honey."

Her father kissed her mother on the forehead. Simone's heart sank. She knew, just as well as he did, that "I'll think about it", was for her mother, no different from saying, "Absolutely without a doubt." The debate went just as every other conversation held between the two. Her mother never really had any power over anything, and they all knew that. He made the money, so he made the decisions. That was the law of the land and her mother's only job was to follow suit. So that settled it. Simone found herself sitting on the examination table of her mother's gynecologist the following week.

"Have you ever had sex before, Simone?" The doctor was a petite, Asian woman with a serious demeanor. She looked straight into Simone's eyes as if she knew the answer to her question without receiving a response. Her voice was pleasant and caring. It was obvious she was trying to ensure that Simone felt relaxed and comfortable. Immediately, Simone trusted her.

Her mother stood opposite Simone, holding her breath in anticipation of her answer.

"No." The lie rolled easily off her tongue. It was automatic and, in a way, the truth. She hadn't had what she considered to be sex. Yes, her father had violated and used her. He had raped and molested her. He ripped her childhood and happiness from her loins. But sex? She had never had sex. Based on her infrequent hearsay, sex was something two people enjoyed. Sex felt good and left you wanting more. Sex was something the boys bragged about and the girls giggled about. She had yet to experience such a thing. She wondered if it was even a reality.

Her mother let out an audible sigh of relief. The doctor asked Simone to lean back on the table and to place her heels in the metal stirrups. She proceeded to examine her. When she was done, she asked Simone's mother to leave the room. She wanted to speak with her daughter alone. She needed to ask some questions that Simone might have been too shy or embarrassed to answer in her mother's presence. Having been through this herself, her mother understood and hesitantly made her exit.

"Now, that your mother has left, I will ask you again, if you have ever had sexual intercourse. Please remember, that I've just examined you and I can see a lot down there."

With her eyes focused on the floor, Simone answered truthfully this time. She had indeed engaged in sexual intercourse. Nevertheless, she followed her confession with a lie. She told the gynecologist that she had a boyfriend and that they had sex occasionally. She pieced the words together perfectly, just as her father had rehearsed her to say. After giving her advice on safe sex and writing the prescription for the birth control pills, the doctor asked her to get dressed and left the room. The examination was over.

I should have told her.

Simone regretted her failure to expose her ugly truth that day. She just couldn't do it. She would not be able to stand the look on her mother's face, could not stand to rip her family apart. She made the right choice, a sacrifice; people do that for others that they love. They sacrifice and Simone was a good person for doing so. She had earned her place in Heaven. She was a good person and would remain so. She popped the tiny blue pill in her mouth and washed it down with a cup of water. It was time for bed. She left the bathroom and entered her bedroom, dropping to her knees at the side of the bed. She said her nightly prayer.

Lord, please take me away. Please end this pain and take my life. I wish to serve you in Heaven as one of your angels, dancing in the clouds and sliding down the rainbows. I just want to be happy Lord and I see no way that I can do that living here in this hell on earth. I want to die and I will do whatever you wish, just please take me tonight. Take me before he comes. I want to pray for everyone I know and love. Please continue to bless everyone with your goodness. When I am gone, please continue to watch over my mother and protect her. Also Lord, I need you to help my father. He is a sick man. He needs you more than anyone and he is sorry for what he does to me. I know that he loves me but he can't control himself. Please help him as I know only you can. In Jesus name, I pray. Amen.

She rose from her knees and climbed into bed. She made sure that she tucked herself in tight, leaving no room for anyone else underneath the covers. Her mother entered the room shortly after to kiss her and bid her good night. She told Simone that she was leaving to attend a birthday soiree for one of her girlfriends, and wouldn't return until after midnight. Simone didn't want her to go, but she kept quiet as she reached up to hug her mother. She held on for a few seconds longer than necessary.

She whispered in her mother's ear, "I love you, Mommy." Simone knew that this would be the night. As sure as she was about every night before, she was of this night. God would answer her prayer and take her before morning.

"I love you too, baby." Her mother hesitated before letting go. She opened and closed her mouth. It looked as if she was about to say something, but decided against it. The two of them were close. Simone rarely kept anything from her mother, but this was different. She was making a sacrifice for the well-being of her family. Everything would work out in time and her mother would appreciate her for her efforts. She always did. Her mother let her go and walked out of the room, turning off the light on her way out.

Now it was time to wait. She didn't know whether or not he was coming that night. She never knew. She always waited to die or to hear his voice, which ever came first. He never gave any hint or indication during the day; he always kept her wondering and waiting.

As she lay still in her bed, looking up at the ceiling through the darkness, she thought about her upcoming encounter with Brandon Stokes. If she lived past that night, she would have something to look forward to in the near future. She let her mind drift to a movie-like scene in which she and Brandon were the only two present at the Homecoming dance. She would flatter him with compliments, laugh at all of his jokes and smile with every word that she spoke. She would playfully toss her head to the side and lightly touch him on his chest. He would love it. He would love *her* and he would ask her to be his girl right there on the spot. They wouldn't need to have sex. Their love would be deeper than that. They would connect on a spiritual level and go on to live happily ever after, such a beautiful scene.

"Hey, baby girl." Her father entered the room about 20 minutes after his wife had left, interrupting her romantic teenaged fantasy.

She jumped slightly at the sound of his voice. He probably didn't notice and didn't know if she was sleeping or not. As she did every night, she lay still, hands by her side, silent. She closed her eyes tight and dreaded his touch. Despite the tight cocoon of covers wrapped so carefully around her body, she felt a chill embrace her as a blanket of cold air invaded the room. After several long moments, he did touch her, reaching under the covers to tickle her feet at the end of the bed to make sure she was awake. She snatched her feet away from his hand as a reflex, still keeping her eyes closed. He wasted no time this night. There was no conversation, no arguing with himself, no tears or words of regret. He remained silent as he unbuttoned his shirt and dropped his pants to the floor. His belt buckle made a soft thud as it hit the carpet and his shirt rustled against his pants. Then he climbed into the bed next to her under the covers. He caressed her face and tenderly kissed her forehead. Then, he pulled her by her waist to bring her closer to him. She felt his erection on her hip. He pressed it against her side. She cringed with disgust.

"You've been taking your pill?"

Simone did not speak. Instead, she just nodded her head in confirmation.

"Good. That's a good girl." He whispered with his face close to hers. His lips touched her ear.

He turned her head towards him, then leaned in to kiss her lips, forcing his tongue in her mouth. Then he climbed on top of her, firmly prying her legs open with his knee. She didn't give much resistance. She never did. There was no point. It was going to happen whether she fought it or not. Nor did she participate. That too did not matter. He took it however he could get it. Her corpselike body would lie frozen, allowing him to use her for his pleasure, while she waited until the torture was over. She didn't cry. She had no more tears left. She was used to it.

He began to kiss her neck slowly, drawing circles in her skin with his tongue. He slid his hand up her nightgown and pulled down her panties, then eased himself inside her, gently, carefully. Still kissing her neck, he grabbed her by the waist and held on as he started to rape her. It was slow at first, but as he continued, his pleasure overpowered him. He began to go faster and harder, thrusting in and out of her small body. He moaned in ecstasy and whispered endearments in her ear.

Then--something happened. It was bizarre and completely unexpected. A strange feeling, foreign to Simone's 14 years of existence, crept inside of her. She felt an intense tingling and a fiery heat begin to rise from her vagina. Her heart was beating rapidly and she felt throbbing between her legs. She lost control of her body and, without warning, began to pump her hips towards her father, matching each of his thrusts. She threw her arms around him and gripped his back, throwing her head back and breathing heavily. Before she knew what was happening, she released a soft, erotic moan while still grinding her hips up and down. It felt good. It was a feeling she had never had before.

This is sex. This is what I've been missing. This is it!

Her father, surprised by her sudden reciprocation, paused and looked down at her sweet face distorted in sexual agony.

A look of bewilderment masked his face. His little girl was a woman, a beautiful, sexy woman. This is what he had been waiting for. She was returning his love. His dreams were coming true and his actions were justified. His confusion turned quickly to an excitement that added to his twisted desire.

He started again, moving in and out slowly first and then gaining momentum. Sweat dripped from his forehead. "That's it, baby girl. Don't fight it. It feels so good doesn't it?" More sexual sounds filled the room. "Give it to Daddy, baby."

His words, meant to encourage her lust, only fueled her shame. Simone snapped back to the reality of the situation with a violent smack. She was having sex with her father!

I am enjoying sex with my father. This can't happen. This is not going to happen. This is his sin, not mine. He is a demented freak, not me!

She opened her eyes and quickly released her grip. Her body froze in shock and fear once again, but this time of her own actions.

"Don't stop now. Come on, baby girl. I know you like it. Feels good doesn't it?"

Just as suddenly as she stopped, she became hysterical. She dug her nails deeply into his back, then pounded on him with all of her strength. She kicked her legs wildly from underneath him, turning her head from side to side in a crazed panic. She jerked her body violently in spasmodic convulsions. She screamed, bit, and cursed. She beat and pounded on his chest, pushing and punching for freedom from under his weight.

"No! Stop! Get off me! No, no, no, no!"

Her father jumped up. Her violent outburst put fear into is eyes. He tried to contain her, holding her hands down, then her feet. He attempted to comfort her and put his hand over her mouth, but she continued in her frenzy. She screamed and cried uncontrollably, twitching and twisting, kicking and punching.

"Simone, please!"

"No, no, no, no, no, no, no, no!" She was in a trance.

He jumped out of the bed. In a panic, he grabbed his clothes and raced out of her bedroom, closing the door behind him. Her conniption did not cease until he was gone.

It's over. He's gone.

Simone lay still in the darkness, looking towards the ceiling, panting to catch her breath. She was sweating. Tears streaked her face. She knew he was still standing outside her door, frozen with apprehension, wondering if she was alright, worried that he had hurt her and terrified of what was to come. She didn't move. She just stared at the ceiling trying to gain her composure.

What happened? Where did it turn from a sin to something I like? When did it change from pain to pleasure? I am dirty. I am just as bad as he is.

She was sick. She was going straight to hell. Then, she felt it again, the throbbing hot sensation between her legs. She shook her head in denial as she realized that, despite her mind's hatred of what happened, her body was calling for more. She placed her hand on her vagina, applying pressure, to stop the throbbing but it didn't work. She was just as dirty and sinful as he was. She was worse, a monster. She turned to her side, pulled the covers close around her body and curled into a tight fetal position, visibly shaking and sobbing.

She whispered, "No, no, no, no, no, no." God had failed her once again, leaving her prayer unfulfilled.

Is there a God?

After several minutes, she finally cried herself to sleep, leaving her question unanswered.

CHAPTER 12

SIMONE'S FATHER

SIMONE'S father was a freshman at the University of Michigan when he first heard the story of Oedipus as told by his Psychology professor. He soaked up the words of this tale with the thirst and enthusiasm of a newborn suckling his mother's breast for the first time. He felt his buddy, Joshua, tap him lightly on the shoulder to pass a note, but the effort was ignored as he shooed him away with a quick flick of the wrist. The rendition of the Greek Myth was enthralling. It was more than an interesting tale and a challenging lesson. It was a revelation.

"It was Oedipus' fate to kill his father and marry his mother. He could not escape it. The oracle predicted it and despite his efforts to defy destiny, he fell full victim to his predestination." Professor Jones paused then slowly looked around the room for what Simone's father thought to be dramatic effect. It was then that he realized she was speaking only to him. He was not sure if it was something that he was imagining or if Professor Jones really was sending him a direct message. Either way, he heard her loud and clear.

For years, his mixed emotions for both his mother and father baffled him. He was thoroughly confused as to why he hated his father only because of the way his mother loved him. The way she looked at her husband, his father, at times -- full of love, forgiveness and even desire -- made him nauseous. It made him want to strangle the man who worked 12-hour days and overachieved at the expense of his family's emotional well being in order to provide his wife and son with the "good life." The boy had daily fantasies of what life would be like if only his father were not around. If only that soft, gentle look in his mother's eyes was for no one but her son. What would that feel like? If his father were gone, what would life be like? His father didn't deserve the warmth of his mother's embrace or the sweetness of her kisses. He was never home. When he was, he barely acknowledged her presence.

As a boy, he would fight back tears of frustration while watching his mother slave around the house only to please a man who never appreciated it. As a young man, he looked on in disdain when his father never noticed when she changed her hair or got a new outfit. He ignored her efforts to woo him with flirtatious charm. He was tired. He was too tired to talk to her about her day, too drained to take her out and too weary to eat the dinner she had prepared to his liking. His mother was miserable and lonely. Her son saw it in her eyes and his own heart broke for her daily.

Twice he had broached what they both knew was the cause of her pain, but both times she brushed him off. He was only a boy and could not possibly understand adult issues. He wanted desperately to show his mother that he was a man -- all the man they needed. He knew that he could provide for them and love her as she deserved to be loved. They didn't need him.

But he knew that he couldn't tell her this. Despite the

strength of his love for his mother, somehow he knew his feelings were inappropriate. He realized he was on the verge of crossing into a forbidden realm, and for that reason, he kept his intense feelings under wraps. While he maintained a grip on his emotions, he nonetheless watched in agony as the years passed with no relief.

When his father finally did leave, he took his mother with him. Simone's father was 19-years-old when his parents died in a car accident. Their sudden death left him, not only in abject grief, but also with unfinished business that would never be resolved. He never had the chance to come to terms with his emotions or to gain complete understanding of what he was going through when they were alive. The irrational hate he harbored for his father and the inappropriate love he had for his mother, festered inside of him until it corroded into a hard, stone lump that weighed heavily on his existence. His lack of insight ate at him until he forced himself to block the memory of any feelings he once had for his parents.

His feelings remained buried until that day. It wasn't until then, sitting in the stadium style seats of his classroom, did he open the locked box of his sub-consciousness and face his demons for the first time. As he listened attentively to Professor Jones explain Freud's theory of the Oedipus complex, he felt a wave of relief from a flash of understanding. As much as it pained him to admit it, he was relieved that his mother was dead. He was safe. She was safe. He no longer had to carry the guilt of wishing his father dead for reasons he could not fully comprehend. They were reasons he did not want to come to grips with, and now that he did, the absence of his parents softened the blow tremendously.

As a young man, his love life could best be described

in the lack thereof. It was never about *love;* it was more of a search and seizure mission. Like a lion on the prowl, he hunted until he found a woman suitable enough to be his prey. Once captured, she served a distinct purpose: to replace his mother. He told himself that he really liked them. He tried to believe the sweet words that dripped from his lips like honey when he cooed and coaxed his conquests. But those soft words of seduction were never sincere. Whoever she was, the woman he was pursuing, was nothing like his mother. She would never be good enough.

He was exceptionally handsome, the type of man women would brag about to their girlfriends and take home to their mothers. His skin was bronze and smooth like satin. His face held a host of piercing dark features, from his onyx eyes, to his ebony hair, and raven mustache and goatee. Standing at six feet three inches, he towered over most of his lovers. He liked it that way. So did they. The women swooned when he entered the room and he took full advantage. Getting them into the bed was never a challenge. It never took more than a few alluring words and a sensual touch on the small of her back to soak her panties right before they dropped to the floor. However stimulating the sex was, from woman to woman, it was never satisfying. After a few weeks of sex and lies, the game was over and he tossed her into the cold of his absence along with his trash on Thursday morning.

For ten years after his parents' death, he walked in and out of meaningless relationships like a mummy awakening from his tomb. There were no emotions, passion, longing or desire. There was no romance, or good old-fashioned courting. It was cut and dry. Once his ceaseless comparisons to his mother made him realize that the woman was not worthy of his time, the game was over, on to the next one. He used his work as a distraction, so staying detached was easy. Gaining momentum and an impressive reputation in the business world, he was able to keep his focus on his work and off his women.

His thirtieth birthday marked a milestone in his life. He knew that he wanted to get married. He knew that he did not want to wander through life without the companionship a "better half" could offer. It took a long and bitter decade, but finally he realized that no one would meet his criteria. His mother was gone and could not be revived vicariously through one of the countless number of women competing for his love.

When he met Simone's mother their encounter was unexpected but it occurred at the right time. He surprised himself by allowing himself to fall in love with her as the months went by. Her bold spirit captivated him and her looks and body met his standards. Their courtship was intense and focused. Thy both felt they did not have time to waste -- leading to a simple wedding ceremony six months after they met. He was satisfied with the solution to his problem. It was a quick fix, something to redirect his focus and keep his mind occupied with the simple task of being a good husband instead of the empty man he had become.

His new wife was somewhat fascinating. She was untamed, sexy and riveting. She was something that he had never had and her freshness mixed with his uncertainty about her intrigued him. Coming from completely different backgrounds, on the surface they did not have much in common, but one thing they agreed on was the desire to start a family. Before their third anniversary, they were expecting a baby. Simone's father was elated that he would finally have the opportunity to prove that he would be a better father and a better man than his father was. His child would never have to wonder if he loved her or try to compete for his time. She would never need or want for anything in life. He vowed to make it a lifelong task to be the ideal father by anyone's standards.

The day Simone entered the world with her eyes wide-open, head full of dark, curly locks and wiggling like a pink glob of JELLO, her father's life changed-- for better and worse. She was undeniably beautiful. From the first day he laid eyes on her, holding her in the hospital just minutes after she had journeyed into the world, he was in love. Some would say that fathers do not have the same instant bond with their newborns as the mothers do. But on that hot and muggy July afternoon, Simone's father and his baby girl defied the conventional wisdom. The look she gave him, with her intoxicating emerald eyes, took hold of his heart with a strength matched only by her smile. The way her miniature nose wrinkled when she yawned and how her perfectly round face flushed a warm rose color when she cried, sent chills through his body that started from the nape of his neck and traveled down to the small of his back. He was in awe of her, but did not completely understand the depth or the reason. He shocked himself with how he obsessed over his baby girl, yet he was unable to control it. His wife was often jealous of the way he held their daughter for hours on end without giving her a chance to look at the child. As a toddler, Simone was his favorite pastime. He potty trained her, taught her colors, numbers and letters and played games with her after work. He took her to Sunday school and Brownie Scouts. Their bond was undeniable. The hold the little girl had on his heart never lifted.

For seven years, Simone's father lived out his promise to be the ultimate dad he vowed to be. For the first half of her life, he was able to hide from himself the real reason he was so infatuated with his beautiful daughter. He kept it from himself, locked in the back of his subconscious. Still, the truth remained lurking around the corner. A revelation was inevitable; it was something that he could not avoid for an entire lifetime. No matter how hard he tried to keep the roots of his feelings submerged in daily father-daughter activities and constant self-coaching, the truth crept to the surface. One day, without warning, it hit him hard in the face.

He stood in Simone's bedroom doorway, watching her sleep peacefully underneath the mounds of blankets her mother insisted she needed to shield her from the night chill. He examined her flawless features as she nestled her head into her pillow in an attempt to get more comfortable. The light wrinkle in her forehead and the mild twitch in her eyelids indicated that she was deep in a dream. It was early in the morning, about 6:00 a.m. The soft streaks of sunlight peeked in through the blinds, grazing her cheeks as a warning that soon it would be time to wake up. He jumped a little as Simone stretched and yawned unexpectedly. He did not want her to know that he was there watching her the way that he was. Although the reason was unclear at that very moment, he was ashamed and uncomfortable with himself. The butterflies in his stomach subsided as he realized that she was not awakening, just merely repositioning herself in order to hide from the sunlight.

Feeling as much confused as he was compelled, he leaned against the wall and raised his eyes to the ceiling. He could not bring himself to walk out of the room, so he told himself if he did not look at her, he had nothing to feel guilty about. He stood there for several moments, wrestling with his own thoughts, asking himself what it was he was really feeling for his baby girl. He demanded the answers to the questions he had been too afraid to confront. Then, she moved again, stirring underneath the covers until her face and half of her torso were clearly exposed. His eyes shot back to her face. She was still sleeping, but he could have sworn that she smiled at him just a little. Although slight, the smile was one that would warm the heart of any proud father in adoration, but for Simone's father, it had the opposite effect.

His heart sank and his breathing stopped abruptly. He tried to grip the wall behind him for support, but his sweaty palms caused him to slip. The sun was now shining brighter, rising in the sky with strong determination. It continued until its piercing rays poured into the room and illuminated Simone's small face like a spotlight.

The recollection of watching his mother during her brief moments of repose almost knocked him over. Simone's father stumbled backward and reached blindly for the doorknob behind him so he could leave. Still in his panic, he never took his eyes off of her. He had managed to turn the knob in a half circle when he heard her soft voice, groggy from fresh sleep and tinged with confusion.

"Daddy?" She slowly sat up in her bed, wiping her eyes with the back of her hand, frowning as she tried to shake herself from disorientation.

He didn't answer. He couldn't speak. He turned and tried to hurry out of the door, hoping she would think his brief presence was still part of her dream. But her words stopped him mid-step.

"Daaaaaady. Where are you going? You have to say good morning. You have to give me a hug and a kissy or I can't wake up."

Simone's father felt the tears rolling down his face. He didn't try to stop them, but he couldn't let her see them. He kept his back turned and remained in place.

"Daddy! Do you hear me?" He could tell from the tone in her voice that she had graduated from half asleep to fully awake.

He felt his knees begin to buckle beneath his weight. He managed to take another step towards the door and was able to turn the knob enough to yank it open. Without turning to see her face, he finally answered, "Go back to sleep. It's not time to wake up yet." The shakiness in his voice did not match the authority of his words. He secretly prayed that she followed his orders, but he did not stay to find out. Finally mustering enough strength to make it out into the hallway, he closed the door behind him a little harder than was necessary.

Blended images of his mother and his daughter merged in his mind. His mother, the woman he had searched his entire adult life for, was alive and haunting him through his only child. After seven years of ambiguity and bewilderment, he now understood what he saw in Simone that caused his obsession. He saw in her what he could never find in any other woman. He found his mother. He thought that leaving the room would comfort him, but it did not. He was not safe and he never would be again. Neither was Simone.

CHAPTER 13

JESSICA

JESSICA asked her husband what he thought about her getting breast implants. He had a bored look on his face as he sat at the kitchen table with his eyes glued to the *Wall Street Journal*. He never glanced up as he answered her question. He had a tone in his voice that told her that he wasn't in the mood for conversation.

"Whatever you want, Jessica. Just don't come back here looking like some freak show."

She ignored his disinterest. *She* was excited. This was going to be a major step in her extreme make over. "Of course I wouldn't get anything too big. You know, maybe just a cup size bigger. A 'D' cup."

"Umm hmm."

"You know my girlfriend, Christine got hers done and she just loves them. She said that Jim just goes wild over her now. He can't keep his hands off of her. They do it all the time."

She watched closely for the expression on his face to change, for him to show any sign of interest in the conversation, to give any indication that her efforts to please him did in some way intrigue him. He did not.

"Umm hmm."

"I've been researching different doctors and I've narrowed it down to three. I have to meet with all of them for a consultation before I make my final decision. Christine said that I should try to get some testimonials if possible too. Then--"

"Okay, Jessica." He kept his eyes on his reading, "I'm trying to read here. If you want to get implants, get implants. Just leave me with some peace and quiet. Do you think you can do that for me?"

She felt a little embarrassed. As usual, she was rambling on and on about something he couldn't care less about. She stood and walked towards the door to leave him to his reading, "Sure, honey. I can do that for you. Just let me know if you need anything."

"Umm hmm."

Wait! He was her husband. Why didn't he care? Why was she the only one excited about this? She was doing this for him, for them. She needed to get her marriage back to normal and needed to have her man back, to have him love her as he once did. She had to have him addicted to her, obsess over her and yearn for her like an addict jones' for his next fix. Why didn't he want the same? Why wasn't he eager to add the fire back into their obviously failing marriage? She was doing everything that she could. She was giving him all that she had. She was dying to get him back. What did he want from her?

She knew why. The answer was obvious. There was someone else. Nausea crept into her stomach and her heart began to beat through her chest. A plum-sized lump rose to her throat, momentarily blocking her air passage. It took several moments for her to swallow and catch her breath. She stood in the kitchen doorway frozen with apprehension. She was frozen from the outside, but her insides were racing. The words of her mother rushed through her head--

"*...And I betcha he cheatin' on ya too. Dey like dawgs, humpin' every livin thang in sight.*"

He was no different. He was no different from their neighbor, Lindsay Hogan's, husband. He had been cheating on her for years with their blonde and busty, divorced neighbor, Clarissa. She was such the obvious choice. The single, young, attractive woman was half that horny bastard's age, with a well-practiced flirtatious smile and the walk to match. Everyone knew Brent was screwing that tramp any time he had a free moment to do so. Lindsay knew it too. Her husband knew that she knew it, and yet still they continued to live their lives as if everything was normal. That was until normal turned into a real live episode of Jerry Springer right in the middle of Cherry Grove Lane.

The whole block was in an uproar for months following the dramatic and embarrassing scenario. All Jessica knew was that little bouncy, blonde, dingbat was naked out on Lindsay's front lawn, drenched in one and a half liters of the red wine that Lindsay used to wake her and her husband up from their little mid-day "nap" in her bed. The whole subdivision watched in horror as Lindsay cleaned that little tramp off with ice-cold water from the garden hose. Brent (by now clothed) stood by completely silent, perhaps afraid of what his maniacal wife would do to him next. It was completely mortifying.

Is that what I have to look forward too? Will I come home one day to find Ross and some cheap whore rolling around in our bed? Will I be the next Lindsay Hogan? Oh God!

She could feel the sweat beads forming on her forehead

as she prepared to ask the lingering question she was not sure she wanted the answer to. She braced herself, holding herself up with one hand on the wall of the doorway.

"Honey?"

"Hmm?"

"I need to ask you something."

"Yes, Jessica?"

"Now, I don't want you to blow this out of proportion or get too angry, but I need an honest answer from you."

She could hear the emergence of irritation in his voice, "What?"

"Well, I was wondering…umm, is there…I mean. Are you umm…"

"For God's sake, Jessica spit it out."

His eyes were still on the *Wall Street Journal.* His voice never raised, but the edge in his tone made her cringe. She was afraid of his reaction, afraid of putting an even bigger wedge between them, but more than anything, she was petrified of what his answer would be. That he would tell her the truth, the words that she didn't want to hear, but so desperately needed in order to validate what she already knew.

"Is there someone else?" There, she had said it. The words flew out of her mouth with the venom of a snake and smacked him right in his face.

His eyes traveled up slowly from the newspaper until they landed on her face. "What did you just say?"

Jessica's confidence faded with every passing second, "I said, Ross, is there someone else? Are you cheating on me?"

She spat the last sentence at him in staccato. She needed some answers and she wasn't willing to wait another minute for them. But she was caught off guard by his unexpected reaction. He started with a smirk that quickly turned into a full-blown smile, followed by laughter. It wasn't a humorous laugh as if in reaction to a joke, or in remembrance of a funny occurrence. It was a derisive, almost callous laugh. It was one that said that he was laughing *at* her. She felt like she was back in high school, standing in the cafeteria suffering the cruel hilarity of her peers with their eyes focused on her dingy clothes, unruly hair, raggedy shoes and pimply face. His laugh told her that she was pathetic, absurd, and should hide her face inside a paper bag. She wanted to run out of the kitchen, out of the house and take her detestable words with her, but it was too late. She had to stand her ground.

Her mother's words taunted her, "*How many other womens he gots, Jessie?*"

"I'm serious. Answer me. I'm tired of living like this. I need to know what the hell is going on. We walk around this house as if we're strangers. You don't touch me, you never want to talk to me, and most of the time, you can barely stand to look at me. I feel like I'm invisible to you. I can't take this anymore!"

His laughter finally ended and seriousness overcame him. "I am not cheating on you, Jessica."

"Well, I don't know, baby, sometimes I think that your mind is elsewhere and it just seems like someone else is occupying your thoughts."

"Look, I'm not about to get into a deep conversation about this. I said that I wasn't and I'm not. The minute that I find someone else, you'll know. You'll be living downriver in a single wide trailer, fighting the roaches for food."

His words pierced Jessica's heart like the sharp tip of a sword. Her past flashed before her eyes, the dilapidated trailer, the roaches, the ragged carpet decorated with years of beer stains and dog pee, and her alcoholic mother passed out on the sofa bed. Was he serious? Would he do that to her? Her mouth opened, but she couldn't gather the coordination to form any words. She managed to keep standing, but her face was distorted in a half confused, half terrified expression.

He stood from the table. After setting his paper down, he walked over to her. His eyes never left hers. She didn't know what to expect. Would he strike her? Was he going to make her leave? Would he throw her out at that moment, leaving her with nothing but the clothes she was wearing? Clothes that *he* bought with *his* money. She would fall full victim to the airtight post-nuptial agreement that he coerced her into signing five years into their marriage. She would have nothing. Well, as he put it, she would have *everything* she had come into the marriage with. She began to plead with him in her head.

Please baby, please don't make me leave. I'm sorry. I'm sorry for disrespecting you. Oh God! What is he gonna do?

He stopped right in front of her, leaving about ten inches between his face and hers. She could smell his cologne, Hugo Boss. She could feel his breath, soft and warm on her nose. He grabbed her waist with a force that made her back cave in. He pulled her closer to him. One arm was around her waist and the other cupped her chin and pulled her face into his. He then did the last thing that she was expecting. He kissed her. It was a deep, passionate, kiss. It made Jessica light headed. It felt so good it was intoxicating. But she was too shocked to react. It ended just as suddenly as it began as he pulled away, almost dropping her like a used Kleenex. His eyes were still fixated on hers. They stood there, staring at each other for, what seemed to be, several minutes. The air evacuated Jessica's lungs; she took in short, deep breaths, wishing for him to give her more of what she had been missing.

Finally, he broke the silence, speaking in a low, measured tone. "Remember where you came from and stay in your place. The moment that you step too far out of bounds, I'll throw you right back where you belong. Do you understand, *Jessie?*"

Jessica, still dizzy from the deceitful embrace, stared at her husband, dumbfounded.

"Do you understand?" he repeated. His voice was icy and condescending.

She nodded slowly. She understood.

He released his hold and took a few steps back, "Now go find something to occupy your time."

Jessica followed orders, leaving her husband in the kitchen to his reading. Her lips quivered and she thought she was about to cry, but the tears refused to fall. She was too frightened, afraid of losing the only man that she had ever loved. She was afraid of losing the life she had grown accustomed to, the feeling she had when she was out in public. She couldn't lose the superiority, the pride, the prestige of being Mrs. Ross Pembroke. She couldn't let it all slip through her fingers. She would not stand by and allow him to leave her lonely, broke and heartbroken. She would do whatever it took to keep what she worked so hard to get.

Jessica walked down the steps to the entertainment room. A few moments later, she heard the front door to the house open and close. The sound echoed off the floor of the foyer. He had left. She stepped behind the bar and opened the liquor cabinet, reaching into the far rear corner to get her half-drunken bottle of Riesling. Then she reached again. This time, to grab a small white envelope, addressed to her husband. Inside was one of the most impassioned letters she would ever read.

Jessica was terrified of losing her man, but was even more determined not to.

Whatever it takes. I'll do whatever it takes.

She would call the plastic surgeons for her consultations that morning. She would make an appointment at the salon the next day to get her hair died strawberry blonde. She would meet with her personal trainer at three o' clock to work on her figure. She was going to make herself beautiful for her man -- a perfect ten, the trophy wife that he deserved. But right then, at that moment. She had to put together the perfect plan.

She grabbed a glass from the bar and poured herself a generous share of her favorite wine. After taking a gulp, she read the letter from her husband's mistress for the 25th time that day. She would get herself together, make herself beautiful for her husband, but first things first. She had to handle her business and get rid of that bitch.

CHAPTER 14

JESSICA

JESSICA sat impatiently outside of the home of Ross' mistress. She positioned her car on the adjacent side street. She had a clear view of the front door to the condominium through her rearview mirror. Her ability to follow Ross and his mistress undetected for days, made her proud and ashamed. The hunger to put an end to the affair and ruin the woman that infiltrated her marriage, took her back to a time in her life she had effectively suppressed for 16 years. It was a time when she was a skinny, white-looking, bi-racial girl in the slums of Hamtramck. When she first recognized that desperate, hungry girl threatening to break through and reveal herself, she fought to keep her down. Jessica wanted nothing to take her back to those miserable days. She had worked too hard to forget the past, but as her marriage grew weaker, her resolve to take the high road diminished. Someone was threatening her. There was too much at stake. This was not something to handle with class and dignity. The situation was well beyond turning the other cheek and fighting fair. This was an all out war.

These black bitches. Always think they can take what's mine.

Jessica had a history with black women that justified her hatred. They always underestimated her because they thought she was white. They thought they could intimidate her because of her color. They were wrong. The rough and rugged life that Jessica endured as an abused and neglected child had hardened her. She wasn't a chump. No one could push her around, not even those black bitches. "Jessie" learned the rules of life early on. It was always about survival of the fittest. Those who lacked the strength and endurance to make it on the streets were eventually weeded out and eliminated. Her mother would whip her ass if she came home crying because somebody else had beat her down, especially a nigger. It wasn't tolerated. By the age of 18, she was hardened and life-scarred, not scared of anyone. No one compared to the cruelty of her mother. After dealing with her all of her life, everything else was simple. If you stepped up to Jessie, be prepared to be smacked down.

When she walked into the Wild Stallion Gentlemen's Club 17 years ago, she was fresh meat, new booty. They started in on her immediately. The black girls, with their nappy hair and huge asses, thought they could scare her. They thought they could bully her into giving them her hard-earned cash. She had to put them in their place, quickly. The main one was Kitty Kat, a tall, light-skinned girl with an old scar on the left side of her face that stretched from her ear to her mouth. She was popular in the strip club, making the most in tips, bouncing and clapping her gigantic backside on the high rollers in the VIP. That was until, Jessie, ("White Chocolate" as her stage name), stole one of Kitty's regulars one night and became his new favorite and recipient of his cash. His decision caused a rift in the dancers and thick tension between Jessie and Kitty. It was on.

Kitty Kat confronted her in the dressing room, "Bitch, I know I didn't see yo white ass over there dancin' on Big Dee in the VIP. Everybody up in this bitch know he my territory."

Jessie stuffed her bag in the locker. She had just finished changing costumes and didn't look up to address Kitty.

"You hear me talking to you, bitch?" The other dancers in the locker room, Strawberry, Peaches, Mercedes, and CoCo, crowded around the two of them to watch the showdown.

Jessie didn't acknowledge Kitty until she was done putting on her Lucite-heeled platform shoes. "Yeah, I heard you. And it should be obvious to you and everybody else up in here that he ain't yours no mo'. He chose me, so step the fuck back, ho."

Kitty's eyes widened in astonishment, as she didn't half expect White Chocolate to have the balls to talk back to her. She looked around the room as if the words she was hearing were mysteriously coming from someone else. She stepped close to Jessie, getting up in her face, "This ain't the trailer park, bitch, or wherever the fuck you came from. Around here, I run this shit, and if you don't watch yo' self, you might get fucked up." Kitty, reached out, gently grabbed a piece of Jessie's hair, and playfully twirled it around in her fingers. She was taunting her, "Now we wouldn't want that to happen would we?" The other dancers, smelling blood, moved in closer, egging on their leader, throwing fighting words into the mix to get Kitty's adrenaline up. They knew she was about to beat the white girl down.

Jessie didn't back down. She whipped her head back to get Kitty's nasty fingers out of her hair. "Might get fucked up?

Ooh is that suppose' to scare me? Don't talk about whatcha might do. Do it now. Let me see whatcha got. Whatcha gonna do? Huh?" She backed up a little, throwing her arms in the air as a challenge, putting some space between her and her rival. Wearing nothing more than a hot pink bikini bra, sparkling Daisy Dukes and six-inch platform heels, she prepared herself for battle, situating her body in a fighting stance.

Kitty did the same. She threw the fist punch and missed as Jessie jumped back low and ducked the blow. Jessie quickly sprang up and threw a right hook that landed hard on Kitty's left jaw. She followed it up with a quick jab with her left fist and hit the bitch in her nose. The one-two combination had Kitty stumbling backwards, but she didn't go down. The other dancers backed up to give the two of them room. Not one of them jumped in to help their girl Kitty Kat.

Jessie seized the opportunity to rush her. With a swift kick to Kitty's gut, she sent her crashing hard to the floor. Strawberry and CoCo hurriedly ran to her side and tried to help her up. But she brushed them off. She was hard. She could handle this herself. Jessie stood back and waited for her to get to her feet. Kitty charged at Jessie with the force of a bull to a matador, only to come face to face with the sharp tip of a switchblade. Jessie swiped hard at her opponent with the knife, but missed her by inches.

"You wanna 'nother scar on your face to match the one you already got? I'll be more than glad to give it to you."

Kitty backed up slowly with her hands in front of her face.

"Where you going? You scared?" Jessie crept towards her, slowly waiving the knife from side to side, "Here, Kitty Kitty Kitty."

"This bitch is crazy," CoCo said to no one in particular.

"That's right I'm crazy, and I'll cut all you black bitches into pieces. Back the fuck up off me!" She turned from side to side waiving the knife at every one of them. They all backed up. Kitty, with her tattered clothes and broken-heeled stilettos, half ran, half limped out of the dressing room. The others followed close behind, leaving Jessie alone with her blade and a victory. No one would mess with her again. They all knew she was fearless. She created a reputation around the club that let everyone know that she would fight for what was hers. It had always been that way, in school, in the neighborhood and in the streets. She handled her business.

When Ross rescued her from that life, she thought she had left those instincts behind. She prayed that she would never have to go back to the hardcore code of the streets. Then this slapped her right in the face, another black bitch trying to take what was hers.

Jessica snapped out of the trance of reminiscence when she saw, from her rearview mirror, the mistress walk out of her home and get into her car. She watched anxiously as she pulled out of her spot in the carport and turned out of the parking lot, crossing right behind Jessica's car to get to 11 Mile Road. She took a deep breath before starting the engine and turning around in the driveway to turn to the left. There was no rush. She knew where she was going. She had frequented this route in the last two weeks. She followed her target to work at an inconspicuous distance. She had business to handle.

CHAPTER 15

SIMONE

SIMONE had never been much of a dancer. Like most teenagers, she was a fan of music videos. It was amazing to see how the girls moved in those videos, popping their butts and gyrating their hips like super sexed up hula dancers. The seductive way they swayed their bodies and rolled their hips, had Simone in awe. She could never dance like that. Even if she could, she would be too shy and embarrassed to actually do it when someone other than her own reflection was watching. She never wanted to draw that type of attention to herself. Of course, she had given the occasional private performances in front of the mirror with a brush in hand and her mother's hot pink stilettos on her feet. She had the steps from Sierra Nightly's, "Desperate in Love" video down to a science, cat crawling on the floor and bouncing her booty to, "Yeah yeah yeah yeah yeah, get it get it." The routine from pop star, Shyanne's, "Give it to Me," was also well practiced. Even though she had the choreography down, she always thought she looked awkward and felt the same. She didn't know how to be sexy, didn't want to be sexy. But, that night was different. It was the night of the Homecoming dance and she was on a mission.

Before entering Stonecreeke Academy's gymnasium, decorated in the school colors of red and gold, Simone determined that she would woo her man, Brandon Stokes with sexy moves and flirtatious smiles. She would pop and lock, roll and bounce, and drop it like it was hot. He would be a blind fool not to notice her. Her dress was perfect, her hair flawless and her shoes and matching hand bag impeccable. It was going to be perfect. He would be the answer to all of her problems, her ticket out of hell. He would be her something to look forward to in her dark life. He would take her mind to a far away place, her sweet escape.

The optimistic idea seemed nice, but standing in the middle of the dance floor with Kristen by her side, Simone felt anything but confident and sexy. Although she looked stunning from the outside in her mint green mini dress, with the iridescent lights from the ceiling bouncing off the gold flecks of her green eyes, she was a nervous wreck inside. The butterflies in her stomach were having a party of their own. She didn't know how to stand, wasn't sure where to put her hands, and for some reason she couldn't seem to catch the beat to any of the songs. All of the moves she had been so meticulous in memorizing had flown out of her head. She was starting to feel ridiculous. The whole idea of attracting Brandon was beginning to seem absurd. She couldn't do it. She wanted to go home.

The music blared from the huge speakers by the DJ's booth. Everyone around her was booty-bouncing, snap dancing and slow grinding. The so-called chaperones were doing anything but. The crowd of young teens looked like they were taken right out of an urban version of *Dirty Dancing*. She looked to her left to tell Kristen that she was going to call her mother to pick her up, but her friend was no longer beside her. She was "the meat" in a sandwich between two 11th grade boys, Darius and Cameron, dancing as if she was on stage at a strip club. Darius was in front of her. She had one arm around him with her hand on the back of his head. Her other arm was behind her, gripping Cameron's pant leg. They were closed in tight, grinding on each other. Her legs were straddled over the leg of Darius and her backside was sticking out, moving in circles and rubbing against Cameron's crotch. Both boys had their hands all over her body. Cameron had a tight grip on her backside and was slowly making his way to her vagina. Darius stayed focused on her breasts, squeezing them to the beat of the song. It was more of a sex simulation than a dance. Simone's mouth dropped open in a shock. She felt dirty for even watching them, but her eyes were glued to the threesome. She barely felt Brandon tap her on the shoulder.

"Hey, baby."

"Huh?" Simone turned around to see Brandon's tall, lean frame in front of her. He smiled down at her with a mischievous bad boy grin. He was cute and he knew it.

"I said, 'hey'. Why aren't you dancing?"

Simone could hardly get her words together, "Umm…I…umm. I don't know. I just….I don't feel like it right now I guess."

"Damn. That's a shame cuz you look good as hell tonight."

"Oh, thanks…I guess."

"For real girl! Yo' body is bangin!" He looked her up and down with exaggerated pleasure. "Ooh shit, baby, why don't you turn back around and let me see that ass."

"What?" His last words took Simone by surprise. She

wasn't quite sure how to respond. She didn't know if she should have just turned around or tried to give a witty comeback to turn the tables. Before she had enough time to figure it out, he grabbed her arm and spun her around in a half turn.

"Oh, hell yeah! It's just right. I can think of a bunch of things I can do to you wit an ass like that." He smacked her hard on her backside.

Simone whipped back around. She didn't like how the conversation was going. This was not at all what she had planned. He was not the boy of her dreams. He wasn't charming and sweet. He wasn't romantic and sensitive. There was no way that he would fulfill her fantasy and take her away from her nightmares. He was a jerk! She just wanted to get away, but he still had a strong grasp on her arm. She scanned her immediate surroundings for Kristen, but was disappointed to see her in yet another X-rated position with her two dance partners.

He ignored the panicked look in her eyes, "So whatcha wanna do after this?"

"Well, after this, I umm…have to umm…go home."

"Home? You not going to the after party at Cameron's house?"

"I didn't know about the after party." She was lying. Everybody knew about the party at Cameron's. His parents were out of town and left him home alone. Kristen made Simone promise that she would go. So the plan was to leave the dance early to go to the party and make it back to the school in time for their rented limo to take them home by curfew. But now, she wasn't feeling too good about the whole plan. She just wanted to get out of there. The walls were closing in on her. The red and gold balloons and streamers looked menacing, as if they were about to attack her. The music was too loud, the room too crowded, and she was starting to break a nervous sweat.

"Come on, baby. You gotta go. We gotta get to know each other better. You know what I mean?"

She knew exactly what he meant and she'd had enough.

"You can roll with me. I got the Mercedes parked right outside. You ready to roll?"

She had to think of a way to stall. "I can't go right now. I have to leave with my girl."

"Go get her then. Shit, I'm ready for a *real* party." He pulled her in closely by her waist and rubbed his erection against her thigh. He whispered in her ear, "You feel me, shorty?"

She pushed him away to put some space between them, "Yeah, I feel you. I'll be right back," she lied.

She turned and walked towards Kristen. The sandwich dance had finally ended and she was talking to Cameron, giggling and a flipping her hair over her shoulder. When Simone walked up, Cameron's eyes darted from Kristen's chest to Simone's face. He bore the same devilish grin that Brandon had as soon as he saw her.

Simone spoke quickly, leaning in close to Kristen so Cameron couldn't hear. "I'm ready to go."

"What?" The music was too loud. Kristen couldn't hear her.

"I said I'm ready to go!"

"Oh yeah! I saw you over there talking to Brandon. I know y'all can't wait to get outta here. Girl he fine as hell, ain't he? I told you!"

"No! I don't want to go with him. I don't want to go to the after party. I just want to leave. I want to go home."

"Go home? Bitch, you crazy? This party gone be live as hell! "

"I'm serious Kris. Come on. I just don't want to be here."

Cameron interrupted, looking at Simone as if she was his next snack, "Damn, baby, you a little too uptight. You need to loosen up. My boy B gone take *good* care of you. Just relax." He reached out to grab Simone by her waist, but Kristen slapped his hand away.

Simone ignored him. "Look, if you're not gonna leave with me, I'll just go by myself. The limo is still outside or I could just call my mom to come get me." She turned to walk towards the door.

Kristen ran after her. "Wait, Si Si damn! What's wrong? Why you trippin?"

"There's nothing wrong. I just want to go home. Okay?"

"Aiight, aiight. Look. We don't have to throw the whole night away. How about this, we go to the party and we stay for about an hour--"

"No, Kris!"

"Okay, okay, okay! Thirty minutes."

Simone looked at her friend with a frown. She was unconvinced." Thirty minutes. No longer!"

"I promise, just thirty minutes. Then we leave. Okay?"

"Okay, but you better not be playing games when it's time to go."

"Trust me. Everything will be okay. Here, drink some of this and you'll feel a whole lot better."

"What is it?"

"Damn! You ask too many questions! Just drink it. It'll make you relax a little. You got yo panties all up in a bunch. Chill out."

"I don't want to get drunk."

"You won't. Just take the rest of this and it'll calm you down."

Simone took her girl's advice. She was tense and jittery, about to jump out of her skin. She didn't like the feeling she was having. Her stomach was turning and her palms were sweating. Her head was throbbing as the overpowering speakers banged deafening bass in her ears. She was jumpy and irritable. If she wanted to successfully endure the next thirty minutes at that party without losing her mind, she knew she had to relax. She took a huge gulp of the red concoction Kristen handed her.

Kristen warned her, "Whoa girl! Slow it down. You keep drinking like that and you *will* get drunk."

Simone's face cringed. Her mouth turned up in a sour expression as the strong drink burned her throat, "I know what I'm doing. Don't worry about me. Just tell me when you're ready to bounce."

Simone had never drank alcohol before. A few of her classmates told her that it was nasty. Her mother told her that it was bad for her. Her father said that it would get her into trouble, but none of that seemed to register at that moment. It wasn't the least bit nasty. It actually tasted just like tropical punch with an extra kick. Just one cup couldn't be *too* bad for her and she knew as long as her girl had her back, she wasn't getting into any type of trouble. After the burning sensation settled in her chest, she took another generous swallow, then another. It was good!

"Ok, I'll leave you alone. Look, I'm about to go get Brandon and Cameron so we can go. Everybody should be leaving soon anyway."

Simone didn't respond. Her face was buried in the plastic cup, gulping down the fruity mix. Her insides were beginning to feel warm and her head felt a little lighter. Her body was getting loose and her eyes heavy. The music that tortured her eardrums before was beginning to sound like her personal theme song. It sounded good. It felt good. She didn't realize it when her hips began to sway to the beat and she began snapping her fingers and bobbing her head. The beat of the music vibrated in her chest and moved through her body like electric waves. She put one arm in the air and grooved to the song as if she wrote and recorded it herself, singing all the words, some correct, some she made up as she went along. She was in a different world and she liked it.

"Yeah, that's what I'm talking about. Shake that ass, baby." Brandon snuck up behind her. Kristen, Cameron, and Darius stood by his side. He stepped up to Simone and wrapped his arms around her from the back, pushing his erection up against her jerking butt so he could feel it rubbing against him.

"Come on, nigga let's go. We can take this party to my house," Cameron was getting anxious. Kristen was all over him, kissing his neck and grabbing his crotch.

Brandon whispered in Simone's ear, "You ready?"

"Naaaaw, I ain't ready yet," Simone was shocked at the sound of her own voice. She was loud and her speech was slurred. She paused for a moment in an attempt to regain composure, but it didn't work, "Krisssy, give me sssome more of dat drank."

Kristen pulled a small silver flask from her purse and emptied its contents into Simone's cup. Simone threw it back with three quick gulps as if it was water.

"Now, I'm ready. Let'sss go!"

"Damn, dog. She a trooper. I know you gone have fun with that. Shit, you should let me hit when you done with her." Cameron's eyes were glued to Simone. He looked hungry, as if he would pounce her within seconds.

"Naw, dog. I gotta keep her all to myself. Ain't that right, baby?" Brandon grabbed her butt under her left cheek. Simone giggled. For some reason everything was funny.

"Oh what, you like my girl now. What the fuck is that all about?" Kristen was pissed, pushing Cameron's hands off her and glaring at Simone through envious eyes. It was hilarious to Simone. She laughed aloud, doubling over holding her stomach. Kristen wasn't laughing at all. She looked her friend up and down, telling her to "shut the fuck up" with her eyes.

"Naw girl! Stop trippin'. I'm just playing with her. Let's roll." Cameron turned around and used his two fingers to whistle as a signal to the rest of the party that it was time to go. Everyone followed and left the gym nearly empty.

Simone, Brandon, Cameron and Kristen piled into the silver Mercedes parked outside of the school. Brandon and Simone were in the front, the other two in the back. They peeled of with hip-hop blaring from the stereo, at least ten other cars followed close behind. Cameron lived in Birmingham, a ritzy Detroit suburb, about ten minutes away from the school, but they got there in six. Brandon pulled into the circular driveway of a massive house. It was huge, about a half size bigger than Simone's home.

Simone's mouth dropped open, "Daaannng! This yo house, Cam? It's sssweet!"

"Hell yeah, my dad is a boss man! Come on ya'll."

Everybody jumped out of the car. Cameron zipped his pants up as he walked up the steps to the front door. Kristen tripped and fell over the last step in a drunken stumble. The other ten plus cars pulled up and parallel parked along the sidewalk. Thirty-five loud, horny, drunk, and hyped up teenagers rushed into the house ready to party. Once inside, Cameron directed everyone down the long pillared corridor. They shuffled past expensive art and African sculptures. The sound of high heels and dress shoes echoed from the marble floors to the cathedral ceiling. The house looked more like a museum than a home.

Cameron directed everyone into the basement. When he turned on the surround-sound stereo system, the party started immediately. Everyone danced with everyone else. The liquor flowed freely and abundantly. Brandon made sure that Simone's cup was full at all times. She had the cup up to her mouth an average of about every 15 seconds. The place was packed. The party was wild. If someone wasn't dancing, they were making out or throwing up. Brandon pushed Simone up against the wall so they could dance close. He had her boxed in the corner with his long arms clutching her tight, grabbing her everywhere his hands could reach.

Simone continued to drink, this time, a green concoction that was sweeter than the first one she had in the gym. She was in a zone. The thumping music took her intoxication to a higher level. The room felt tilted. The walls were spinning in slow motion. Her and Brandon's bodies were grinding hard and slow to a sexy R-rated ballad. Brandon pushed her dress up to her upper thighs and lifted her left leg to wrap it around his back. He needed to get closer so she could feel how hard he was. She did feel it, and she liked it. It seemed to Simone that everyone else in the basement had disappeared, leaving her and Brandon alone to their erotic lovemaking dance.

"Damn, baby. You feel so good. I can't *wait* to hit it."

Simone didn't hear him. She was lost in her own world, floating and spinning with the walls. The lights were off and it was hot. She was sweating as her body rubbed against his. Sweat and spilled punch ruined her dress. Her hair had fallen out of the neat up-do her mother had so carefully coiffed. It was wet and frizzy, sticking to her back. Brandon kissed her on her neck, licking the salty sweat from her skin. All of it, everything felt so good. Then all of a sudden, she felt a strong uncontrollable urge to pee.

"Ooh! I gotta peee. Where's the bathroom?"

"Right down that hall. Don't take too long. I got something for yo fine ass when you get back."

She rushed into the crowd pushing and stumbling until she got to the hallway. She could barely stand up straight -- partially from being drunk, but also from trying to walk with her legs crossed so she wouldn't pee on herself. She used the wall as her support as she continued down the hall. The bathroom seemed to be miles away. But eventually she made it.

She pushed the door open, almost falling once inside. She knocked over some candles and a decorative soap dish on the countertop. She ripped down her stockings and panties and plopped down on the toilet seat right as the first drop of urine escaped her bladder.

"Ahh."

After her long overdue release, Simone sat there with her

elbows on her knees and her chin in her hands. She was too drunk to get up and too befuddled to do anything other than try to count the tiny blue dots on the hand towels hanging on the wall in front of her. She would get to three before they would all blend into one big blob and she would have to start over.

One, two, three, dangit....
One, two, why do they keep doing that!
One, two, three, four....

She hadn't realized that she'd fallen asleep until she felt the impact of her body hitting the cold, white tiles as she crashed to the floor. The collision jolted her eyes open in a dazed confusion. She had to get up and get out of the bathroom. She had to make it back to Kristen so they could leave. She knew she was excessively drunk and it was time to go. After several attempts, she managed to reach a standing position, stumbling and threatening to topple over the whole time. Feeling proud of herself, she pulled up her panties and her ripped stockings. The task left her exhausted. She leaned her body against the bathroom wall, waiting until she had enough energy to make it to the door and out into the hallway. Then she heard a knocking, thumping sound on the other side of the wall. The knocking started at a slow and steady pace, then graduated into a rapid tempo, getting louder with each thump. Simone thought she heard voices on the other side, so she put her ear to the wall to get a better listen.

The first voice belonged to a girl. "Oh shit, ahh, oh shit. Damn, baby. Fuck me. Fuck me harder. Oh oh shit. Yes!"

There was another voice, this time a guy. "Yeah bitch, take that shit. You nasty bitch. Aye dog, you getting this? Get over here on this side and tape it from this angle."

The girl: "Oh Cameron, damn! Oh it feels so good! Oh shit! Fuck me! Yeah, just like that! Ooh!" That time, Simone recognized the voice. It was Kristen.

There was a second guy, "Come on, dog, let me hit it. You been fucking her forever! It's my turn. Come on!"

"Wait nigga, I'm about to bust a nut all over her face. Make sure you get this shit on the tape Dee."

"Ha ha! Yeah, I'm getting it. Shoot her in her eye."

Simone couldn't believe what she was hearing. She had to get out of the bathroom. She had to save her girl. Kristen probably had no clue what was going on. She was drunk beyond comprehension. They were video taping her. They were running a train on her! She had to get them out of there. She rushed out of the bathroom and started banging on the door of the room where she heard the sounds.

"Open this door right now! Open the door! Kristen! Kristen, it's me. Tell them to open the door! Let her out. Let her out!"

"Damn, baby what took you so long? You were in there forever." Brandon was behind her, his eyes were half closed, his body swayed back and forth, threatening to fall on her.

"Tell them to open the door. Please! I have to get my girl out of there!"

"Step back, shorty. I'll tell 'em."

He knocked on the door, "Hey ya'll come open the door. It's B." After a couple of seconds, Darius opened the door. His pants were unzipped and loose around his waist. The video camera was in his hand. Simone pushed past him and entered the room, not noticing Brandon closing and locking the door behind him as he followed her in. She did a quick scan of the huge guest bedroom. On the wall opposite her, was a large overstuffed couch. On one end, there was a girl Simone didn't recognize, passed out in a drunken stupor. Her homecoming dress was pulled up around her waist exposing her naked bottom half. On the other end of the couch was a senior. Simone recognized her but didn't know her name. She was performing oral sex on Jeff Coleman, the captain of the basketball team. He sat on the couch with his head laid back and eyes closed.

On the adjacent wall, were two twin beds sitting side by side against the wall shared by the bathroom. The bed furthest away from Simone was neatly made, the corners were tucked and it was topped by about a dozen pillows, fluffed to perfection. On the other bed, she saw Kristen, on her elbows and knees. She was naked with her face buried in the pillows. She was still having sex with Cameron. He was pounding her small body from behind, calling her nasty, disrespectful names and smacking her on her ass.

Simone was horrified and speechless. She couldn't move. She wanted to scream and yank Kristen out of the bed and run out of the house, but her feet wouldn't do what her brain told them to do. Darius walked back over to the side of the bed and continued to tape Kristen and Cameron. Jeff lifted his head. The girl's lips were still wrapped around his penis. He yelled across the room to Brandon, standing behind Simone.

"Whassup B? I see you got yo' girl. Whatcha waitin' on? Get at her."

Brandon immediately followed orders and grabbed Simone by her arm, spinning her around violently. "Come here you drunk bitch." He grabbed her by her neck and forced his tongue down her mouth. It was disgusting. Simone gagged as the taste of liquor and vomit invaded her mouth.

Simone tried to push him away, but it only made him more forceful. He lifted her off the floor, took a few steps and threw her on the made up bed, knocking half of the pillows onto the floor. Simone screamed as she landed on her back.

"Shut the fuck up!"

Brandon had a fire in his eyes. He was charging at her with a look on his face that told Simone that he was going to rape her. He pulled her by her legs to the end of the bed. Her legs wiggled frantically, trying to break free. She sat up and tried to grab and scratch at his face, but she couldn't reach him.

She screamed and cried, begging for mercy, "Please no, please. Just lemme go!"

Brandon ignored her pleas, "I said shut up, bitch!" He raised his left hand over his shoulder and struck Simone with the back of his hand. She fell backwards on the bed. The salty taste of her own blood dripped into her mouth from her freshly busted lip.

Darius, still standing by Kristen's bed, dropped the video camera and yelled at his friend, "Yo B! What the fuck you doing, dog? You bout to rape her? Yo, nigga chill out! It ain't that deep!"

Brandon couldn't hear his boy scolding him. He had one thing on his mind and nothing was stopping him. He unzipped his fly and dropped his pants to the floor, then jumped on top of Simone. His chest muffled her screams. She kicked and punched, gasping for air. He kissed her on her neck and pulled her panties and her stockings off. The girl who was orally servicing Jeff lifted her head from his lap and stared at the two tussling on the bed. She didn't say anything. She looked frozen in shock. Jeff grabbed the back of her head and slammed it back down, "Mind your business, ho." She did as she was told.

Darius rushed over to Simone and Brandon, lying on the bed, "B, nigga you trippin'. Get off her. Man, this shit ain't worth it, dog! All our asses could go to jail. Get the fuck up!"

"Shut up nigga! She just playin'. She want it. She been wantin it all night. She just like it rough."

Simone interjected, "No, please, please no I don't want it. Please lemme go." She was no longer screaming. She was losing her voice. Her words were half drowned out by her tears.

Darius pushed Brandon off her. He fell to the floor, but jumped back up like a spring into Darius' face, "What the fuck you doing, Dee?"

"Look nigga, I'm not tryin to hate, but come on dog, you drunk! She's screaming and fighting and shit. That's not a good look. What if she goes to the police or something? She just a silly bitch man, don't throw your life away for some bullshit."

"Man, fuck you!" Brandon turned around and got ready to jump back on the bed, but Darius grabbed him from behind, putting him in a chokehold. Simone, hopped off the bed, grabbed her panties, then ran to the bed Kristen was on. She and Cameron were done having sex. They were laying on the bed on their way to sleep. Kristen's face looked calm and peaceful despite the crude and disgusting things she had just done. They were oblivious to the fact that Simone had come within seconds of being raped. Brandon continued to struggle with Darius until they fell to the floor.

"Come on, girl! Get up. We gotta get outta here. Get up!"

Cameron glared at her with disgust, "Bitch, you betta get away from me unless you want some too."

Simone stayed persistent, ignoring him, "Kris, let's go girl. He tried to rape me!"

Kristen laughed with her eyes still closed "I ain't going nowhere. Get the fuck outta my face. He *should've* raped yo stupid ass. Come up in this bitch like you betta than everybody."

"What? What are you talking about? Look, you're just drunk. Come on let's go!" Simone grabbed Kristen by her arm and tried to drag her out of the bed, but Kristen pushed her away.

"Get the fuck off me! Touch me again, I'll beat the shit outta you."

Cameron chimed in, "Man, get yo stuck up ass outta here. Bougie bitch."

Simone was completely astounded. She stood still for a moment, soaking in what was happening. Kristen, her girl, her best friend, was not her friend at all. She didn't have her back. She was never there for her. She hated her just as much as she did the day of their confrontation. It didn't matter that she was drunk, Simone heard absolute sincerity in her voice and she knew that she was alone.

After a moment, she snapped out of it. She stole a glance at Darius and Brandon. They were still struggling on the floor. Brandon was still fighting for freedom from Darius' vise grip, but Darius was bigger, stronger, and more importantly, he was sober. Brandon was no match. Simone didn't wait to see who would win. She didn't stick around to see if Kristen would come to her senses. She didn't care if anyone else in that house was raped or hurt that night. She couldn't afford to stay to find out. She had to get out.

She charged out of the room and pushed past her over-charged, sweaty classmates. She bumped into, what seemed to be, every person there as they rocked and bounced to the roaring music, knocking Simone upside her head. She rushed up the stairs and out of the door.

It was a cold autumn night in Michigan. The tempera-ture was barely 40 degrees. It wasn't until her teeth started to chatter that she realized that she'd left her coat and purse in Brandon's mother's Mercedes. Thankfully, the doors were unlocked. She grabbed her belongings from the passenger seat and ran for her life.

Cameron's house was on the corner. She ran down the adjacent street. She had no idea what street she was on, but she recognized the lights and busy traffic of Woodward Avenue about four blocks straight ahead. It was Saturday night, about midnight. The Downtown Birmingham scene was bustling with nightlife. Partygoers, -- mostly couples in their mid to late twenties -- staggered in and out of "The Blue Martini", "The Corner" and the other upscale bars and nightspots on or near the strip. Simone had no idea where she was going, was clueless as to what she would do, but the bright lights were a savior calling her to safety from the dark, wooded streets that surrounded Cameron's house.

She couldn't call her parents to come get her because she wasn't where she was supposed to be. Running helplessly through downtown Birmingham, with raggedy hair, torn stockings and a busted lip would be impossible to explain. She had no plan, no way out. So she continued to run.

She ran to leave the whole nightmare behind her. She ran faster to keep her mind racing so she wouldn't have to think about her best friend's betrayal, her dream man's false pretenses, or the sour liquor that was sloshing around in her stomach, inching it's way up to her throat, forewarning a massive vomit. She ran until the heel of her silver pump got stuck in a crack in the sidewalk and snapped off the bottom of her shoe. It made her trip and stumble into a nearby bush. The bristles and branches scratched her legs, tearing her stockings even more. She hadn't made it to Woodward Avenue yet; there was still one block to go. Simone quickly removed her shoes from her feet, holding them in her left hand, and continued to run, ignoring the pain from the sticks, rocks and leaves, tearing into her feet with each step.

Then finally, she was on Woodward, immersed in the bright lights. The clawing darkness was behind her. As she began to feel more comfortable, she reduced her pace to a slow walk. The walk would have told anyone, who may have noticed her, that she was lost and confused, but no one noticed her at all. No one cared that she was barefoot, or that her hair was a frizzy, matted mess. No one was concerned with her bloody lip or her bloodshot eyes. They all walked past her, in their own party buzz, unaware of her horrible Homecoming night.

No one noticed as she walked through the door of Paradise restaurant on the corner of Thirteen Mile and Woodward, and headed straight to the bathroom to relieve herself of the red and green mixed drinks fighting inside her stomach. She ran into the last stall of the dingy bathroom and let it all out after dry heaving for about five minutes. The bathroom was empty and it smelled of cheap potpourri mingled with old urine. The stench caused Simone to heave once more to rid herself of the remnants of the alcohol.

After flushing the toilet, she went to the sink to wash her hands, but paused as she caught sight of herself in the mirror. Beyond the runny mascara, tear-streaked cheeks, bloodshot eyes and dried blood on her lip, she was still remarkably gorgeous. Her roasted almond skin was impeccable, her nose and mouth in flawless proportion, her face in perfect symmetry, her emerald eyes were piercing, her hair, although disheveled, exquisite. She was breathtaking; her beauty was an aberration.

It was the first time she had taken a good look at herself in months and it enraged her. Her breathing became heavy and her body stiff. She squinted her eyes in a glare and her lips became a tight, thin line. She was appalled, but she couldn't peel her eyes from her own reflection. She was captivated, trapped. It wasn't until the thought of her father crept into her head, did she snap out of her trance. Rage convulsed her entire body as she lashed out on the image that stared back at her. Growling with a painful anger, she beat the mirror ferociously with her fists. But it stood strong, refusing to shatter under the blows. It made her pound harder and harder until her fists ached from the impact.

Desperate to destroy her reflection, she frantically turned in circles, searching the bathroom for something to break the glass. Finally, she found it. A white metal trashcan sat in the corner by the door. She quickly snatched it up, shrieking to boost her strength, and struck the mirror with a blunt force.

It cracked into a spider-webbed pattern, but that wasn't good enough. Her eyes were still staring at her, taunting her. They grabbed and pulled at her. It was torture. She had to escape those eyes, those menacing, treacherous eyes. With another wild scream, she hit the mirror again. This time, she achieved her goal. Hundreds of pieces of glass flew out from the mirror and landed all over the floor, in the sink, in the stalls and on the counter.

Simone stared at the broken glass all around her with immense disappointment. It was still there. Although, she could no longer see the cause of her suffering, her pain remained. It spread through her body like a virus. It twisted and turned, branching off into every corner of her being, completely consuming her. She cried on the inside and out. She was frustrated, desperate to numb her remaining anguish. With her back against the wall, she slumped to the floor, letting her body fall, like a rag doll, in an awkward position. Her legs sprawled out in front of her. One bent backwards, the other straight ahead. Her arms lay lifeless by her sides.

She sat there absorbed in her own misery for several minutes before she noticed a throbbing ache in her right arm. She examined her arm and found several small cuts from the shattered mirror. The sight of the blood beading on her skin was soothing. The pain of the wounds was diverting, comforting and calming. It hurt, but it was a good hurt. The hurt consoled her and tranquilized her distress. She felt a flush of satisfaction as she reached to grab another piece of the shattered mirror, calling to her from the bathroom floor.

Anxious to escalate the euphoric feeling, she used the sharp edge of the glass fragment to slice the underside of her forearm. It was a small incision, not deep enough to cut through an artery, not wide enough to cause intense bleeding, but just enough to release some of the misery that festered inside of her. She released six months of abuse as it dripped slowly from her arm. She cut herself again, then again, then six times more. Each laceration brought her an intoxicating sense of contentment and control. She had control. The pain that directed her life was now subdued and she held the key of restraint in her hand. It was time to take back her life, to stop surrendering to her torment. She was in control. Her tears dried away and she relaxed. She closed her eyes and allowed herself to enjoy the pleasure of her self-mutilation.

The bathroom door swung open hard and hit the wall with a thud. A short, overweight, dark brown woman stormed in, holding a large serving spoon in her left hand. Simone sprang up from the floor and stumbled before catching her balance against the wall.

"What the hell is going on in here? What did you do to my bathroom?" The woman shrieked.

With panicked eyes and jittery hands, Simone snatched her coat from the floor and ran towards the open door, pushing the woman aside. She ran into the dining area. Behind her, she heard the woman scream for someone to call the police, but Simone was out of the restaurant before anyone could take action. She sprinted wildly onto Woodward Avenue, into the middle of ongoing traffic. The blaring horns and cursing screams of angry motorists pushed her to keep going. She bobbed and weaved and didn't stop until she reached the other side of the street where she crouched down to catch her breath and clear her mind.

When she looked up, she saw the illuminating neon sign of The Blue Martini, a popular nightclub. Young bar hoppers and wannabe socialites spilled out of the door, staggering and laughing after a night of intoxicating music and drinks. When Simone noticed a few of them glaring at her in mixed expressions of shock and pity, she realized her bloody arm was exposed and threw on her coat to hide the evidence of her shame. She felt hopeless and alone. Unaware as to what to do or where to go, she closed the coat tightly with her hand, and sat on the edge of the sidewalk, facing the parking lot.

The next hour, for Simone, was a blur. She woke up at home, in her own bed the next morning. She was naked under the covers. Her dress, stockings and purse lay tossed on the opposite side of the bedroom in a heap. She remembered two young women helping her to her feet outside of the club the night before, but she could not recall their names or faces. They had asked if she needed to go to the hospital or if she wanted them to get the police. Simone cried that she just wanted to go home, that was all she wanted. So there she was, at home. She did not remember how she got there, didn't care. She was home.

CHAPTER 16

RYAN

"EXCUSE me. How much is this bag?"

"The Canvas? I believe it is $885.00. Give me a moment and I'll check for you."

"Thank you." Ryan bit her bottom lip in an attempt not to wince at the sound of the outrageously high price of the handbag she had been admiring. She was in a high-end boutique, feeding her destructive impulse to shop. She had learned from her therapy sessions that the habit was a side effect of her depression.

"Okay, here we go. I was right. It is $885.00. Would you like me to wrap that up for you?" The sales woman was a short redheaded, white woman in her early twenties. She was extremely bubbly -- a little too bouncy and cheery for Ryan's liking. She found her body language, her voice and mannerisms to be presumptuous.

"Um… I don't know. I think I'll keep looking for a while. Thanks for your help." She walked away from the woman before she succumbed to the overwhelming urge to slap the ridiculous smile off her face. She placed the handbag back on the shelf and moved towards the back of the store. She feasted her eyes on yet another tantalizing bag. This one was leather, not canvas like the first, so she knew it would cost more. Not really wanting to hear the answer, she flagged the sales associate, walking past her and asked for the price. He was better than the first woman who helped her. He was a black guy, more calm and down to earth. He seemed a lot more laid back and easy going than his co-worker did. He didn't have an unnecessary bounce in his step or the jumpy hand gestures. He didn't speak with an exaggerated high pitch at the end of his words. He was, what she considered to be, normal.

"Excuse me, Sir. Can you tell me how much this bag is?"

"Sure, that's $2,230." The sales clerk let his eyes travel from Ryan's flawlessly made up face to her busty chest, then down to her curvaceous hips. He licked his lips as he lifted his eyes back up to meet hers. It was obvious that he liked the view before him.

Ryan rolled her eyes, aggravated by his obvious gawking. Damn! Could she go anywhere without being treated like a piece of prime cut meat? "That's too much. You all don't have anything on sale?" She wasn't sure why she'd asked the question. She knew herself well enough to know that she was going to buy the bag regardless of the price and she knew the store's policy well enough to know that they never had sales.

The sales clerk visibly relaxed his posture, obviously feeling more comfortable, and allowed himself to be slightly flirtatious. Ryan hated that. "Come on now, you know we don't have no sales up in here, but if you let me take you out to dinner, I can get it on my store discount for you."

The irritation she'd felt when speaking to the other sales associate crept up inside of her and exploded out of her mouth, "Look, I didn't come in here for anything other than a handbag. *Anything* else that you think you have to offer me, I am not interested in. I have a man and I am more than capable of purchasing this bag, as well as dinner, on my own. If I can't, he will. Now, please take this to the counter so I can cash out."

"Ooh, you a feisty one. I like that! Look, it's cool if you have a man. I can just be your friend. You know what I'm saying?"

Ryan was losing her cool, "What exactly is it that you don't understand? I do not want to be your friend. I do not want to go out with you. All I want is for you to do your job and ring up the bag for me. Do you think you can do that?"

He did as he was told, but his hopes were still high, believing her harsh rejection to be nothing more than a friendly game of hard to get. She slapped her credit card down on the counter to pay the hefty price for the bag, then turned to leave, but was prevented from doing so as she felt the dry, rough skin of his hand wrap around her wrist.

"You make sure you come back to see me *real* soon," he leered.

Ryan snatched her hand back, repelled by his rude persistence. She couldn't come up with any words and she didn't feel as if he was worthy of the time it would take to say them, "Ugh!" It was all she could manage to utter as she walked out of the store, swinging her hair along with her hips.

Somerset Collection, for some, was more of a status symbol than a mall. If you wanted to be seen and at least give the illusion that you had money, you shopped at Somerset. The architecture was beautiful, the atmosphere elegant, and the prices high. It consisted of two buildings located across the street from each other, connected by a glass skywalk hovering over the busy traffic of Big Beaver Road. The building on the North side of the road was usually the more crowded of the two, housing the more mainstream, affordable shops and boutiques.

Ryan was on the South side that Friday evening and was annoyed to find it just as crowded as the North side. She saw several people that she knew. People from work, friends of friends, and people she used to know from high school years ago. She did not stop to talk to most of them. Only the few who actually stopped to get her attention did she take the time to acknowledge. She wasn't a talkative, sociable person at all. She wasn't mean; she just didn't want to be bothered. Ever. Some would call her a bitch, but Ryan considered herself to be very selective, one who chose her time and words carefully and didn't waste either on those who were less than deserving. There was nothing wrong with that. Nevertheless, for some reason, people always took it upon themselves to approach her. To try to engage her into meaningless conversations about their kids, what they were doing with their lives and how much they hated their jobs. The bored, disinterested look on Ryan's face never seemed to deter them.

Katrina, Ryan's supervisor from her old firm, bumped into her as she was entering one of the department stores.

"Ryan? Is that you? Oh my goodness, I haven't seen you in about three years. How have you been?"

Ryan, forced her best fake smile, "Oh, hey Katrina. It has been a long time. I'm doing great. How have things been?"

"Oh, you know me. I'm just doing everything I can to try to keep that zoo they call a firm in order. You remember how it was."

"Girl, you know I do. I--" before she could finish her sentence, Ryan's body was jolted forward as someone violently pushed her into Katrina from the back. Her shopping bag nearly fell to the floor. The push, harsh and blunt, was obviously deliberate. Ryan whipped around to catch a good look at the perpetrator. It was a woman. She was white, in her late thirties or early forties, about 5'2" with bleached blond hair. She was an average looking woman, on the verge of being pretty, but her lips ruined her chances. They were extremely puffy, pumped full of collagen. She looked as if she was part mallard with her lips spread wide and stretched out like Daffy Duck. She was dressed in expensive clothes and had an air about her that exuded superiority.

She turned around to face Ryan as she continued down the hall. Her stilettos click clacked on the tile floor, "Oh, excuse me."

Ryan stared into the woman's face and tried to conjure up any trace of recognition, but she failed. She had never seen her in her life. However, the sarcastic apology told Ryan that the woman knew who *she* was. Either that, or she was incredibly mistaken. Whatever the case, Ryan wasn't going to let her get away that easily, "What is your problem? I know you saw me standing here."

The woman stopped and spun around to face Ryan, "Excuse me?"

"You heard me! What is your damn problem? Do I know you?"

Katrina, sensing the negative energy in the air, began to back her way into the department store and leave the scene. "Well girl, it was good to see you. Later." Ryan ignored her farewell as she walked away.

Ryan's eyes tightened as she glared at the woman who pushed her. The duck lipped woman stared back, but she stayed in her place. "Oh, no problem at all. It was purely an accident. Again, I apologize." The woman gave Ryan a smile that seriously lacked sincerity. She turned back around and continued to walk away, this time faster than before, almost in a trot.

Ryan, was heated, "Oh you think you're just going to bump me and keep walking like nothing happened? Just who in the hell do you think you are? Hey. Hey…!" Her challenging words were lost in the crowd of shoppers rushing in and out of the department store. The woman had disappeared somewhere between the makeup counter and the shoe department. Ryan decided against her first instinct to follow her and give her a well-deserved beat down. Dr. Gloria had taught her to count to ten when she felt a rush of anger rising, in order to calm herself. That shit never worked, so she popped a Xanax instead.

Go with what you know.

She took the pill dry as she did most of the time, as her pill popping was often spontaneous and urgent. There was no time to waste looking for water. She needed relief quickly, on the spot. As she waited for her high to kick in, she picked up her cell phone and pressed the speed dial number one. After two rings, Anthony answered the phone.

His voice was groggy, as if he was sleeping, "What's up, baby?"

"Hey, what are you doing?"

"Waiting on you. When are you coming over here?"

"I'll be there in a minute. The mall is packed."

"Well make sure you hurry up. I miss you, baby. I can't wait to see you."

"Aw, I miss you too. You got something for me?"

"You know I do. Come over here and get it."

Ryan let out a devilish schoolgirl giggle, "Ooh what is it?"

"I don't know. You might not be able to handle it."

"Try me."

"You'll just have to find out when you get your fine ass over here."

"Ooh, I can't wait, I'm leaving the mall now. I'll be there in 20 minutes. Oh, I almost forgot. I bought this new handbag and I need $2200 to cover it."

"We'll see when you get here. Depends on how good you can handle what I've got for you."

"Oh don't worry. I'll have you giving me *all* your money." They both laughed before hanging up the phone. Ryan felt wetness between her legs as she relished the arousal overcoming her body. She almost sprinted through the mall and into the parking lot. She had forgotten all of their recent arguments. The five times he had stood her up without calling in the last two months were a distant memory. The outrageous stories and excuses were erased from her mind. The countless emotional mind games were absolved from her brain. All she could think of was riding her man on his butter soft leather chair in front of the big, picture window overlooking the Detroit River. She was so excited, she almost squealed as she jogged to her car.

The drive to his loft, in Downtown Detroit, was unusually smooth. It was the weekend, so there weren't nearly as many cars on the freeway as there were during the week. The music from the stereo was blaring as Ryan glided in and out of traffic. The speedometer never dropped below 75 miles per hour. It was snowing outside, the first snowfall of the season, but it wasn't sticking, so she didn't have to slow her pace. It was about 7 o'clock in the evening. Standard time was already in effect. It was beginning to get dark as the sun set in the distance, activating the automatic headlights of her Beamer. She grabbed her purse on the passenger seat as she heard the text-messaging alert go off. She took her eyes off the road for a second to retrieve her cell phone and read the text from Lauren, reminding her of their hair appointment the following morning. Ryan texted back, keeping a view of the road ahead in her peripheral vision.

Before she could hit the green button on her phone to send the message, a charcoal colored Range Rover drove up close behind her. There were about two feet between the two cars as the SUV tailed her.

Ryan cursed the driver of the Rover, screaming to her rearview mirror, "What the hell is wrong with you? Get off my ass!" She made an earnest attempt to divert her trailer, pressing down on the brake pedal to slow her speed to 40mph, hoping the other driver would become impatient and go around her. But the SUV stayed close, slowing its pace to match Ryan's. Ryan sped up and switched from the far left lane to the middle, regaining her momentum and climbing back up to 75 mph. The SUV stayed close. She switched back to the left lane then crossed all the way over to the far right, but she couldn't shake him.

"Okay, you want to play games? Let's see how far you want to take this!"

She decided to give chase, slamming on the gas and increasing her speed to 80, then 90, up to 100, but the Rover never let up. She turned down the radio, needing her full concentration. The booming bass blaring from the speakers was a serious distraction.

The two cars rode past five exits on the freeway, maintaining a speed well above the legal limit. She looked into her review mirror to catch sight of the driver, but couldn't see past the tinted windshield. She cut in front of a minivan, barely avoiding a collision, in hopes of loosing her tormentor. It didn't work. The minivan switched lanes giving the Rover the chance to move back up on Ryan's tail.

"What the fuck! What is going on?"

She was being followed at a dangerous pace of 110 miles per hour. The roads were slick and wet from the slushy snowfall. It was dark and Ryan's night vision was blurry. She was prescribed to wear eyeglasses when she was 10 years old, but had been neglecting the obligation since she was 16. The streetlights reflected off the wet road. The glare further impaired her vision. She was nervous, not sure if someone was intentionally trying to hurt her or if it was just a sick game. Either way, she wanted it to end. She made one last attempt to lose her pursuer. She switched lanes again, this time to the far right, keeping her speed at a steady 105 miles per hour. The Range Rover followed. Ryan was confused and equally afraid. Her fingers tapped uneasily on the steering wheel. She picked up the phone to call Lauren, hoping her best friend would be able to calm her nerves, but her dialing was interrupted as the bright rays of the Rover's high beams blinded her.

"Oh shit!"

She dropped the phone. It made a small thud as it hit the floorboard. She needed to pull over, needed to slow down, but she could do neither. She couldn't see a thing. The bright incandescent lights glared from behind, illuminating the inside of her car. She bit down on her bottom lip to prevent herself from crying, knowing the tears would hinder her vision even more. The Range Rover was still on her ass, bright lights blazing.

Ryan jerked the steering wheel in desperation to dodge traffic, barely missing the cars in front of her. She switched from the right to the middle lane, then to the far left and back to the middle trying to escape the Rover's glare. The SUV stayed in close pursuit, leaving only a couple of feet between them. Ryan honked her horn to warn the other drivers on the road to get out of the way. She had come close to colliding with a black Mustang on her right, barely missing it by only a few inches. Finally, the Range Rover moved to the left lane, giving Ryan some relief from its high beams.

She looked to her left and squinted her eyes in an attempt to focus and identify the driver. She failed. The crazed motorist was indistinguishable through the tinted windows. His image was nothing more than a black profile. Ryan could tell that he was wearing a hat and a large goose down coat, but that was as much as she could decipher. The driver looked on straight ahead. He never looked at Ryan, never giving her the implication that he knew or recognized her. The way he sat stiff in the driver's seat, was robotic, both hands on the wheel with the seat at a 90-degree angle. He kept his pace, riding along side of her BMW.

Ryan seized her first opportunity to slow down. She cruised over to the right lane, taking her foot off the gas and giving a red Toyota the chance to pull up in the middle lane, coming between her and her stalker. She pressed down on the brake pedal, but it wouldn't budge. She pressed again, but got the same resistance. The brakes were stuck. In a panic, she stomped the pedal, pumping down on it with her right foot, trying to force them into action. It didn't work. Her hands were sweating and her heart was beating profusely. She could no longer hold back the tears. They rolled down her face, taking her mascara with them. She took a quick glance at the floorboard, hoping to diagnose the brake problem. She saw that her cell phone was lodged under the pedal.

"Shit!" She slid down in her seat, trying her best to keep at least one eye on the road. She kicked at the cell phone to loosen it from under the brake pedal. She missed it on the first and second try, but was successful on the third. She let out a large sigh of relief and wiped the tears from her face with three quick swipes, then pressed down on the brakes. The feeling of the car slowing soothed her. She slid her body back to an upright position. She took a deep breath to calm her nerves, then looked to her left to locate the Rover. The Toyota was no longer by her side. She saw the Rover in the far left lane. She silently prayed that it stayed there, but it didn't. He jumped into the middle lane. They rode side by side for about ten seconds before he grabbed the wheel and made a sharp turn to the right, swerving into Ryan's lane, ramming the driver's side of the BMW.

He's trying to force me off of the road! He's trying to kill me!

There was no time to go into shock and no time for tears. Ryan reacted. In a millisecond, she turned her wheel hard to the left to avoid falling into the huge ditch bordering the freeway. The BMW and Rover connected; they rode joined at the side until the Rover let up and moved back over to the far left. But before Ryan could regain her composure, he came back with a swift sideswipe, slamming into Ryan's driver's side. The BMW fishtailed as the Rover sped up and continued down the freeway, leaving Ryan behind, spinning out of control.

Ryan screamed as the car whirled dangerously close to the edge of the freeway. Her heart was beating uncontrollably. Her eyes bulged out of their sockets. The other cars on the road swerved frantically, honking their horns, trying to maneuver safely around the twirling BMW. Amazingly, no one hit her. After three full 360-degree turns, the car came to a halt. Ryan sat frozen in her seat. She couldn't move, couldn't breathe. Her mind was unable to process the thought that her life nearly ended just 15 seconds prior.

She had her own unique relationship with God, one that hardly involved prayer, unless she wanted something. But that day, at that moment, she was deeply and truly thankful to the Lord, thankful for her life, and she told Him so repeatedly. She promised that she would try to be a better person. She repented for her sins and praised His name. She promised that she would continue to pray from that point on. These thoughts lasted just as long as it took her to say them, but she did sincerely mean it at the time. She slowly pulled her maimed car over to the shoulder of the freeway and stepped out to inspect the damages.

"Oh my God!" Tears welled up in her eyes as she stared at the crushed driver's side door. It was completely smashed, like a crumpled piece of paper. She thought about calling the police to report the incident. That's what any responsible, sensible person would do. After all someone did just try to end her life, but her better judgment told her not to. She didn't get the license plate number of the Rover and she had no way to identify the driver, but most importantly, she was driving on a suspended license. She had gotten a ticket for speeding back in August and couldn't remember to pay it for the life of her. She couldn't risk calling the police and getting arrested.

"I'm fucked!"

She held herself in a tight embrace, as her shivering body reminded her that she was outside in the middle of a cold Michigan autumn. She got back in the car and drove the rest of the way to Anthony's place. She rode in silence, paranoid, constantly checking the rearview mirror for her attacker, but he never reappeared.

When she got to the building and pulled up to the security gate, she breathed a sigh of relief. She would explain the terrifying, near-death experience to her man and he would take care of everything. He would comfort her. He would cradle her in his arms, kiss her forehead and reassure her that everything would be okay. He'd pay for the insurance deductible on her car and give her one of his cars to drive while hers was being repaired. He would make everything okay. The guard at the security gate recognized her and allowed her to proceed.

She parked her car inside of the parking structure and took the elevator up to his floor. Before her knuckles could touch the knocker, the door swung open. Anthony stood holding the doorknob, blocking the entrance.

Ryan jumped up to hug him, "Oh my God, baby! I'm so glad to see you. You won't believe what just happened to me."

"What took you so long to get here?" He looked and sounded angry. His body was stiff and he did not return her embrace.

"That's what I was about to tell you. Somebody just tried to kill me on the freeway!"

"Oh really."

The sarcasm in his tone told Ryan that he didn't believe her. She released her clasp and frowned at him. He still stood holding the door. He wasn't going to let her in.

"Yeah, really. Are you going to let me in so I can tell you about it?"

"Let you in?"

"Yes. Let me in."

"I don't think so."

"What?"

"Come on, Ryan, somebody tried to *kill you*?"

"What? You saying I'm lying?"

"I don't know. I don't know what you were doing. Maybe, just maybe, nobody tried to kill you at all. Maybe, you were with that guy you were flirting with at the mall."

"What?"

"Don't act like you don't know what I'm talking about."

"I'm not acting. I *don't* know what you're talking about."

"Oh, so you don't remember going into that store in the mall and throwing yourself at that loser who works there. You don't remember asking him to use his store discount or holding his hand at the counter?"

"Wait, that's not how it happened. He was trying to flirt with me, but I told him--"

"You think I'm stupid don't you? I know a lot of people, Ryan and those people go a lot of places. Everywhere you go, you represent me. You embarrassed me today, acting like a ho. You might as well have fucked him right there in the store."

"What the hell are you talking about? That is not what happened."

"That's not what I heard."

"And how in the hell do you know? You saying that you have people watching me?"

"I have a lot of people who care about me and look out for my best interests, and right now it is not in my best interests to be with a ho. I certainly wouldn't marry one."

He'd never talked to her like that before, never called her disrespectful names. He had never looked at her with hateful eyes. Ryan was looking at a different person. This wasn't Anthony. This wasn't the man who had swept her off her feet a year ago. He wasn't the man who used to bring her flowers every other day and leave love notes on her door. This wasn't the one who rushed to take care of her every need and canceled his plans to spend long nights with her, then whisked her away on spontaneous tropical vacations. He wasn't the man who looked into her eyes and told her he would kill and die for her. This was not her man. This was someone else standing in his shoes, wearing his clothes, invading his body and using his voice.

She was confused, hurt and offended. But even more so, she was tired. She was tired of the accusations, tired of being stood up when they were supposed to go out, tired of the long drawn out excuses and the lies that accompanied them, tired of him not answering her phone calls and never calling her back. She was tired of him treating her like shit. The last four months were hell. He had changed on her with no warning, blindsiding her like a deer in headlights.

Ryan took a deep breath before speaking. She wanted to make sure she was calm and tried to be careful not to scream her words. She needed her message to come across seriously, clear and to the point. "Look, Anthony. I don't know who told you what, but I was not with any guy. And I am not going to stand here and listen to you disrespect me and try to make me feel like I did something wrong when you and I both know that I didn't."

"I don't know shit. I don't know what you do when I'm not around. You hang out with your girl all the time, listening to her dog me out. Letting her convince you to see other people and you're so stupid listening to everything that she says. She's just a lonely ass ho and she wants you to be a lonely ho right along with her. Stupid."

Her enforced calm was quickly wearing off, "Where in the hell do you get off talking about Lauren?"

"She's a ho."

"She's not a ho! And what does she have to do with this conversation? This is about me and you."

"Yeah, what about me and you?"

She threw her hands up in the air, "You know what, Anthony? There is no me and you."

"Watch your mouth. Don't say stupid things that you don't mean."

"I know exactly what I'm saying. I'm sick and tired of your bullshit. I'm done waiting up for you in the middle of the night. I'm done listening to your ridiculous lies. I'm done listening to you put me down. I'm just done. You're not worth it."

"*I'm* not worth it? Why in the hell do you think I never have time for you? Why do you think I treat you differently than I used to? Because *you're* the one who's not worth it. I deserve better and I intend to find better. Now are you done? I have things to do."

He was unbelievable. It was as if he was talking to someone he didn't know, some random chick off the street. It was so ridiculous. It almost made her laugh.

She smirked, "Yeah Anthony, I'm done." She turned her back and walked away. Before she took her second step, he had slammed the door. It was over and she was never going back.

CHAPTER 17

RYAN

RYAN stared at the phone, using her imaginary teleki-netic powers to will the damn thing to ring. He hadn't called. She hadn't heard his voice in a week. She had checked the phone for damages, taking it up to the nearest repair shop for an inspection. She thought that maybe his number was mysteriously blocked. Her phone was only allowing calls from Lauren and her mother to come through, along with a couple of unsolicited calls from miscellaneous people she would barely acknowledge as friends. Most calls went unanswered. All text messages were unreturned. Voicemails were ignored.

She didn't feel like talking, didn't feel like explaining to anyone why she hadn't been to work in five days or why she'd lost almost five pounds in one week. She couldn't bring herself to explain why she didn't think it was necessary to comb her hair or change her clothes or why she couldn't sleep at night and spent her mornings crying uncontrollably. She couldn't find the energy and couldn't hold her tears long enough to make her words comprehensible. Instead, she stayed isolated in her condo with the windows closed. The only source of light was the soft glow of the TV screen as it aired a crime investigation show marathon.

She wore old bleach-stained jogging pants, once black, now gray. Her oversized T-shirt was one of Anthony's, long forgotten. It still held a hint of his cologne and she sniffed it every now and then to feel closer to him. She had never washed it. Her hair was a mess. It had lost its luster and shine. She had it pulled back in a sloppy ponytail; raggedy strands fell in her face as evidence of her nightly tossing and turning. Her eyes were swollen from her continuous tears. Under her arms, reeked a musty stench, from her crotch, a fishy odor. She hadn't showered in days. She was a mess, to say the least.

Emotionally drained and mentally numbed, she lay lifeless across the sofa in the living room. Her eyes darted from the TV screen to the phone, then back to the TV again. Twice she thought she heard the phone vibrate, the buzzing sound jumped off the cocktail table. Both times she'd sprung up from the couch to answer it. But of course, it wasn't him. It was just the sound of some sick maniac on TV butchering his neighbor with a chainsaw. The second time it was only her imagination.

Next to the phone on the cocktail table, lay an empty half gallon of chocolate ice cream. Next to that, was a near-empty pizza box, accompanied by three bottles of cherry cola, a half-eaten bag of cookies and candy bar wrappers. She had fallen completely apart and it would take two armies, a forklift and a truckload of super glue to put her back together. When she dumped him, it was a real good idea at the time. It made sense. She wasn't happy. She was being falsely accused and disrespected. She deserved better. She was worth more. She was a strong, independent, intelligent, black woman. She didn't have to take any shit off of a man. She didn't need some good for nothing bastard making her feel like she was worthless, making her feel like she was nothing. So she did what any respectable woman would do. She kicked his ass to the curb.

But if that is what she was supposed to do, why did she feel like less than nothing. Her insides were empty. Her self-esteem was non-existent. Nothing in the world mattered anymore.

She'd finally come to the realization that she was the reason why they weren't together. *She* was the one that had changed. She nagged him all the time. She was demanding. She cursed like a streetwalker, screamed like a lunatic, and her temper was out of control. She had a fucked up attitude, was self-centered and selfish. She was sarcastic and mean. She had pushed him away. She pushed and pushed until she forced him to change. No wonder he stood her up constantly and never answered her phone calls. It didn't take a genius to figure out why he never wanted to spend any time with her. She understood why he didn't help her with her bills like he used to and why he'd come over her house late at night to fuck her then leave without spending the night like he used to. It was clear why everything she said to him made him snap and snarl at her. Why in the hell would he want to marry someone like that?

She now realized her mistake and hoped that it wasn't irreversible. She just needed a chance to plead her case, to tell him that she was sorry. She was stupid for leaving him. He was a good man and he deserved better. She would give him better, everything that he needed and 100% more. She would tell him all of that as soon as he picked up the damn phone!

She had called him at least fifty times a day. He never

answered. Sometimes he sent her straight to voicemail. His mailbox was full from the countless messages she had left. His executive assistant at the office was screening his calls, and after Ryan threatened her life, the bitch started hanging up as soon as she heard her voice on the other end of the receiver.

Her pills were no longer working. She popped about three or four Xanax a day, but the high no longer comforted her. Her anxiety was increasing. Her stomach was doing cartwheels. She kept taking the drug to keep her sane, to keep her from suffering the withdrawals.

The phone rang. Once again, she hopped up from her resting place to look at the caller ID. Her heart was beating fast and she held her breath as she picked up the phone. It was Lauren. Her heart dropped and the tears began to flow. She slammed the phone back down on the table and laid down on the couch. It rang again, about fifteen seconds after the first call. It was Lauren. She called again, then again. The phone jumped and danced to the vibration on the table as her best friend continued to call. She called four more times. It was driving Ryan crazy.

She screamed at the phone, "Stop it! Stop it! Shut the fuck up!" She grabbed it and pushed the red button to turn it off. But if the phone was off, she would miss his call, so she quickly turned it back on. Finally, the buzzing stopped. Lauren had given up. As soon as she laid her head back down on the pillows and began to immerse herself in its comfort, she heard a knock at the door, a repetitious banging, like someone trying to tear the door down. Paranoid that the attacker from last week was back to finish the job, she jumped to her feet and armed herself with the lamp from the end table at the edge of the couch. Then she heard yelling from outside.

"Ryan! Open this damn door! Are you okay? Are you in there? Ryan, please! Open the door!" It was Lauren.

Ryan didn't make a move towards the door. She put the lamp back down and dropped herself on the couch, covering her head with the pillow to drown out the banging and the screaming. She whispered, "Just go away. Please just leave me alone." Ryan knew that Lauren wouldn't just go away. She hadn't heard from her in days. She had missed their hair appointment last Saturday. She wasn't answering her phone calls. When she did, it was a short conversation that began and ended with "I'll call you back." To go from countless conversations throughout the day to none at all was a noticeable difference and an obvious indicator that something was wrong. The banging continued.

"Ryan, if you don't open this door, I'm coming in." The knocking stopped. The next thing Ryan heard were keys jiggling in the door. She sat up on the couch and stared at the door.

What is she doing?

The door swung open and Lauren stormed in, dropping the keys on the dining room table. She was tall. Statuesque. Her hair was cut in a short, cropped style, light brown with golden blonde highlights to match her sun kissed skin. She had a keen sense of style, one that paralleled Ryan's. She wore a tapered, tan leather jacket, thin brown sweater, skinny jeans with a gold belt and tan, leather boots to match her jacket. She looked like she had just stepped out of a photo shoot. It was annoying. She ran to Ryan's side on the couch, "What is going on with you? What happened?"

"How did you get a key to my house?" Ryan didn't want her there, didn't want her to see her the way she was. She buried her head in the pillows, hiding her face. She didn't look up as she spoke to her.

"I got it from your mother."

"You asked my mother for a key to my house?"

"What else was I supposed to do? I keep calling and you never answer. When you do pick up, you sound like you're dying." She looked around at the filthy condo. From the living room, she could see the dishes piled up in the kitchen sink and the mounds of paper stacked on the dining room table. Shoes and miscellaneous items were scattered on the floor. She flinched as the odors rising from Ryan's slovenly body drifted under her nose. She scrunched up her face and placed a slim hand over her mouth and nose. "What's wrong? Tell me what happened. It looks like you haven't left this couch in days!"

Ryan's eyes filled with tears as she prepared to tell her story. She hadn't repeated what happened to anyone, hadn't heard the dreaded words come out of her own mouth. To say them would mean facing reality and dealing with it head on and she didn't know how to do that. She would rather live in her own world of isolation, where she romanticized her relationship and drowned herself in guilt and blame. Her only chance for salvation was the slight possibility that he would take her back. She wasn't ready to hear someone say that wouldn't or shouldn't happen. She shook her head to fight the side of herself that wanted to tell her secret. She kept her mouth closed.

Lauren sat on the couch next to her, pushing a few magazines out of the way. She grabbed the TV remote and turned down the volume. She placed a gentle, consoling hand on Ryan's back. "Ryan, you know you can tell me anything. You know that. Please just tell me what's wrong so we can fix it. What happened?"

Ryan turned to face her. "We broke up." That was all she said. That was all she needed to say for Lauren to understand why she was falling faster than a ton of bricks off an 80-story building. Lauren's eyes averted as she processed what she was hearing. It was something she had never heard before. Not Ryan and Anthony, not since they'd started dating. Ryan sensed her state of discomfort and saw her struggling to put together some supportive words.

"He dumped you?"

"No, I broke up with him?"

Lauren's eyes grew big, her body stiff. She was shocked. She made a weak attempt to suppress a smile of delight. "What happened?"

"I don't want to talk about it."

"Okay, we don't have to talk about it right now. We need to get you cleaned up and out of this house." She grabbed Ryan's arm and pulled her to an upright position. She used all of her strength to try to force her off the couch, but Ryan remained stationary.

She started crying again, "I fucked up, Lauren. I fucked up the whole relationship. I made him feel like less of a man. I was always screaming at him and tearing him down. He didn't do anything to deserve that. Now he won't return my phone calls. I don't know what to do."

"Ryan, leaving him was the best thing you could've ever done. Look at you. Look at what you've let him do to you. You're a mess! He didn't treat you right and he pushed you to leave. You didn't do anything wrong. Yeah, you may have screamed and cursed and got mad a few times, but look at the reasons why. He was treating you like dirt. You don't treat someone you love like that. Not unless you want to lose them."

Lauren didn't know what the hell she was talking about. She didn't have a man and wouldn't be happy until Ryan shared the same fate. She had to shut her down immediately, before her negative attitude contaminated her and blocked her path to her goal. "You just don't understand. You never do. You don't know how it was between me and him. You don't know how deep we were, how we felt about each other. You have no clue."

"You're right, I don't understand and I don't have to. What I do know is what I see right now and what I've been seeing for the last four months. You're not the same person you used to be. You used to be happy. You used to love yourself. Now look at you. You're depressed, shutting yourself out from the rest of the world. You're irritable as hell, exploding at everyone around you. No man should make you feel that way. You need to pick yourself up and learn that you don't need a damn man to complete you. Until you figure that out, you'll never be happy."

"Here you go with this self help Iyanla Vanzant meets Oprah, holier than thou bullshit. I don't need to be lectured. I don't need for some bitch who doesn't have a man and hasn't had a man in the last three years tell me how to handle my relationship. I don't need a preacher, I need a damn friend and it is obvious that you don't know how to be one right now. Look, just leave me alone, okay. I just want to be alone. I have to figure out how I'm going to get my man back."

Lauren's back stiffened. She closed her eyes for a moment and took a deep breath before speaking. She was trying her best not to lash out. She spoke carefully and slowly. "I'm going to let that go because you're upset. I know this is hard for you right now and you may be saying things that you don't mean. So, I'll ignore that."

"No, don't ignore it. Listen very carefully and let it sink in. I'm sick and tired of you judging me. I'm tired of you talking shit about Anthony and talking shit about things you know nothing about. I'm sick of it and I don't want to hear it anymore."

Lauren's light brown skin turned red. She clinched her hand together and banged an angry fist on the cocktail table, "Do you know how stupid you sound right now? You're defending a man who treats you like shit! He doesn't give a fuck about you. He never did. The only reason why he was still with you was because you were stupid enough to listen to his lies and put up with the games."

"Get out of my house!" Ryan stood up and yelled, pointing towards the door. She was fuming. If Lauren didn't leave at that second, she was liable to slap her in her face.

Lauren stood up to meet Ryan eye to eye, "Look I didn't mean that, okay? Let's just calm down and talk about this."

"I said get the fuck out!"

"I'm not going anywhere! You can yell and scream and get in my face all you want, but I'm not leaving." She started to weep. "I love you, Ryan. You're like my sister and it hurts me to see you suffering like this. I just want my friend back, the Ryan that I used to know. You are such a beautiful person and he doesn't appreciate that. I just wish you could see what I see in you and just learn to love yourself again."

Ryan couldn't say anything. She didn't have the energy. She felt defeated. Her best friend's words hit her hard, grabbed at her heart and yanked the tears from her eyes. All she wanted was to be happy. That's all she wanted. It didn't matter how she got there, she just needed it to happen fast. She dropped her head and let the tears drip to the floor. Lauren wrapped both her arms around her and held her with the type of embrace only the closest of friends could share. Ryan's tears stained Lauren's jacket as she cried on her shoulder. Lauren held her and let her cry. Neither of them said a word.

Their sister-to-sister moment was interrupted by Ryan's vibrating phone on the cocktail table. Ryan was the first one to break the hold, but Lauren managed to grab the phone first. The look on her face as she glanced at the caller ID told Ryan exactly who was calling. Ryan leaped at the phone, trying to snatch it from her hands. Lauren almost fell backwards as Ryan pounced her, but managed to keep the phone just out of reach.

"Stop playing, Lauren! Give me the damn phone!" Ryan grabbed her wrist and shook her arm to make her drop the phone, but her grip was too tight.

"No." The phone continued to buzz.

"Bitch, I will seriously hurt you. Give me the phone!"

"I said no." Lauren was three inches taller than Ryan. Her boots added an additional two. Ryan was not going to reach the cell. They struggled back and forth for the next few seconds, swaying, stumbling and threatening to fall, until the buzzing stopped. They froze, staring at each other with heavy breathing. Hate and determination flooded Ryan's eyes. If Lauren thought it was a game, she was about to lose.

Ryan caught her breath. "Give me the phone now!"

"Ryan, you don't need him."

"Give me the phone right now!" She was screaming so

loud her neighbors could hear her through the walls. She didn't care what they thought. All that mattered was that she got her cell phone so she could call her man back before he changed his mind.

He wants me back. What else could he possibly be calling for?

He was calling to forgive her, to make everything right and to tell her how much he loved her. She had to call him back before he changed his mind. Ryan and Lauren continued to glare at each other, woman to woman. Both desperate -- one to save her best friend, the other to feed her twisted emotional addiction. Neither was willing to give up. Neither was backing down.

Lauren's breathing was heavy. Her face stern, "You don't need him Ryan. You're better than he deserves."

Before Ryan had time to threaten Lauren's life, before she had time to tell her she would break her fingers, maim her limbs and tear her head off if she didn't let that phone go, it vibrated again. Lauren held her grip on the cell, then turned and sprinted for the front door. She tripped over the leg of one of the dining room chairs and almost made it to the front hall before Ryan tackled her from behind. They both crashed to the hard wood floor. The phone went spinning towards the wall. It was still buzzing. Ryan used Lauren's head as support as she crawled over her and pushed herself up from the floor. She almost ran into the wall as she stumbled her way to the phone and flipped it open.

"Hello? Hello, Anthony?"

Lauren was back on her feet. Sternly she commanded, "Hang up the phone, Ryan."

Ryan ignored her, "Hey, baby. I was so worried that I'd

never hear from you again. I'm so sorry for how I acted and what I said."

"Ryan, please! Hang up the phone!"

"Hold on for one minute okay? Don't hang up." She snapped her head around to face Lauren's scolding eyes, "Shut up! Can't you see I'm on the phone? Just get out okay? Get the fuck out."

Lauren stared back at her with tears of fury and frustration running from her eyes. She had been defeated. The power of Ryan's love addiction was too strong. It had completely taken over. Nothing in the world mattered more than getting that high. Her friendship, good counsel and caring were no match. "Okay, Ryan. I'll leave, but just remember the next time he breaks you down, I won't be there to pick up the pieces. We're no longer friends."

"Yeah, whateva. Lock the door on your way out. Thanks." She went back to her phone conversation, "Sorry about that. I miss you so much, baby. I need you. Will you ever forgive me?"

Lauren turned on her heel and walked out of the house without another word, locking the door behind her.

Ryan continued to plead her case. The sound of Anthony's voice was soothing. The way he said her name was arousing. How he said he missed her and loved her was intoxicating. Everything was alright. Just like that, in a matter of seconds, he returned Ryan's shattered world to wholeness and rightness. She had her man back.

CHAPTER 18

JESSICA

Hey Baby,

It's about 2 o'clock in the morning and I can't sleep. So I thought I'd go old school on you and write you a good old fashioned love letter to make you smile . Where do I begin? It's kind of difficult because I have so much on my mind, but it's so hard to put all of my emotions into words. I guess I'll start by saying that I love you. You already know that I love you, but I don't think you know how much. I don't think you know all of the things you mean to me and everything that you do for me. You complete my existence. Before I met you, I felt so alone, like something significant was missing from my life. I wasn't sure exactly what it was and I didn't know how to fix it until I saw your face. When I met you everything made so much sense. Everything came full circle for me and I knew then what my purpose in life was, it was to be happy with you. Everything I do involves you. Whether I'm doing it with you, for you, or with you on my mind. Everything revolves around you. What I feel is stronger than love; it's a connection so deep that it would be an injustice to try to put it into words. You are my life. You are my world and I will do anything to protect our bond.

I constantly think about our future. Marriage, kids, a big house and a dog. I know that sounds corny as hell , but when I look into your eyes, that's what I see. I see my future. You say that you want to spend the rest of your life with me. I get chills every time I think about that. I believe that we are destined to be together. To think that out of this whole world in its entirety, that I've managed to find you, that God sent you to me, it's a miracle. I am thankful everyday because at times I feel like I don't deserve you. Everything that you do for me, the time we spend together, the trips, the flowers, the friendship, your sweet words, the mind blowing sex (the money helps too), it's almost overwhelming. You go beyond to make me happy. You go out of your way to make me smile and I just want you to know that I appreciate you. I love you and I would do anything for you. You're my man, my friend, and my soul mate. I will never do anything to destroy what we have. Always remember that.

After all of that, I'm finally getting sleepy. So I'll end it here and I'll talk to you in the morning.

Love Always,
Ryan

RYAN Stephenson lived in Southfield in Cadillac Condominiums, located on the North side of 12 Mile, three blocks west of Greenfield Road. Her address was 25662, the fifth door if turning on Clearview Street and going right to enter the complex. It was the third door, coming from Fairview Street and entering from the left. She lived alone, no kids no pets. The condo was moderate in size, no more than 1500-1700 square feet. It was a sardine can. She drove a small, new, dark gray BMW. PLJ 004 stamped her blue and white Michigan license plates. From the looks inside her car, she was messy. Dust and stains from recent snow and rainfalls covered the gray paint of the car. Inside the car were four half-empty water bottles. Two were in the front cup holders, one on the front passenger floor, and one in the back on the floor behind the driver's seat. She was wasteful. On the back seat, lay numerous old newspapers and fashion magazines, some clothes and two pairs of shoes. In the front passenger seat, were more papers and a couple of envelopes. It looked like mail, bills. She was a slob. The driver side door was severely smashed. She was a reckless driver. She worked at an accounting firm in Troy on 14 Mile and Crooks Rd. She usually got into the office around 9 o'clock in the morning. Most mornings she was late by ten or 15 minutes. She would leave by 6:30 in the evening. She always left on time. She had not been to work in the past five days. She was careless. She got her hair done in Detroit, at a salon on Eight Mile Road near Hubbell Street. She went on Saturday mornings with a friend, tall, slender woman with short hair. They stayed there for at least four hours, sometimes longer. She was very high maintenance.

She regularly refilled prescriptions for Xanax and Wellbutrin. She was crazy, a serious pill popper. She also had a shopping addiction; her mall of choice was Somerset in Troy. She was broke. She couldn't be making more than $80-85,000 per year in salary, yet she shopped at the most expensive stores at least three times a week. She was irresponsible.

She was medium height, about 5'5" or 5'6." She graduated to 5'8" or 5'9" with her hooker-heeled stilettos. She was dark black like dark, unsweetened chocolate, about three shades darker than Ross' peanut butter complexion. Her hair was medium length; she wore it in a razor cut bob a little past her shoulders. It was straight, jet-black, and undoubtedly permed. She had small, almond eyes, long lashes, full lips, and a smooth complexion. She was fat, probably around 140-150 pounds. Her waist had to be about 27 inches. Her legs and thighs were huge, like two turkey drumsticks. Her ass was ridiculous. It looked like two balloons stuffed inside her too tight jeans, gasping for air and fighting for freedom. She dressed like an expensive whore. Her "True Religion" jeans were tight enough to cause a chronic yeast infection. Her breasts happily spilled out of her Donna Karan or BCBG blouses. And her shoes, well there was nothing negative to be said about her shoes. She had an awesome shoe collection. She managed to get one thing right.

She was nothing like Jessica. They were complete opposites. Ross would have a heart attack if he saw his wife dressed like a call girl. He would hyperventilate if she allowed herself to balloon into the obesity that was 140 pounds. He would gag if she cursed and carried herself in the uncouth manner that Ryan did. What did he see in her? How could he be with someone like that?

Jessica folded the letter and carefully placed it back into the envelope. The information she was able to gather about his mistress just by following her around for a few weeks was priceless. And Ryan had no idea.

Ross was equally clueless. Men were so dumb and careless when it came to cheating. It was almost as if he didn't care if Jessica had found out at all. The letter wasn't hidden in a locked box. It wasn't tucked away inside a cabinet or stashed in his briefcase. Jessica found the evidence of adultery in his car, in plain sight. In fact, it literally dropped in her lap. Gas prices were rising at an insanely rapid rate and Ross constantly fussed about the $75 weekly deposit he made into the Range Rover's gas tank. He reasoned that he would not be the successful and financially secure man he was today if he squandered his hard-earned money on senseless sunken costs. So he took the keys of the gas guzzling SUV from Jessica and replaced them with those of his more conservative Lexus sedan. The day the letter dropped from the sun visor of the Lexus, Jessica gritted her teeth and held her stomach as she watched Ross ride off in his new Mercedes S600. So there it was, in her face, staring at her with truth and conviction. It was her proof that her man was giving himself to another woman, a younger woman, a real *black* woman. The letter was addressed to Ross. The name was his, but the address was not. She'd followed the MapQuest directions to 1247 Woodward Avenue, The Motor City Lofts in Downtown Detroit. He had a loft she knew nothing about.

He had a separate life, an identity outside of their marriage. He was someone else when she was not around. He was Ryan's man. Ryan was in love with him. She wanted to marry him and have his children. Ryan wanted to be Mrs. Pembroke.

Jessica couldn't let that happen. She could not stand by and watch her marriage fall apart. Nothing would come between her and her husband. She would do whatever it took, even if it meant spending hours parked outside of Ryan's condo, waiting for her to leave so she could follow her to work, to the grocery store, to the mall and the salon. If it meant, digging through her trash in the middle of the night to gather as much information as she could about her personal affairs, she would do it. If it meant "accidentally" bumping her in the mall to get a good look at her face, sending anonymous pictures of her flirting with the store clerk to Ross from a cell phone number he didn't recognize, or forcing her off the road on slippery, snowy nights, she would do whatever she had to do. She grew up in a world that taught her to fight for what was hers. That was exactly what she was doing, fighting, and she wasn't going to back down until victory was hers. Whatever it took.

Jessica sat in the car outside of his building. She had been there for three hours, waiting, smoking her second joint. She was waiting for that slut, waiting for Ross, waiting for anything to happen, anything to fuel her fire. The last time she had seen her at his place was a week prior. It was a short visit, right after the "accident" on the freeway. She ran to him like the pathetic little home wrecker she was. Jessica should have killed her. She should have ended the game at the moment and knocked her ass off of the road and out of their lives. She should have, but she didn't. She froze. She wasn't sure why. Maybe it was a combination of things. Maybe her conscience got the best of her and that little, white, angelic Jessica on her right shoulder won the battle with the little, red, devil Jessica on her left. It is possible that she had gotten a little scared of the consequences of her actions. Maybe she was afraid that Ryan may have survived the accident and would have been able to identify her. There is a chance that for one brief moment, she told herself that what was happening to her marriage wasn't Ryan's fault and she didn't deserve to die. Maybe with Ryan out of the picture, Ross would just replace her with another woman. Maybe the fault was with him, not Ryan.

But more than likely, it was none of the above. More than likely, Jessica was just stupid and froze up like a coward, letting that slut continue on her full court press to ruin her marriage, giving her another day to destroy her life. She was stupid and gutless. It would not happen again. An opportunity to wrap this whole thing up would present itself in the near future and she would take full advantage.

It was a little past six in the evening. The sky was dusky with the first signs of nightfall. Jessica hated how it got dark so early in the evening. It was so depressing. More suicides occurred in the winter than any other season of the year. With darkness blanketing the sky as early as 6 p.m., she could understand why. It put her in a somber mood. Sitting silently inside the Lexus, slouched in the driver's seat with the chill of cold, dark air creeping through the crack in her window, she was reminded of her past.

• • •

She went back to when she was 18, when her name was Jessie and she used to run outside to escape the cruelty that was her drunken, God- forsaken mother. She would hide inside the old beat up Cadillac stationed on the other side of the trailer park. She leaned back in the driver's seat so her mother could not see her through the windows. It was the "community's" car. It didn't run. It hadn't worked as long as she could remember, but Carl, the greasy, old, retired mechanic who lived two trailers away from hers, worked on it everyday, as if he could somehow bring it back to life. It was a rusty, reddish-orange color. The inside reeked of mildew and motor oil. She could feel the foam bursting from the worn leather seats, rubbing against her thighs as she slouched further down and Wanda's slurred curses drew nearer. She could hear the dead grass crunching under Wanda's feet. Her strides were unstable with no rhythmic step to her walk. She stumbled her way around the lot, screaming for her daughter to come out and get her ass beaten.

"Jessie! Jessie! Bring yo' dirty nigger ass ova here!"

Her calls went unanswered. Jessie could hear the sound of a glass bottle crashing to the ground, then her mother's drunken, obese body colliding with Ms. Bessie's front gate.

"You little, slutty cunt! You ain't think I'd find out did ya? You ain't think nobody knowd you was a dirty little whore? Well I know. Bring yo filthy ass outta here. I can smell yo stankin' pussy from here."

Jessie's body tensed as her mother's voice crept closer to her hiding place. She clenched and unclenched her fists as she prepared for Wanda's arrival.

"Jessie, you little slut. How long you been poppin' yo nasty pussy and shakin' yo ass for money? Huh? You hear me, bitch? How long you been ho-in' around? Answer me!"

Her voice was right outside of the car, near the passenger side. Jessie closed her eyes and wished herself to another place, another life. But the wish didn't come true.

"You ain't think I knowd did cha? Yeah, I know." She paused to catch her breath, "Everybody knows you a dirty, cock suckin' whore. Shakin' yo ass out there sellin' yo pussy. Everybody knows. Everybody den seen't cha. Dat's where you been gettin' dat money from ain't it? You hear me, bitch?"

Wanda knew exactly where the money was coming from. She knew how long Jessie had been stripping at the Wild Stallion too. She knew because every night, for the last month, Jessie would come home from the strip club and hide her tips in a new, creative spot. Every night, she'd count her three, four, and five hundred dollar fortune, then awaken in the morning to find it cut down to barely $100.

Wanda knew because her brother Charlie was in the club on Jessie's second night there. After she refused his request for a lap dance, Jessie knew he would run his big mouth the next day. That is exactly what he did, telling anyone who would listen that his only niece was a good for nothing whore.

Jessie's employment was the reason why Wanda was able to buy the good liquor instead of her cheap gin or Mad Dog 20/20. Jessie was the reason why Wanda was able to go down to the local bar and put $50 on the card game and another $50 on lottery tickets. Wanda took Jessie's money every night as if *she had* been the one on that stage, taking off her clothes, sliding down that pole, and grinding her hips against those sweaty, drunken fools who whispered crude demands in her ear. Wanda stole Jessie's money every night, leaving her with a fraction of what she had rightfully earned.

It was time for it to stop. The night before Wanda began hunting for her in the trailer park, Jessie had gotten tired of her mother taking advantage of her. She was fed up with shaking her ass every night in that hot, stanky, smoky club, then waking up in the morning with nothing to show for it. That night, she took her $546, stuffed it in her panties, and slept with it on her. Early the next morning, she went to the nearest bank and opened a savings account. When Wanda realized there was no money, she went on a rampage.

Jessie heard her opening and closing cabinet doors, flipping mattresses, and snatching clothes out of the drawers. She tore the cushions from the sofa bed, kicked up the rug, and rearranged the small number of canned goods in the kitchen pantry. She was out of breath and bent over in pain when she started shouting her only child's name.

"Jessie! Damnit, where da hell are ya?"

When the search for her daughter began, Jessie was outside, in the back of the trailer, sitting in a lawn chair with her feet propped on an empty milk crate. She was on the cordless phone, engaged in a deep conversation with Dwayne, the owner of the Wild Stallion. He was telling her that she had a future at the club. She just needed to learn how to expand her horizons. He explained to her in his soothing, fatherly way, that she could make the real money outside of the bar with private parties. Jessie was the hottest piece of ass in the place and he was getting many requests for her services elsewhere. If she made $500 a night in the bar, she would make a minimum of $1500 doing parties. The best part was, Dwayne would only take a 25% cut of the profits. You couldn't beat that anywhere else in the business.

"Yeah, baby. You going places. Ya know what I mean? You got the talent, the body, and the brains to take this thing over. Ya know what I'm sayin'? Just stick with me, baby and I'll make yo ass a star." Dwayne had a way of making everything sound so simple, like dancing was what she was born to do. She was a natural and nobody could do it like she could. When he talked to her, he made her feel so strong and confident. He made her feel beautiful and safe.

"You really think I can make that much?"

"Shit yeah, girl! And you know what? You can do more

than that. The real pros out here gettin' more than two grand a night. All you gotta do is a little extra, you know what I mean? You know, a few special favors here and there, and bam, you paid."

"Now wait a minute, Dwayne, I ain't sellin' no pussy. I ain't no hooker."

"Calm down, baby. Ain't nobody talkin' bout prostitution. Just a few "special favors." You know, suck a few dicks, lick a coupla balls. You know, that type a thang. Ain't no big deal."

"I don't know about all that, Dwayne. I mean, I just wanna dance, you know?"

"Look, you a grown-ass woman and you gone be out there with some grown-ass men. Jiggling yo titties and shaking yo hips ain't gone cut it. Now you said you wanna make some money right?"

"Yeah."

"Then do what the fuck you gotta do to get it." He softened his tone, "You would be in complete control, and if you get scared, I'll be right there for you the whole time. I won't ever leave your side. Aiiight?"

Jessie heard the front door to the trailer swing open then bang shut. She flinched at the sound of Wanda stomping around in the front yard.

"Look Dwayne, I gotta go okay. Everything sounds good, but I have to talk to you about it tonight, alright?"

"Aiight, you make sure you bring yo ass in at seven. See ya later, baby."

She pushed the "End" button on the cordless phone to disconnect the call. Keeping the phone in her hand, she ran to the opposite side of the trailer park towards the old Cadillac, plopped herself in the driver's seat and slammed the door shut. There she sat as Wanda continued to revile her with the most derogatory names her limited vocabulary would allow.

"You little nigger bitch! Where da fuck you at? Huh? Bring yo ass out here."

Just as her mother's voice began to fade as she turned around to make her way back to the trailer, the cordless phone in Jessie's hand rang. Wanda whipped back around, turning on her heels to rush in the Cadillac's direction. She ran to the driver's side of the car, "Found ya, ya little bitch!"

Before she could reach her fat, stubby, pig arms into the window to yank her daughter out by her frizzy hair, Jessie flung the car door open. It banged against Wanda's stocky legs, causing her to fall hard to the ground. The drunken woman made her best effort to regain her balance and pull herself to her feet, but before she had made it half way up, Jessie was out of the car, standing over her. She had her foot in the air, ready to come down hard on Wanda's heaving chest. Wanda grabbed her foot before it landed on her breast and yanked with all the force her drunken state would permit. Jessie came crashing to the ground, landing on her ass. She quickly popped up and put herself in a squatting position, giving herself leverage to pounce on her opponent. She leaped and landed on her mother, holding her neck in her hands with a vise grip, powered by vengeance and a death wish.

"I should kill you right now! I should fucking kill you! I hate you!" Jessie's chokehold grew tighter with every syllable.

Wanda let out loud, gagging, grunting sounds as she gasped for the air that was quickly escaping her lungs. She clawed and scratched at her daughter's face, fighting desperately for freedom. But Jessie was stronger. She was younger.

She was in shape and she was sober. She was going to commit murder right there on the dirt-patched grass of their trailer park home. She was going to kill her mother and they both knew it. Tears streamed down Jessie's face as the realization of her fate took hold of her.

She screamed, "I hate you! You fat bitch. I hate you. Die!"

Wanda's pasty face started to turn blue, and her eyes rolled to the back of her head. But just seconds before she slipped into unconsciousness, Jessie's hands were violently pried from her neck.

Jessie was snatched up from the ground and she stood over Wanda's inert form with her arms gripped from behind. Carl's huge, greasy hands handcuffed her wrists with no promise of letting go. Wanda looked up at her daughter with no signs of recognition. She didn't know the girl, the woman, who stood before her. She didn't recognize the violent rage that had overcome her. She wasn't used to her fighting back. She was afraid. Jessie met her stare with a matched intensity. Hate spewed from her eyes.

There were no words, just heavy breathing. Carl broke the silence, "Now I don't know what the hell is goin' on here and maybe I don't wanna know. But Jessie, maybe it's best you take a walk or somethin' to clear yo mind. This here is yo mamma and you can't let thangs get outta hand like that."

Jessie spoke softly in between slow, deep breaths, "Carl, let me go." She never moved her eyes from Wanda's bloated face. Her mother stared back at her. Her face held an expression that told Jessie she was afraid to move. She was afraid that if Carl let her go, Jessie would kill her.

Carl's grip didn't loosen, "Now Jessie, if I let you go, you promise me you gone take a walk and get on outta here? Ya hear me?"

"Yeah, Carl. I hear you. Just let me go. I'll let this old bitch sit here and drank herself to death. I ain't *neva* comin' back." The old man reluctantly released her arms and stepped back. With heavy breaths and staggered steps, Jessie turned around and walked away. She was leaving it all behind: Her mother, the trailer, the liquor, the abuse, the only life she'd ever known. She walked away from it all and she would never go back.

Wanda gained back some of her bluster as she screamed at her daughter's retreating back, "You little whore, you ain't goin' nowhere. You ain't got nowhere to go. Don't nobody give a fuck about you."

Her words had no effect on Jessie. The words that usually tore her down like a bulldozer, didn't even slow her stride. She had a new life ahead of her and money to make. The next time she planned to see that fat bitch, she would be in a pine box.

• • •

A chill surged through Jessica's body as she reminisced on her past. It was so long ago, a different life, a different person. It felt like she was remembering a movie she had once seen years ago. That wasn't her, not anymore. Her husband had polished, crafted and refined her into a remarkable and admirable woman. She was Jessica Pembroke. Jessie Wolinsky had died when she left Hamtramck on the day she tried to kill her mother.

Jessica looked at the digital clock on the dashboard. It was nearly 7 o'clock and there was still no sign of Ross or Ryan. The sky was black and the four-hour stakeout was beginning to take a toll on her. She yawned and stretched before turning the key in the ignition to get ready to make her way back home. As she pulled out of her parking space, she felt the soft vibration of her cell phone on her thigh through her purse. She put the car back in park and glanced at the caller ID. It was a number she didn't recognize.

"Hello?"

"Hello, may I speak with Mrs. Jessica Pembroke please?"

"This is she. How may I help you?"

"Mrs. Pembroke, this is Margaret Fletcher. I am the night manager calling from Maple Village Retirement Community. Ma'am, I regret to inform you that your mother, Ms. Wanda Wolinsky...."

"Yes, what about Wanda?"

"Well, I'm sorry Ma'am, but she passed in her sleep. We approximate the time of her death at six-fifteen p.m. I truly am sorry for your loss."

Jessica held the phone in silence. Her heart didn't skip a beat. Her breathing didn't lose its rhythm. It was as if someone just called to tell her that her dry cleaning was ready for pick up.

"Hello? Mrs. Pembroke?"

"Yes?"

"We would need for you to come down to the center to fill out some paper work. Of course, you could come whenever you feel up to it within the next forty-eight hours. Again, I am sorry."

"Okay."

"Okay?" Margaret Fletcher sounded confused.

"Yes, that's fine. I'll be there tomorrow morning. Thank you for the call."

Jessica ended the call, flipping her small, black cell phone closed and throwing it back into her purse. She took one last long, slow drag of her joint, before putting it out in the ashtray. She then checked her makeup in the rearview mirror, wiping the pink lipstick from her two front teeth with her finger. Since the collagen injections, that had been a constant problem. She smeared a fresh coat of gloss over her luscious pout, raked her fingers through her strawberry blond locks and sucked in her cheeks to show herself what she would look like once her cheek implants were in place. After turning on the radio, she popped in Lorraine Dubois' Greatest Hits CD and drove home in silence.

CHAPTER 19

SIMONE

"MOM, I'm going upstairs to take a shower and get ready for bed."

"Ok, sweetie good night."

"Good night, Mom. I love you."

"I love you too." Simone bent down to reach her mother, sitting in an overstuffed chair in the living room, and kissed her on her cheek. Her mother returned the affection with a loving embrace.

Her mother was the first to pull away. She held her daughter's face in her hands and inspected her features with a frown in her brow. "Is everything okay, baby?"

"Yeah Mom, everything is fine."

"You sure? You seem--sad. Like something is on your mind."

"No, nothing at all."

Her mother pulled her face in closer. She smoothed her fingers over her forehead and rubbed her cheeks with her palms, "You look pale."

"Do I?"

"Yes, you look sick. Honey, you sure there is nothing

wrong? You know a mother can tell when there's something wrong with her baby."

Simone pulled away from her and stood straight. She held her mother's hands in hers as reassurance. "Mom, trust me, everything is fine. I'm just a little tired that's all. I had a long day at school and I need some rest."

Her mother wasn't convinced and it showed in her expression.

"Really. I promise. I'm fine. Okay?"

"Okay, if you say so, but I'm keeping my eye on you. I don't want anything bad to happen to you. And we can't have you walking around with people thinking there is something wrong with you. It's really a bad reflection."

"I know, Mom. You worry too much. Good night."

Simone proceeded upstairs to her bedroom. She was exhausted. It had been a painfully long day and she needed relief, quickly. She climbed, what seemed to be, five thousands steps of the winding staircase with a sluggish, tortoise-like pace. Once in her room, she stretched her arms as far as they would go before collapsing down on the bed. She didn't bother to undress and had forgotten about the shower. It would have taken too much energy. It did not take longer than two minutes for the oversized, goose-down comforter to seduce her into an instant sleep.

But her sleep hadn't lasted long before the phone on her nightstand rang. The sound jolted Simone awake. She was hesitant to answer it; half of her was afraid of who was on the other end and the other half was just too tired to reach. She didn't receive many phone calls and didn't have many friends. She decided that whoever it was, they weren't worth the strength and effort it would take to stretch across the bed and reach for the phone, so she just stared at it until the ringing stopped. She closed her eyes once again. This time, it was just a matter of seconds before the ringing phone interrupted her sleep again. Frustrated with the constant interference, Simone quickly rolled over the bed and snatched the phone from the receiver. The caller ID read "Private Caller", offering no indication as to who was on the other end. She answered the phone, sounding slightly annoyed. It was her private line so she didn't have to use the same formality and professional tone as she would with answering the main line to the house, "Hello."

"Yeah, is this SiSi?"

"Yeah, this is SiSi. Who is this?"

Simone heard a sigh as the caller hesitated before answering, "Um, this is Darius."

"Darius? Brandon's boy?"

"Yeah, look I was just calling to umm…make sure you was aiight after you know…the other night at the party."

"Oh, I'm fine."

Simone could hear his discomfort on the other end of the line as he struggled to produce words of concern.

"Good, cuz you know, what Brandon did, I mean what he was tryin to do….that shit wasn't cool man. I just wanted to let you know dat."

"Yeah, I saw what you did. Thanks for lookin' out."

"No problem. I mean, I ain't no "Captain-save-a-ho" or nothin' like that, but I just couldn't let that shit go down. Not like that. Aye, you ain't gone call the police or nothin' like that are you?"

The thought had never occurred to her. "No, I'm not tellin' *anybody*."

"Good lookin' out cuz that could be a bad look for all of us, you know?"

"Yeah, I know. Don't worry about it."

"Aye, you know yo girl, Kris talkin' some ill shit about yo ass."

"What do you mean?"

"She was tryin' to tell everybody at school that you was out there, you know like them other girls was. She said some dirty shit about you. Tried to make you look like a real ho. But yo I squashed that shit quick."

"You defended me? Why? You don't even know me that well."

"I know, but I know you not like that. I guess I just felt bad, you know. I saw how shit happened with y'all and I just felt like I had to say something. Aye, but don't think I'm soft or nothin' like that! I was just lookin' out fo you cuz it seemed like nobody else was."

Simone was baffled. What was his angle? Why would he look out for her? She was nobody. He must have wanted something from her. He had to be just like everyone else that used her for their own selfish motives. Stunned and skeptical, she struggled with a response. "Uh, I don't really know what to say right now."

"You ain't got to say nuthin'. Like I said, I was just makin' sure you was aiight. Aye if anybody starts fuckin' wit you at school let me know. I got you."

The sudden sincerity in his tone made Simone break out in an unexpected smile. *Maybe he is for real.*

"Okay, Darius. Thanks. Thanks a lot."

"Aiight, later. I'll see you at school tomorrow."

Simone placed the phone on its cradle and stared at it

as if it may jump up at her. She wasn't sure of what had just happened and she wasn't sure if she trusted his intentions. She had someone to look out for her. That was something that was incomprehensible at the time. God didn't even look out for her, why would Darius? She didn't know whether to trust him or beware. Still, the thought that he may be for real was enough to lift her spirits, if only just a little.

The uplifted feeling was brief, however, as the reality of the moment set in. It was bedtime and her father may be visiting soon. The thought of what might come lifted her from her bed and dragged her into the bathroom. She started the shower, making the water as hot as she could tolerate without scalding her skin. She flinched as the steaming water hit her, but her body quickly adjusted to the temperature. She let her hand lightly graze her lower abdomen, the area right below her belly button. Her fingers traveled up and down, softly touching her morning cuts. There were eight lines stretched horizontally across her skin. The cuts were already beginning to heal themselves. The rush she had felt that morning was long gone. Her constant pain returned.

Her mind was racing with thoughts of that day, the stares she got when walking through the halls of school, the isolation she felt during lunch when no one sat next to her, the whispers she heard as she walked past Kristen and her new clique and the disgusted looks on the girls' faces as she entered the classrooms. It all made sense now. They all thought she was a ho and her only chance for redemption was Darius. Still, she felt hopeless.

She stood still in the shower and let the water hit her face. Her tears blended with the drops, sliding down her cheeks and off her chin. She reached on top of the shower door and retrieved a small razor blade, her salvation. Her heart skipped a beat as she anticipated her satisfaction. Sitting down on the shower bench positioned in the corner of the stall, she propped her leg on the ledge. A loud sigh of pleasure and pain escaped her as the blade sliced her inner thigh. Her tears magnified as she cut herself. Eyes closed, her sobs let out a month's worth of frustration and self-hatred. She only opened her eyes for a moment to see the blood and water mix rush down the drain, taking her problems with it. As always, it soothed her. It gave her a high and told her that everything was okay.

It was easy to hide the cuts. It was cold out so she had a reason to wear long sleeves, oversized sweaters, and pants. The only time she undressed was in the privacy of her own bedroom. No one could know her secret. No one could find out. They wouldn't understand. They would think she was crazy. She knew that she wasn't crazy. She was far from normal, but crazy? No, she wasn't crazy. She was damaged. She made eight small incisions on her right inner thigh before leaving the shower. Once back in her room, she dressed in her night clothes and got into the bed. Sleep came rather easily. She didn't say her prayers. She hadn't said them in a while. She knew that God wasn't going to take her to Heaven. He did nothing to redeem her. She had figured that out weeks ago when she recalled her countless, unanswered pleas to the Lord for some type of mercy. She knew that she was alone and the only one there for her was Simone. She had to rely on herself to heal her own wounds. God was not the answer. Her heavy eyes closed and sleep took her through a window of unconsciousness.

Within a half hour, the door opened and closed. The soft sound of bare feet walking across the carpeted floor caused

Simone to stir in her sleep. He didn't say anything, just walked slowly over to her bed. He did not sit down. His daughter was awake, but didn't open her eyes. She sensed his presence, smelled his scent. He was standing over her, watching her. She could feel him standing there. She was afraid. But it wasn't the same fear she'd felt before-- the natural fear that would overcome any 14 year-old girl whose father raped her.

No, it wasn't the same. She was afraid of herself, of what she would reveal to him. She was afraid of her own thoughts, of the great possibility that her body would betray her again if he touched her. A part of her wanted him to touch her, to make her feel that hot, burning sensation that pulsation between her legs just like the last time. That terrified her.

He hadn't made any late night visits since it happened. Her father stayed away from her as if she carried a contagious decease. Two Fridays had passed since that night and he hadn't said more to her than "Good morning", at breakfast and "Good night", in the evening. A piece of her was disappointed that he hadn't come to visit in two weeks, but a bigger piece was excited that he was finally there. Simone squeezed her eyes tightly as she erased those thoughts from her head. No matter what her body felt, no matter how those pieces of her were forming together to cause her to consider ridiculous, indecent thoughts, her brain told her it was wrong. It was disgusting and forbidden. There was no way that she would allow her body to act on the dirty thoughts her mind was fighting to suppress. There was no way. The covers crumpled as Simone crossed her legs tightly, locking them at the ankles.

As if her movement was his cue, he finally spoke, "Do you ever feel like you just want to die, Simone?"

She didn't say anything. His question made her body tense up. It was unexpected, a scary question to answer. Yes, she wanted to die. Every second of her miserable teenage life, she wanted to disappear into the world of the unknown. She wanted it so desperately and for so long, that she didn't remember what it felt like to not want it. Of course she wanted to die. Of course she did. But she didn't tell him any of that. She said nothing.

"I guess that was a dumb question, huh?" He let out a slight, nervous laugh. "Of course you do. Why wouldn't you? You probably think that I don't know what I've done to you. What I'm *doing* to you. And you're probably right, for the most part. I mean, I can't imagine what you're going through right now. There is no possible way I could guess what it's like to be you. But I figure death has to cross your mind every once in a while."

Simone turned her head to face her father. He stood next to the bed with his back against the wall. She still did not speak. She wanted to hear what he had to say without interruption.

"I don't know what happened, baby girl. Everything was perfect. We had the perfect family, the perfect house in the perfect neighborhood. We had everything. Could've had our own reality TV show", that nervous laugh again. "I just couldn't hold it in anymore. I couldn't fight it. I know you'll never understand, and I don't expect you to. But it was something I couldn't control. You know what I do every night?"

Simone remained silent. It was a rhetorical question.

"I pray to God every night that He takes my life. I do that every night and I wake up every morning, pissed that it didn't happen. I don't know what else to do. I don't know how to make this stop. The only way is to… die."

Simone's stomach tightened as she figured where her father was going with his monologue.

"I've thought about killing myself. I think about it a lot. Do you ever think about that?" It was another rhetorical question. He knew the answer. "If I'm gone, you'd be safe. You and your mother would be free to live a normal life. You wouldn't have to worry about your daddy coming to hurt you anymore."

Simone shifted in the bed.

Her father's voice quivered as he made a weak attempt to keep from crying, "I love you, baby girl. I love you so much. I love you enough to give you that peace, to give you a chance. I'd give anything to make you happy. I'd give my life."

Simone's eyes widened. He was actually talking about committing suicide! He sounded as if he was going to take his own life that night, at the moment.

"What are you gonna do, Daddy?"

He snapped his head in her direction as if her presence startled him, then looked away just as suddenly, "I don't know, baby girl. I know something has to change. Something has to happen. We can't keep going on like this." Without another word, he walked out of the room, leaving Simone alone in her bed, stunned by his unexpected revelation.

He's going to kill himself for me.

Already, she missed him.

CHAPTER 20

ANTHONY

ANTHONY sat alone on the hard concrete curb at the corner of Ballanthyne Road and Fordcroft Street. With his elbows on his knees and his head in his hands, he could feel the pressure of his temples banging against his skull as he fought back tears of lifelong anger and frustration. In 1977, a 13-year-old black boy sitting awkwardly outside in the middle of the night in Grosse Pointe was enough to bring negative attention to the scene. But the added offenses of his bloodied nose and badly soiled clothes, caused the residents of one of Michigan's most affluent neighborhoods to peek suspiciously out of their windows and to lock their doors in a mixture of fear and disapproval. Anthony's mother had given him countless warnings about wandering outside alone in the neighborhood. Their family was a rarity in the area and those racist bastards were looking for any reason to catch a little black boy and make an example out of him. Always eager to please his mother, Anthony usually followed her rules, but on this particular night, nothing mattered beyond the banging in his head and the flashbacks of the horrific scene he had just encountered.

Something told him not to sneak out of the house that

night. He had second-guessed his plan at least three times before he had actually gained the courage to follow through with it. After all, he knew exactly what he was going to find. There was not much of a point in going, but still he needed a confirmation. He needed something to hang on to when he thought he might get weak and give in to his enemy. He needed a visual image to fuel his fury and stoke his hatred. So he went.

He followed his father out of the house that night. It was eleven o'clock, an hour past his bedtime. An hour ago his mother had just kissed him goodnight and turned out the light. She told him that she was going straight to bed because it was the end of a long day and she just wanted it to end. It seemed like every day was the same for her. He did not know it then, but looking back on those early years, he realized that his mother was depressed and she medicated herself with tears and sleep. That particular night was no different.

He waited until he heard the door of the master suite close at the far end of the hall, and then slowly slid out of his bed, careful not to make the floor creak beneath his feet. He stole a quick glance at the alarm clock on the nightstand to see 11:03 p.m. flashing back at him. He had to hurry if he wanted to catch his father before he left.

Carefully, he slipped on his jeans and grabbed a pair of sneakers without making a sound, then tiptoed out into the hallway. No one could have suspected what he was up to. He was proud of himself. The staircase was at the end of the hall, right past his parents' bedroom. Standing just a few feet away from the door, he could hear his mother's soft sobs as she cried into the pillows. The sound left him momentarily frozen with indignation. He wanted to open the door, rush in to hug his mother, rock her in his arms, and tell her that everything would be okay. It would all be over shortly. He would handle it and take care of everything like a man. But there was no time for that. He only had a few minutes to execute his plan or he would miss his opportunity. He allowed the same sounds that temporarily restrained him to propel him forward in his scheme. Anthony knew that his father was in the study, on the far West end of the house, so he would not hear his son creeping slowly down the stairs. He would go on undetected as he snuck into the kitchen and slipped out of the side door into the cool, summer night air.

Once outside, the feeling of cold concrete beneath his feet reminded Anthony that he was barefoot. After quickly slipping his sneakers on, he retrieved the spare key to his father's Jaguar from his jean pocket and used it to unlock the back door. He knew his father kept the key inside of the top drawer of his desk in the study and Anthony was able to swipe it earlier that day unnoticed. He climbed onto the floor of the backseat and carefully closed the door before laying flat on his back. He silently prayed that the darkness of the night, would keep him hidden and his plan unobstructed. A few minutes later, Anthony felt a slight chill as the front driver's door opened and closed. His father started the engine and backed out of the driveway. Anthony's blood rushed and his heart began to beat uncontrollably in anticipation. He felt a wave of adrenaline overcome his anger and fear and he had to clutch his stomach and close his eyes in order to keep his insides from racing. He silently repeated his own words of encouragement in his mind to quiet the doubt that was beginning to take over.

You have to do this. You have to be a man for her. You will save her. You will get rid of him. Everything will be better. You are a man. You are the man. It's all up to you.

The car stopped, interrupting Anthony's thoughts. He held his breath as he listened to his father remove the keys from the ignition and exit. He climbed to his knees and peeked out of the window to watch his father walk up the winding driveway of a medium-sized, brick home and ring the doorbell. After a few seconds, the silhouette of a woman opened the door. Anthony felt the pain of certainty twist his stomach into a bow tie, as his father greeted the silhouette with a kiss before entering the house and closing the door behind him. It was time for Anthony to make his move. He waited a few moments to make sure his father and the woman had time to settle, then he slowly crawled out of the car. Feeling like a spy for the CIA, he crouched down to stay out of view of the front bay window, crept up the driveway to the house, and ducked just below the windowsill.

Anthony could hear the grass and bed of flowers crunching beneath his feet as he struggled to catch a good look into the house. He was in an awkward position, but with a quick peek, he was able to catch a glimpse of his father and his mistress cuddled on the couch in the living room. They were glued together in a tight embrace. She threw her head backward against the back of the couch in what seemed to be ecstasy. His father's hand was hidden underneath the bottom of her negligee, and from the way she thrust her pelvis towards him and let her legs fall open, Anthony had a good idea of what his fingers were doing there.

After watching for only a moment, he couldn't take it anymore. The whole scene made him want to vomit on the pink and purple tulips surrounding him. The memory of his mother crying herself to sleep alone and in the dark flashed in his head. He clutched his eyes tightly to block out the image, but it didn't work. Fury carried him to the front door and, without any conscious thought, he banged on the door with the force and authority of gangbusters. He heard faint voices on the other side of the door as the two adulterers scrambled to readjust their clothes and rush to the door. Anthony didn't stop the banging until the door flew open and he saw the confused faces of his father and an attractive, unknown woman staring back at him.

Panic coursed through Anthony's veins as he realized that he had no idea what to do. The actual reality of catching his father in the act of cheating on his mother overwhelmed him. He had been so consumed with the strategy to get there, that he had neglected to plan in the event that he made it that far. Anthony's blood ran cold as he watched his father's expression morph from confusion, to worry, and then settled on rage. However terrified he was at the moment, he refused to let his terror show. He managed to keep a stern face as he stood eye-to-nose with the man who was so causally and callously tearing his family apart and destroying his mother -- the enemy.

"What are you doing here?"

The angry words from his father were more of a demand than a question. Anthony felt the tears bubble up inside of him, but could not manage to speak.

His father stepped out of the house, closing the screen door behind him. His woman looked on from inside. "Do you hear me talking to you, boy? I said what in the hell are you doing here?"

Anthony swallowed the hard lump blocking his air

passage. He gathered his thoughts and stuck his chest out. He could not be afraid. He had come all this way; it was too late to back down. "No! What are *you* doing here?"

His father looked behind him at the woman standing in the doorway as if he was checking to see if she had heard the outrageous demand the boy had made. He lifted his finger to tell her to give him a moment and she closed the door to leave father and son alone on the porch. He slowly stepped towards his son until his mouth was almost touching his forehead. Anthony titled his head back to make sure they were eye to eye.

His father spoke in a slow, measured, almost patient tone, "What I'm doing here is none of your damn business. I don't know how you got here, but you have about a half a minute to get your ass back home before I make you wish you never came."

"It's none of my business? Is it Mom's business, huh? Is it her business that you're sneaking out in the middle of the night to be with some slut when you should be at home with your family?" The words Anthony spoke were bold, but the tremor in his voice revealed his apprehension.

His father stepped in even closer, "Boy I'm going to tell you one more time to get the hell out of here, now!"

"I'm not going *anywhere!*"

"What did you say to me?"

"I'm tired of you cheating on my mama!" Before he knew it, tears started to run down Anthony's face. "I saw you! I saw you kissing that woman, that slut! I'm telling Mama! I'm telling her and we're going to leave you. I hate you! *We* hate you!"

Anthony's father, standing at six feet four inches, and

weighing 220 pounds, towered over his meek son still suffering through the growth spurts of puberty. With one swift move, he grabbed Anthony by his neck, lifting him two inches off the ground. Neither of Anthony's parents had ever physically restrained him, so he went into a shock. The only thing that pulled him out of his trance was the feeling of cold, wet grass scrapping his back as he hit the ground. The force and anger his father used to toss him into the air and onto the lawn, was of a caliber Anthony had never seen before. With his eyes wide in trepidation, he watched as his enemy charged toward him and stood over his shaking body.

"Get up," his father commanded.

Anthony didn't move.

"I said get your ass up! You want to step to me like a man, then fight like one."

His knees were shaking as Anthony stood slowly to his feet.

His father clasped his throat with his left hand again, "Now, you and your mother aren't going anywhere. You will not tell her about any of this. Do you understand?"

Anthony twisted his face in disgust and infuriation. He wasn't sure whether to give in to his fear and retreat, or to let his anger take control and attack. When his father released his hold, he decided on the latter. Feeling like he had nothing to lose, he drew back his hand in a fist and swung as hard as his lanky body would allow. He missed. His father laughed at him in a way that made him feel embarrassed. In an effort to redeem himself, he threw a punch with his other fist, but his father stopped it in mid air as he caught his fist, twisted it backward and used his free hand to backhand Anthony hard across his face. The boy stumbled backward, but didn't fall.

He could taste the salt of his own blood in his mouth as it ran from his nose. He stared at the man he no longer recognized as his father, standing in front of him. His father watched with pure hatred in his eyes as he let out another menacing chuckle.

"You think you're a man, huh? Coming over here acting like you're all big and bad. Take your ass home before you get hurt even more and I'll act like none of this happened in the morning."

Anthony looked up at the bay window and saw the mistress peeking out from behind the curtain. She quickly closed it when she noticed him staring back at her. He directed his attention back to the enemy and watched in frustration as his father turned his back to him and slowly walked back up the walkway to the porch and disappeared behind the door. Anthony figured there was no use in furthering this exchange. He had lost the battle, but the victory of the war would be his. There was always tomorrow.

He turned and started running. Looking up at the street signs, he knew he was no more than a mile from home. He ran until the reality of what had just happened hit him with a blunt force and caused him to sit down on the curb in an effort to regain composure. Alone and finally feeling comfortable enough to give in to his emotions, Anthony let the tears flow freely down his face with his head in his hands. He made a promise that night to never be like his father -- the enemy. He would never make his wife and child suffer only because he was too weak to suppress temptation. He was a better man than his father ever was and ever would be. In time, he would prove it. He repeated his pep talk to himself until he noticed the headlights of his mother's car pulling around the corner, ending her frantic search for her only child.

• • •

Twenty years passed and Anthony's hatred for his father never abated. He kept his promise, and four years into his marriage, he lived up to it. Refusing to drag his family through the heartache and proving to himself that he was twice the man his father was, he successfully fought off the countless advances of women dying to be "the other woman" for a successful, married, black man. In his head, he was in a constant battle with his father. With each day, week, month and year of self-control, he was able to force the enemy's ways out of his system. He was not his father's son. He was his own man, independent of that man's legacy. His father may have been able to beat him in the flesh, but Anthony would not allow him to conquer his state of mind.

As the years pressed on, Anthony was saddened as he slowly began to realize that the fight was never with his father. It was a battle within himself. His father's blood flowed through his veins. He was a part of him, always was and always would be. Despite tireless attempts to brainwash himself into monogamy, he became the only type of husband he knew how to be. He turned his marriage into a reflection of the only example of holy matrimony he had been exposed to.

His first affair occurred just days after his fourth wedding anniversary. He didn't put up much of a fight. His resistance was low from years of tireless self-combat. The day he slept with an office assistant at his firm, he did so with no thought or emotion. He told himself, if he remained detached, then the crime would be reduced from first degree to second. If he never called her again and pretended like it didn't happen, maybe he could slide by with a misdemeanor, but the plea bargain he had constructed in his head was quickly rejected as his penis made the final decision as judge and jury. The adulterous relationship continued for a year before she began to pressure him about leaving his wife and making their relationship "official." It was apparent then, that it had gone too far.

Leaving his wife was not an option. It was too complicated and messy and he did not have the time for that type of disruption in his life. He moved on to one of his clients, then another, and two more after that. The affair with his accountant went on for almost two years and ended with a restraining order preventing the crazed woman from coming within 100 yards of him. It was a near-fatal attraction. The only thing missing was the boiling bunny on the stove.

Learning from his past experiences, Anthony knew he had to be more clever if he wanted to continue to feed his destructive habit. Cheating was no longer a virus he desperately wanted to cure himself of. It was becoming a way of life, something that he expected of himself and took pride in when done successfully. He began to lie to his women about his marital status. He rented a swanky new loft downtown with a view of the Detroit River, so there was no chance of anyone stopping by his home and disrupting his family. He became an entirely different man, leading an entirely different life. He was the bachelor-stud of the year.

By the time he met Ryan at Starbucks, he was a master of the game: his every word was calculated; his moves were predetermined; even his thoughts were contrived. He had conquered her before he had spoken his first word. The way she moved her curves when she walked, smooth and slow like sweet molasses, caught his attention almost immediately. She was fiery, had a little attitude going on. It only intrigued him more. It only took one January and half of February (a short month) before he had her professing her love for him and giving him sole claim to her pussy. The sex was electric and her conversation was stimulating. She had class. She knew how to command attention and she didn't take any shit off of anybody. He whisked her away on spontaneous trips and bought her expensive gifts. In return, she performed erotic strip teases and told him she was his. Her body was intoxicating and her bedroom skills were unmatched. He would not allow himself to love her, but he *was* infatuated. He lost himself in between her dark chocolate thighs and indulged in her sweet kisses. She gave him what he sought. All she needed in return were empty promises of marriage and commitment, which he gave abundantly. To her he was her man. To him, she was an exquisite pussy – his preferred service provider of the moment. Sometimes he surprised himself at how neatly he had compartmentalized his life. He had successfully conquered the task of having his cake and eating it too.

But after a year, the affair with Ryan began to spiral out of control. Even with his separate identity, the balanced scales of married and bachelor life were beginning to swing wildly. She was becoming hip to his lies and no longer settled for his bullshit. She constantly questioned his motives and his whereabouts. The pressure to keep up the ruse was beginning to irritate him. They began to argue almost daily. She was becoming erratic and short tempered. She screamed and cried as a part of her nightly regimen. He would not admit it aloud, but he knew it was because she was having trouble dealing with his sporadic presence in her life. She knew when he was lying to her. He could hear it in her quivering voice, as she demanded an explanation. The only thing she seemed to hold onto was the slight chance that he would marry her. She had become obsessed with the idea. She brought up the topic whenever there was a pause in the conversation. She was so desperate to get married; she failed to see that he was no longer present in the relationship. Things were beginning to get dangerous. Her actions were becoming unpredictable. It was time to cut Ryan loose before things went any further.

CHAPTER 21

RYAN

IT was a cold Friday evening. The channel four news told Ryan that it was only 30 degrees outside. It felt like two below. It made her wonder what it would be like to move to Miami or Southern California. What was it like to go through the whole year without any snow? Those people had no clue what a real winter was, a Michigan winter. Hell, it wasn't even winter yet. It was still fall. The temperature plus the wind chill factor had Ryan's teeth chattering and she wasn't even outside. Just the thought of walking out there and that frost hitting her face, gave her chill bumps. That was why she was thankful for her little surprise weekend getaway to Vegas. It could not have come at a better time. It was time for her and her man to get reacquainted. It was well overdue. It would be nothing but a weekend full of sex, good eating, sex, clubbing, sex, shopping, sex, gambling, and more sex!

A week had passed since their reconciliation. He took her back with no hesitation. Well, that wasn't completely true. She had to serve up some groveling along with a side of "Baby, please forgive me. I'll do anything" and hot sex for dessert, before he finally cracked and gave her another chance. It felt as if she had been holding her breath for seven days until he finally said those words, "I forgive you." His words were magic, as if he waived a wand and everything was okay.

Her second chance was enough to have her floating, but the surprise trip was a bonus. He'd called her last night and told her to pack her bags because they were going to the city of sin for the weekend to see if they could live up to the name. She had packed as if they were staying for two weeks with one suitcase with enough clothes for her to change three times a day and another with the shoes to match. A third bag held her toiletries and hair care items. Then there was a fourth, it was empty, for the new things she would come home with.

She piled her luggage by the front door. Anthony was due any minute. It was 6:45 and the flight left at 8:30 in the evening. She peeked out of the window just in time to see him pulling up in his new Mercedes. It was such a sexy car for an equally sexy man. Her heart rate sped up as she let the excitement of what was to come overwhelm her. She opened the door before he had a chance to knock.

Her ridiculously wide smile greeted him at the door, "Hey, baby!" She felt like a little girl in her excitement.

"What's up, babe?"

She stepped back to let him in the door, "Well, I'm ready to go. I've got everything packed. I checked and double checked and I don't think I'm forgetting anything."

His eyes shifted. He looked down at the floor and walked past her in the foyer, "So you're all ready to go, huh?"

"Yeah baby, I'm so excited. I mean, I know we've had our problems, but I feel like this will be really therapeutic for us. You know?" Ryan checked her bags for the fourth time. She thought she may have forgotten her flat irons, but she was relieved to see that she hadn't. Satisfied that she really did have everything this time, she waited for Anthony's response.

"Did you hear me, baby? I think this will be really good for us."

"Yeah, I heard you. Look Ryan, about this trip…"

"What's up?" Ryan walked over to her man standing in the dining room of the small condo. She could tell that whatever he was about to say was not good.

"Um…We're not going to be able to make it."

"What do you mean? We have plenty of time to get to the airport. It only takes 30 minutes to get to Metro from here."

He finally looked her in the face, "That's not what I mean."

Ryan sensed where the conversation was going. She had heard it too many times before -- just in different versions. There was the time he was supposed to take her to his colleague's wedding reception. At the last minute, he told her that he decided that he didn't really want to go. He would just pop in for a minute to show his face then leave shortly after. There was no need for Ryan to go with him for that. He would pick her up after he left. After four hours of waiting, fully dressed and teary-eyed, sprawled out on the couch, she finally accepted the fact that he just was not coming. It wasn't until he arrived at ten o'clock the next morning that he told her he *did* go to the reception without her and stayed all night, too drunk to leave and too polite to tell his associates that he had other plans. She couldn't verify so she *had* to trust.

Then there was the time the De La Hoya vs. Mayweather fight was showing on pay per view. Anthony was a boxing fan, so Ryan told him that she paid the $50 fee to see it on cable. She bought a fifth of super premium vodka, some snacks and a sexy-ass teddy from Vicki's Secret so they could have their own round-by-round bout after the televised fight. After several text messages and promises that he was on his way, he never showed up. The next day he apologetically explained that he had taken some cough medicine for a nasty cold he was trying to fight off and didn't realize that it was the PM medication instead of Daytime. Before he knew what happened, he had awakened from the morning sun shining on his face.

Yeah, Ryan knew where the conversation was going. She knew it all too well. The familiarity of it smacked her hard in the face. He was bailing out on her. Something "came up."

"What in the hell do you mean then?"

"There you go with that bitch-ass attitude. I don't need that shit right now."

"Tell me what's going on, Anthony."

His demeanor changed. His back stiffened and his face hardened. He switched from apologetic to defensive within milliseconds.

"Look, something came up. I don't have to explain shit to you, not if you're going to have a funky-ass attitude about it. I thought I told you about that. I told you to keep your attitude in check."

"You have *got* to be kidding me. Are you serious?"

He didn't answer. His clenched mouth and scornful eyes told Ryan that he was not playing.

She tried a different approach. "Okay, I'm sorry for jumping the gun. Just tell me what happened and maybe we can work it out. Maybe we can still go. We just have to figure some things out, okay? Just tell me what it is."

"I didn't want to tell you because I knew you would

think it was bullshit. I didn't even want to go there with you tonight."

"Whatever it is, baby, I'll believe you."

"Okay, my credit card was stolen."

"What?" What does your credit card have to do--"

"It has a lot to do with it! Somebody stole my Platinum card! They've already run up like $3000 worth of charges on that thing. I'm not going anywhere until I get that shit cleared up."

"Wait, I must be missing something here. We're not going to Vegas because your credit card was stolen?"

"That's right."

"Babe, you have like a hundred different cards and you have a ton of money in the bank. Call the credit card company and tell them what happened. They'll close the account and issue you a new card. It doesn't have to interfere with our plans," She desperately smiled.

"I'm not going anywhere until I find out who has my card and where this three grand charge is coming from!"

"Anthony, you sound ridiculous!"

"If it's somebody I know, I'm kickin' some ass."

"Baby, please. Let's not let this ruin our trip. We need this. Just take a different card and we'll worry about the stolen one later. You can call the credit card company while we're in Vegas. They won't even hold you responsible for the charges. Come on!"

"Look, I know you're disappointed, but this is more important than some stupid ass trip, okay. We're talking about my money!"

Ryan had heard enough.

This has to be the most ridiculous excuse yet. It doesn't make the slightest bit of sense. He's gotten sloppy with the lies. Must of thought of this one while walking from his car to the front door.

She could feel her face getting hot and her stomach turning into knots. Her hands began to shake and her knees felt as if they would give in.

He was intrigued and afraid. He had never actually witnessed one of her breakdowns before.

"You okay?" He instinctively moved in closer to her and reached a hand out.

She felt herself explode on the inside before the eruption reached the surface. She let it out with a hysterical scream. Her words were barely decipherable.

"You mutha fuckin' lyin' ass piece of shit!"

"What did you just say to me?"

"Oh my God!" Ryan frantically paced the floor with her hands clutching her hair, and sweat beading on her forehead. "You're lying! Stop lying to me! Stop fucking lying to me!"

Anthony took a few steps back with a look on his face that said his fear was beginning to match his anger.

"Crazy bitch!"

Tears rolled down her face. She shook her head frantically, trying to fight them off, "I hate you! I hate this shit! You don't love me! You never loved me! Lying ass piece of shit!"

Her insides were racing and her heart was banging. Her breaths came out in short jagged spurts. She was falling apart from the inside out. She crouched on the floor before him, still holding her hair in her hands. Tears of rage spilled from her eyes. She shook her head in doubt, refusing to believe that this was actually happening to her.

Anthony turned and headed towards the door in a

half walk, half trot, but managed to keep his voice low and controlled.

"I don't need you in my life right now, Ryan. You are crazy as hell and I hope that you find the help that you need, but you and me? We're over. Don't call me anymore, don't text me. If you see me on the street don't even look at me. Act like you never met me."

He never raised his voice. The whole time Ryan had known him, he had never yelled at her. He was always so controlled and emotionless. His calm tone fueled her fire. It threw her straight over the edge. She popped up from her crouching position and charged at him, knocking over the suitcases stacked by the door. His hand was on the knob as he was preparing to leave, but he wasn't going to get away that easily. She jumped at him with arms and fists swinging wildly. When she landed, she was on top of him, straddling him, with his back pinned to the floor. She struck his face and his chest with closed fists, screaming like a banshee. Her face was twisted into knots and her hair was wild. She gritted her teeth and clawed at his face.

Taken off guard by her sudden attack, Anthony did nothing to defend himself at first. He took each blow like a soldier, wide-eyed and opened-mouthed from shock. Ryan showed no signs of letting up anytime soon.

"I hate you! You fucking liar! You never loved me! You were never going to marry me! I hate you!"

Anthony snapped out of it. Quickly assessing the situation, he grabbed both of her wrists with one hand to restrain her. With strength that trumped Ryan's ten-fold, he sat up and threw her back against the nearest wall. She bounced up like a spring and pounced him again before he had a chance to get to his feet. This time he was prepared, blocking her blows to his face with his forearm. Again, he grabbed her wrists with his left hand, then her neck with his right and rolled her over on her back. They switched positions. He was on top of her now. She kicked and squirmed beneath his weight, but it was worthless. He was too strong. They stayed on the floor. He held her there until she grew too tired to struggle.

"Are you done now?"

She didn't answer. Her loud sobs spoke for her. When it seemed to be safe, Anthony slowly stood to his feet. He never took his eyes off her as he stepped over her crumpled body to make his way out of the door. Ryan didn't move. There was too much going on in her head, too many thoughts and regrets flooded her mind and weighed her down.

"I'm leaving now, Ryan. It's over. It's finally over. Goodbye."

He adjusted his tie and walked out the door as calmly as he had entered, leaving Ryan on the floor drowning in her own self pity.

It was over for good. She had no one, no man, no friends, no one. She was alone and she had no one to blame but herself. She did this and maybe she even deserved this. There was nothing left to do but tear herself apart. As she lay on the floor, she felt everything inside of her break and shatter and she welcomed it. She needed it. There was nothing left. Several seconds passed before she finally picked herself up from the floor. Drunk from the adrenaline of the fight, she stumbled to the bathroom to retrieve her poison. After popping a Xanax, she walked back into the living room and plopped on the couch.

She picked up the phone and stared at it hesitantly before

finally dialing seven familiar numbers that she hadn't dialed for a while. Lauren answered on the third ring, "Hello."

Tears made Ryan choke back her words. There were a million things she needed to say to her best friend. She owed her a lengthy explanation. She owed her a profuse apology with an expensive dinner, a new pair of shoes, and her first-born child. There was so much to say, but words failed her. She summed everything up in three simple words.

"I need you."

Lauren voiced no hesitation, "I'm on my way."

CHAPTER 22

JESSICA

IT was surprising to Jessica how easy it was to get a gun in the state of Michigan, maybe it's that easy in every state. She wasn't sure, but she knew it only took a valid picture ID and a background check that only took 48 hours to complete, before she was holding the cold, heavy steel in her hands. The weight of the 9mm Smith and Wesson gave her a sense of empowerment. She felt like a bounty hunter on her way to catch a criminal. She sat alone in the entertainment room caressing the gun, feeling its power in her hands. It felt so damn good. She allowed herself to get lost in a vision of sweet, intoxicating revenge. Her fantasies had her so drunk with promises of redemption, that she didn't hear Ross calling to her from upstairs.

"Jessica, let's go!" He sounded irritated.

She snapped out of her reverie, hid the gun behind the bar, and trotted up the stairs to meet her husband.

"Coming, honey!"

• • •

The church was breathtaking. The immense cathedral

ceiling, adorned with an elaborate mural, was high enough to reach Heaven itself. Intricate paintings of bible stories beautifully embellished the walls. The floors were made of marble. The mix of golds, creams, and deep reds gave the illusion of walking on the Red Sea. The stained glass windows also told stories of worship, betrayal, and God's miracles. There were flowers posted on the ends of each pew, covering the alter, and drowning the chocolate-colored, cherry oak casket. There were many pinks and white too with a little bit of blue mixed in as well. It was absolutely beautiful. It was disgusting.

Jessica shifted uncomfortably in her seat as the Pastor gave his unrealistic rendition of what a great woman sister Wanda Wolinsky was and where she was going in her afterlife. He didn't even know her. "Sister" Wanda Wolinsky had never even set foot in a church throughout her entire miserable life. It was too much. Too *good*. The extravagant church, the elaborate floral arrangements, and the hundreds of sorrowful faces seated in the pews behind her, all made her stomach turn into knots. She crossed and uncrossed her legs, cringing at every positive word the Pastor spoke to describe Sister Wanda Wolinsky.

"This is not a time for mourning, people. No, this is a time for celebration. We must rejoice in honor of Sister Wanda's homecoming. She is going home to be with our Lord and savior Jesus Christ!"

Jessica was having a hard time keeping still. She wanted to leave. The display, the whole thing, was ridiculous. It was a preposterous performance. The pastor looked as if he was about to keel over. Sweat rolled down his face in rivulets. The nurse followed every other word with a quick swipe to the Pastor's forehead with a white handkerchief. The "Yes Lord's" and the "Amen's" from the congregation hissed in Jessica's ears like poisonous snakes.

"She was a good woman, Lord, with a kind heart. She gave life all she had to give…"

Blah, blah, blah. Jessica could barely stand it anymore. It took all of her will and a small prayer to keep her from walking out of the huge, polished, wood doors. She impatiently tapped her fingers on the back of the pew in front of her.

"Stop it. You are fidgeting around like a child, Jessica. What is your problem?" Ross' hushed whisper clearly portrayed his annoyance. He bumped her on the thigh with his knee to warn and reprimand.

She whispered back, "This is ridiculous, Ross. I mean come on, all of this for Wanda? That bitch--"

"Watch your mouth! You are in a church."

"Whose church? We've never even been to this church. This is like something out of a movie with all these flowers and these people, acting like they give a damn about a woman they don't even know. You'd think we were at Elvis' funeral or something."

"It's your mother. Show some respect!"

"Mother. Hmph, that's a good one."

"Look, I have an image to uphold. I can't let people think that I don't take care of my family. My secretary spread the word around the office that my mother-in-law died, so a few associates of mine came through to show support. No big deal."

"No big deal? This place looks like Taj Mahal! She doesn't deserve any of this. I think I'm going to throw up."

Ross glared at her with the disapproving eyes of a parent

to his child, "Shut up and be still before you make me angry. If I have to speak to you again about your behavior, it will be a huge problem when we get home. Do you understand?"

Jessica put her head down. She was out of line and the last thing she wanted to do was make him mad at a time when their marriage was already so fragile. She decided to stick it out until the end. How long did funerals last anyway? They had been there for about an hour already. It couldn't be too much longer. She mentally zoned out for most of the service. She caught the last few words from the Pastor who looked like he was melting on the pulpit.

"We are living in our last days. The time is now to get right with the Lord. Don't wait until you're on your death bed, begging for forgiveness and looking for a place behind Heaven's gate. Don't wait until judgment day. The time is now. Who will join Sister Wanda in Heaven and walk with the Lord? Who will live a life of righteousness? The time is now. It's your turn to make that change."

On cue, the massive choir seated behind the pastor in their red and gold embroidered robes, rose to sing, "His Eye is on the Sparrow." The lead singer was a plump, black woman with a voice like thunder. It was emotional and moving. Her vocals sent vibrations throughout the sanctuary. Sniffles echoed throughout the congregation as the soulful rendition touched the hearts of several of the attendees. It made Jessica roll her eyes. When the song was over, everyone stood as the pastor recited a prayer. She didn't listen to that either. She kept her head up and allowed her eyes to wander until they landed on the stained glass window to the left. An illustration of David and Goliath adorned the window with bright colors. Her body jerked as Ross yanked her hard by the hand to get her to regain focus. She followed his implied order and bowed her head in a simulation of prayer.

"Amen."

The lengthy prayer ended in unison. Even Jessica managed to mumble out an "Amen" in an attempt to show her sincerity. She turned and scanned the enormous congregation. She recognized several faces in the sea of black suits and dresses. There was no one to remind her of the faces she hadn't seen in years. She didn't see any of the faces she'd forgotten and had pushed out of her mind. There were no traces of the people she knew when she was a poor, seemingly white trash strumpet with ragged clothes and unkempt hair. No one knew that she used to shake her ass in an old, smoky, strip club that had since burned to the ground. She didn't want to see those faces. She didn't want them to remind her of what she once was and who she was afraid she still might be. But none of them were there. No one who actually knew her mother would show up to her funeral. Maybe old, greasy Carl with the rusty, orange Cadillac would've come. But Ross' secretary had arranged the funeral, so she knew that no one from her past would have been notified. They would have destroyed his delusional image of his ideal family, and his perfect homemaker, raised by the perfect mother, in the perfect little house in a modest, small town in Michigan. As Ross told the "Official Story", his wife came from humble beginnings, but she was ambitious, beautiful and smart. He saw a spark in her eyes when they first met 16 and a half years ago at a black-tie event thrown for his colleague in celebration of his making partner at the firm.

No, these people in the church did not know her. They didn't know about her abusive, alcoholic, pathetic excuse for a mother. They didn't know that Ross forced her to put Wanda into one of the best adult nursing care facilities in the area to be properly cared for because that was his image of "what decent, respectable families" did. He would not have his mother-in-law living in the slums, trapped by her own filth and desolation. It made *him* look bad.

They had no idea that Ross, a young law associate on the rise, with tailored suits and manicured nails, bearing a striking resemblance to his late father, the honorable Judge Lawrence Pembroke, met young Jessie as a stripper at a bachelor party for one of his college buddies. They had no idea that he paid her $1000 for a lap dance, while she straddled his pelvis, grinding in small circles on his groin and after grilling her about her background, he took her under his wing and transformed her from Jessie Wolinsky into the classy and refined Mrs. Jessica Pembroke with finishing school, grammar and etiquette training, and a bachelor's degree in Sociology. Ballet and modeling classes corrected her posture and enhanced her poise. He spent thousands of dollars on an extensive wardrobe, manicures, pedicures, facials and hair upkeep -- His own Stepford wife. She was a woman so desperate to leave behind the only life she had ever known, that she was willing to give up her own identity and live in the shadows of his existence. The attendees at the funeral didn't know anything about the way he had trained her to be the epitome of the all-American wife, the kind that was decorously seen and not too often heard, the kind that was book smart, but also smart enough to know her place -- behind her man.

She glared at Ross' profile as he focused on the pulpit.

Why aren't I good enough?

After all the work, the training, and the effort, why was

she still not good enough for Ross? What did she have to do? She did everything he wanted. She acted the way that he demanded of her. She put on the performance he made her rehearse for their entire marriage and she did it well. Still he treated her as if she were nothing. He was having an affair and living a separate life. Nothing she could do would make a difference. No amount of schooling, polishing, or refinement would change how he felt about her. It would never change who she was. None of it mattered anymore.

Her fixation on Ross hardened as she felt herself grow aflame with anger and frustration. Once again, she looked around the church at the strangers filling the pews. Jessica glowered at the ones she had dined with during the occasional business/family outings and holiday parties. She scowled at those with whom she'd tapped crystal flutes of Dom Perignon and mingled on the golf courses of the Detroit Athletic Club, sharing political jokes and fake laughs. These were the men and women that, after 16 years, Ross still did not trust her around. He always stayed close to her, hovering to ensure she did not say the wrong thing or give the wrong impression. Despite the rigorous etiquette classes she took, he'd still watch her closely while dining to make sure she'd use the correct fork for her salad and the right spoon for her soup. These people didn't know her. They had no clue who she was. They were ignorant of the desperate life she lived behind the closed doors of the mansionette that sat on the corner of Cherry Grove Lane and Cambridge Avenue. Yet, they were all there, each of them, ready to offer a hand on the shoulder or a soft whisper in the ear as assurance that they *really* did care. She rolled her eyes and let out a deep, aggravated breath.

This is stupid and I need to put them all in their places.

The Pastor paused and eyed the congregation before encouraging friends and family to share their kind words and memories. Jessica looked up at the pulpit as if she was waiting for approval. Her mother was dead now; there was nothing to bring her down. Nothing mattered anymore. Her marriage was crumbling around her, and the life she worked so hard to gain was shattering. It meant nothing. It never did. The money, the cars, the house and maid, all of it was just a facade. No one knew who she really was and who she always had been. It was time to let them all know. It was time to let Ross know. She was done to death with the masquerade.

Jessica stood slowly to her feet, clutching the pew in front of her with sweaty palms. She felt Ross reach for her arm and try to pull her back down, but she snatched away before he could get a good grip. She ignored his angry whispers as she walked towards the altar. He had no control or authority over her. She felt propelled by a tidal wave of emotion and, for that moment, she could not be constrained. She walked past her mother's open casket without looking at Wanda's withered body. As she approached the three steps to the pulpit with caution, the Pastor greeted her with an exaggerated smile.

"Sister Pembroke, please share with us. We all know you loved your mother dearly. Bless us with a few kind words."

Jessica looked at him blankly and managed to contrive a smile. He stepped to the side to give her room to position herself behind the podium. She placed her hands on the lectern and focused her eyes on her husband as he sat in front of her, menacing her with his eyes. It only empowered her as she felt the adrenaline rush to her head and the hatred flood her heart.

"My mother was a drunk bitch."

The gasps from the congregation resounded throughout the sanctuary. Jessica saw the Pastor rushing towards her in her peripheral vision, but she shot him with a look that dared him to try her. He reluctantly eased back and she continued, "She used to beat me because my father was black. She used to call me "Dirty Nigger Bitch," like it was my first, middle and last name."

Ross shifted in his seat and looked nervously at the congregation out of the sides of his eyes.

"I hate that bitch! She was never good to me. We were poor white trash living in Hamtramck. What did *he* tell you? He told you I was from Ferndale? Farmington Hills? Well guess what ladies and gentlemen?" She threw her arms in the air in an exaggerated presentation, "It was none of the above. That's right."

The room was silent. She had the full attention of the crowd as they stared at her with wide eyes and mouths agape. Even Ross was thunderstruck with shock.

"I was a stripper. I bet you he didn't tell you that. Did you, honey? Did you ever tell your esteemed colleagues how we met?"

Ross jumped to his feet and started towards her. He crept nervously across the floor as if he were walking barefoot on hot coals. His eyes held a host of emotions that all seemed to visibly intertwine into revulsion. Jessica thought she recognized a hint of fear and it pleased her. He spoke to her through clenched teeth, "Jessica, you shut your mouth. Get down before you make a fool of yourself."

She smirked, "Make a fool of myself or make a fool of *you*? That's all you care about isn't it? Your *image*, your *creden-*

*tial*s. It was never about me." Her bottom lip quivered against her will, "Did you ever even love me?"

He continued to creep slowly towards her, "Jessica I won't tell you again to shut up."

"Tell them, honey. Tell them how you met me. Tell them who I am."

He paused and looked around at the expectant faces, now hungry for blood and thirsty for the kill, as they waited for an answer. He opened his mouth, but failed to form any words.

"Tell them that we met at a bachelor party when I gave you a lap dance. Tell them how you watched me all night, and then tipped me a thousand dollars while I shook my ass for you. A far cry from the "black-tie" story isn't it, sweetie?" Jessica laughed a cold chuckle. The looks on the faces of the attendees ranged a full spectrum of emotions: shock, shame, pity and eagerness to dish some more dirt. The way Ross seemed to shrink in his own humiliation like quicksand was riveting. She was starring in the "Jessica Pembroke Show" and she relished every moment of it; the show was not over yet.

"Wanda Wolinsky doesn't deserve any of this. She isn't worth the dirt she'll be buried under." She looked down at the cherry oak box containing her mother's corpse and smiled, "This has been a long time coming." She stretched her body over the pulpit as far as she could lean. She closed her eyes for several seconds to gain the courage to do what she felt she had to do. Finally, she took a deep breath, opened her eyes, then hocked and spit in the dead woman's face. The slimy mix of mucus and saliva hit Wanda on the bridge of her nose and slid down the leathery skin of her cheek. Jessica smiled at her great aim and precision and fought the urge to do it again. The congregation went into a frenzy. Some of the grievers stood, others gasped, while few clutched at their chests and covered their mouths in shock.

Ross rushed to the pulpit, taking the three steps in one leap. He reached behind the lectern to grab his wife by the forearm. She violently snatched free from his clutch and pushed past him without making eye contact. She left Ross and the Pastor standing, openmouthed, at the pulpit. She could hear Ross' stammering words in an attempt to redeem himself in front of his peers. As Jessica sashayed down the center aisle, she ripped the ribbon from her hair that held her neatly crafted bun and let her wild tresses fly behind her like a cape. She never looked behind her as she stormed out of the oversized wooden doors of the church. Nothing mattered anymore. Nothing was holding her back.

CHAPTER 23

JESSICA

ROSS slammed his fist on the kitchen counter, "You ungrateful bitch! You will pay for that scene you made today. Do you have any idea of the damage you've done?"

Jessica sat at the table in the breakfast nook. She gave her husband an amused look while she sipped on a cup of tea, "How was the burial?"

"Don't you play coy with me. Have you lost your mind? After everything I've done for you, this is how you repay me? You humiliate me in front of my peers. You smear my name in the mud."

"I--"

"Shut up!" He moved in closer to the table so he was able to look directly down on her. "You don't know how to act. You don't know your place, how to play your role. You're hopeless. Your actions today were inappropriate and you've proved that you are nothing more than trash!"

"That's all you care about. It was never about me. Everything was for you. Everything was to make you look good. Why did you even marry me, Ross? Why didn't you get some bougie bitch from a respectable family and a good school? Why a dirty stripper?"

"Watch yourself Jessie --"

"Answer me!"

"I didn't marry the woman I see in front of me right now. I married the woman I fell in love with, and she disappeared a long time ago."

"After everything I've done, everything you put me through to be the perfect wife, I'm still not good enough."

"You're weak. Without me you would be nothing but what your mother made you. I taught you how to act, how to dress, how to be a lady, and you didn't know what to do with it. You don't have a mind of your own. You wait for me to tell you what to do. You don't make a move without my approval. You're so weak and dependent, it disgusts me."

"That's what you wanted."

"No, what I wanted was the fighter I met at that party. That's who I thought I was marrying. I did you a favor, giving you the life you would have never had a chance to live, but you lost yourself in the process."

"You don't love me."

"Nor do I respect you."

Jessica set her mug down on the table and stood up. "Is that why you're cheating on me with Ryan? Because you 'don't respect me'?" she mocked.

Ross frowned in confusion, but she knew he was well aware of what she was talking about.

"You didn't think I knew did you? I'm not stupid Ross. You don't think I know about the loft downtown? I know. I know about all of the fake business trips and all the lies. Yeah, I knew about all the other women too."

He smirked, "Can you blame me?"

"How dare you."

"Like I said, you're weak. Just like my mother. She let The Judge run her life. She didn't live for herself. Everything was for and about him. I hated her for it. You're just like her. No mind of your own."

"I'm still the same woman I used to be."

"You're right, you've always been pathetic; I just didn't see it. That was my fault. Now Ryan, she's a real woman." He turned away from her and let out a menacing laugh. He was taunting her and she knew it, yet she couldn't prevent his hateful words from piercing her through the heart.

"Stop it!" She slammed the coffee mug down on the breakfast table. It titter-tottered in response.

Ross turned around to face her, "She has fire. She's a *real* woman. Ryan knows how to stand up for herself and speak her mind and still make me feel like a man."

"This isn't about Ryan. It's about you!"

"No, she was different than the rest of them. She's special. That's who I should've married. Maybe I still will after I get rid of your ass."

The thought of Ryan taking her place, her home, her husband, and her life made Jessica visibly shudder. She wouldn't let it happen, not after all the work she had done to get to where she was. No one would take that from her! Ross thought she was weak, but she still had plenty of fight left.

"You can't leave me! We have sixteen years. You can't just turn your back on that. I worked hard for this! I've earned this life!"

"You obviously weren't happy with your life; you threw it all down the drain at the funeral when you acted like a complete fool. You have nothing. You are nothing and you're about to get a rude awakening, 'Jessie'." He spit her birth name out at her like venom.

Jessica looked in his eyes for any sign of a bluff but she saw none. It made her sick to her stomach, but she was still in love with him. He was her knight, her salvation. No one would take that from her. She reached out to touch his arm, but he dodged the soft gesture. "What about our daughter?"

Jessica noticed him avert his eyes at the mention of their little girl. She wasn't sure of what to think of it so she decided to dismiss it.

At that moment, both of their attention turned towards the kitchen doorway as they watched their daughter walk into the kitchen, holding an empty glass in her hand.

"Hi, Mom." She lowered her head and mumbled a greeting to her father, "Hi, Daddy."

"Simone!" Jessica rushed to her daughter and hugged her with a tight squeeze. "How are you, baby?"

"I'm fine. Just came down to put my glass in the sink. Is everything okay with you two?"

Ross shuffled awkwardly back and forth.

Jessica answered, "Of course, sweetie, everything is fine. Your father and I were just finishing up a conversation."

"How was the funeral?"

Ross turned swiftly on his heel to walk out of the kitchen. "Just be glad your mother didn't let you come," he answered over his shoulder on his way out.

Jessica called out to him as he walked away, "Where are you going?"

He ignored her as he made his way into the foyer. She flinched as she heard the front door open and slam shut. Jessica turned to Simone, "Honey, go up to your room and finish your homework. I'll be up later to see if you need any help."

"Are you sure everything is okay, Mom?"

"Yes, baby. Now go ahead."

Simone did as she was told, looking back at her mother for a final sign of reassurance. Jessica gave her a weak smile.

When she was sure her daughter was in her room, Jessica ran downstairs to the entertainment room in the lower level of the house. Ducking behind the bar, she reached inside the same cabinet she hid her weed and Riesling. Her fingers fumbled over bottles and whatever else was stashed there before they found the gun.

She let out a sigh of relief as she clutched the weapon close to her chest. It was the answer to all of her problems. Ross called her weak. She wasn't weak. She was a fighter and she'd fight till the death to keep and protect what was hers. She couldn't let Ross leave her. What would happen to her? What would happen to Simone? Simone needed her mother and father as constants in her life to grow into a healthy adult. They would make it through this. All families had trials. Theirs were no different. They'd get counseling and Ross would get over his anger for what she did. She just had to handle her business and put things in their proper place, starting with Ryan.

CHAPTER 24

SIMONE

"HELLO, Simone. How are you today?"

"I'm fine, Dr. Gloria."

"That's good to hear. Are you feeling any differently since our last conversation?"

"No, not really."

"Well, have you given any thought to what we've talked about?"

Simone shrugged her shoulders.

"You seem to be rather down. Is there a reason for that, something out of the ordinary?"

"No."

"Okay. Well, I see that you have a notebook there. Did you take me up on my suggestion and start a journal?"

"Yeah."

"How did it make you feel to write your thoughts down on paper and get your feelings out in the open?"

"I don't know. It was kind of draining. It made me cry a lot. It makes me cry every time I write in it."

"That can be a good thing, Simone, to let your feelings and your pain air out. Let it out so it's not bottled inside of you. What type of things did you write about?"

"I wrote a lot about my family and how we used to be when we were happy. And about the kids at school and what happened with Kristen. Stuff like that."

"Did you write about things that we haven't talked about here?"

Simone put her head down, locking her eyes on the red and silver notebook sitting on her lap. There were plenty of secrets she had revealed to the notebook that she hadn't shared with the therapist.

"Yeah."

"Did you write about why you think you cut yourself?"

She nodded her head.

"Do you want to tell me about it?"

She didn't look up as she shook her head to make it clear that she was not ready to go down that path.

"We don't have to talk abut it if you're not ready. But I know there is something deep down inside of you. Something is bothering you. Something that has happened or may still be happening to you that's causing you to do this."

Simone's eyes began to water and she watched silently as a few teardrops stained her notebook. The therapist handed her a tissue to wipe her face. She took it.

"Cutting is a form of self-mutilation and there are many different reasons why people choose to harm themselves in this way. Sometimes, it's a means to cope with stress, whether it's academic or social." The therapist looked hard at Simone's face and body language for some type of response to what she was saying. When she saw none, she continued. "Sometimes, it's done to release internal pain from abuse or molestation."

That last word sent a sharp pain through Simone's rib

cage. She closed her eyes tightly and held the notebook to her chest.

"Sometimes, it makes you feel better to feel the pain on the outside instead of on the inside. Right?"

Eyes still closed, Simone nodded her head in agreement.

"Makes you feel like you're letting the pain out with the blood."

She nodded again.

"I need for you to know, Simone, that you are not alone with this. There are millions of teenage girls out there just like you, who feel the same way that you do. I know a lot of times it may feel like you're all alone and no one understands what you're going through. But you have to understand that this does not make you weird or strange. You are not alone."

Wiping her nose with a piece of tissue, Simone didn't look up. The ends of her hair, draped over her shoulders, were getting soaked from her tears.

"Did someone hurt you, Simone? Is someone still hurting you?"

Another nod.

"Is that what you wrote about in your journal? The person who is hurting you and what he or she is doing to you?"

Simone opened her eyes, lifted her head, and said, "Yes."

"Simone, why do you think your mother sent you to me for counseling?"

"Because she caught me. She caught me cutting. Delores told on me after she walked in on me one morning by accident. She saw me cutting in the bathroom. That's where I do it. I was doing it to my arm. She told my mom right then and there even after I begged her not to. It was horrible."

"You think your mother sent you to me because she loves you and she is concerned about your health and well-being?"

"She sent me because I'm perfect."

"What do you mean by that?"

"She thinks I'm perfect. She has worked so hard to make sure I was this perfect little princess. It's like she has something to prove to somebody or maybe even herself. That's the way she sees me. She even sends me to Sunday school every week just because that's what 'good respectable' girls do. To find out that anything has gone wrong is a reflection of her and is regarded as *her* failure. She freaked out when she found out. I thought she was going to have a seizure. I know she loves me. I know she only wants what's best for me; I just don't think she'll be able to handle it if I fall below her expectations."

"Does she know why you cut yourself?"

"No."

"What about your father? Does he know?"

"No. He can't know."

"Why is that? Do you think he would be angry with you?"

"I begged my mom not to tell him. Cried and begged. She said she would keep my secret for now if I agreed to go to counseling. Then we'd both tell him together when I was ready."

"Why don't you want your father to know?"

"I didn't want my *mother* to know either. I didn't want anybody to know."

"But now that your mother knows, why not your father too?"

"You know my father. My mom told me she found your business card in his office."

"Yes, I did know your father in the past, but you have to trust me when I say anything that you tell me is held in the strictest confidence. I will not tell your father, or anyone else, no matter who it is. I promise you that."

"He can't know."

"Simone, is your father the one who hurts you?"

There was no response. Again, she dropped her head. She couldn't bear to look Dr. Gloria in the face while thoughts of her father's body on top of hers flooded her mind. Shame overwhelmed her petite frame and her tears flowed once again. The small room grew even smaller. The cream-colored walls and the ivory lovelorn blinds closed in on her. An unseen vacuum sucked the air out of the room. Simone thought that she might start to hyperventilate, but it was all in her head. Her brain was beginning to get cloudy with images of her and her lover. No! No, he wasn't her lover; he was her father. The pictures flashed in her head like Polaroids.

Snap. He softly opens her bedroom door.

Snap. He walks across the room to Simone as she lies in her bed.

Snap. He lifts the covers at the end of her bed and tickles her feet.

Snap. He pulls the covers down to expose her body.

"It *is* your father isn't it? Simone, you can talk to me. You can let it out. Whatever you say here stays here. It is strictly confidential."

Snap. He kisses her on her forehead, her neck, and then her lips.

Snap. He climbs on top of her.

Snap. He uses his knee to pry her legs open.

"I know it hurts. I know that it's hard, but the only way

to recovery is to get your fears out in the open. To confront the pain head on so you can defeat it and learn to heal and move on."

Snap. He enters her. He rapes her. He steals her innocence and leaves her wounded beyond repair. He leaves her to heal herself through self-mutilation. Her father, the man who was supposed to protect her, had ruined her. He desecrated the sanctity of her being. He was a monster.

But so am I.

"Simone?"

She could barely hear Dr. Gloria calling her name or remember where she was. Her eyes were closed once again. She shook her head, trying desperately to shake those snap shots out of her memory. The warm, salty tears rolled down her face uncontrollably. Then she felt it coming on. The urge, the undeniable craving to relieve herself of her agony began to take over. She needed to cut. It was like an itch that had to be scratched. She quickly scanned the room for something, anything that would satisfy her hunger. She saw a pen on the desk where her therapist was seated, but decided against grabbing it and using it to stab herself. The Dr. would have stopped her and blocked her way to relief.

"Simone, what is going through your mind right now?"

Dr. Gloria's soft voice made Simone realize what she was thinking about doing. She was acting as if she was insane.

Am I insane?

She looked up at the honey brown woman with tears and desperation in her eyes. "I just want it to stop. I just want all of it to go away."

The Dr. took Simone's hands into hers, "Simone you will

make it through this. We will work together and beat this thing."

"I don't want to hurt myself anymore. I don't want anyone to hurt me anymore." Her words were barely audible through her tears. Her pleading sobs filled the room. Dr. Gloria handed her some tissues to wipe her eyes, but the tears continued to flow. She wrapped her arms around Simone, holding and rocking her like a newborn baby. Simone's breathing was raggedy, the way it gets when the crying is too hard and you're trying to make it stop. No words were needed. They rocked together until the tears stopped.

They stayed there like that until time was up. It was an hour-long session (really 50 minutes), and another troubled soul was seated outside of the office awaiting sound advice and self-preservation. Simone had made a breakthrough of sorts that day and Dr. Gloria would need a few extra minutes to document the visit in Simone's file. She released her embrace and stood to her feet.

"I'm so sorry Simone, but our time is up."

Simone nodded her head and stood as well.

"I want you to know that you can call me anytime." She scribbled a number on a business card and handed it to Simone. "It doesn't matter when, day or night. You call me if you feel like you need to talk. You can call my cell phone if there is something you want to say, you can tell me. Off the clock. If you feel the urge to cut, you call me, Simone. I'm here for you. Will you do that?"

Simone nodded again before walking out of the room, taking her notebook with her. She walked past a young man seated in the waiting room. He stood as he saw her pass, and then walked towards the door of the room she'd just left. He was a rather short man. Nothing stood out about him. He looked normal, like nothing could have been wrong with him. There was no telling what secrets he would bestow or what pains he had to confront so that he too could move on with the rest of his life.

She kept her head down out of shame of what went on behind the closed doors of that tiny office. It felt like everyone could look at her and read the story of her life right off of her forehead.

"Excuse me, Simone?"

She heard the receptionist behind the counter but didn't want to stop. Her focus was on the door so she tried to keep going. Her mother was waiting outside for her and she told herself that was the reason she was rushing. It wasn't because she didn't want anyone to look at her or because she was too embarrassed to face anyone.

"Simone! Wait one moment please. We will need your mother to fill out a few forms for you. Just a few that we missed on your fist visit."

Annoyed, she decided to turn around and acknowledge the woman, "What?"

"It will only take a moment for me to print out a few documents for you to take to your mother. You can bring them back on your next visit. It's really just standard stuff. Please have a seat."

The receptionist hurriedly shuffled through piles of paper until she finally found what she was looking for. Simone sat down in one of the chairs in the waiting room. She sent her mother a text to tell her that she would be out in a moment. A moment passed and the documents were ready. She grabbed them from the woman behind the desk, who was apologetic for taking up her time. Simone politely acknowledged her apologies and headed outside to her mom's car.

After her emotional encounter with her Dr. Gloria, Simone had decided that she would tell her mother everything about what her father had done and about his plans to commit suicide. She would tell her everything. She needed to know. Her mother loved her and would do anything for her and she deserved to know. Her father needed help. He needed to be restored back to the father he used to be. It couldn't happen if secrets were kept in the closet.

Yes, she would tell her mother but not right then, not that day. She wasn't ready. *They* weren't ready yet. When the time was right, she would bare all and everything would be okay.

CHAPTER 25

RYAN

RYAN pulled her rental car into the parking lot of the all-too-familiar short, brown building on Thirteen Mile and Orchard Lake Road. A week ago, the mere sight of the building would have exhausted her, but today she was optimistic and excited to walk through the glass double doors of Frontier Counseling Center. Today she was ready to be restored and resurrected. She had begun to wean herself off the Xanax, reducing her dosage to one pill per day. That was the only way to do it without suffering severe withdrawal and anxiety attacks. It was the painless way out.

Her other addiction would be easier to conquer. She quit love cold turkey, leaving it cold and wet at the curb where she had kicked it. There was no telling when she would relapse in the future, but all she had was that moment. She couldn't allow herself to worry about the future. There was no sense in dwelling on the past. For now, she was a woman on a mission of restoration, and her focus was on herself.

That was the pep talk she had given herself before walking into the counseling center. It was all about a better Ryan Stephenson. It was about a Ryan who loved herself and didn't need a man to make her happy or to complete her and make her whole. What she needed was sanity and closure and she intended to get it. It was a new day and the beginning of a new life.

She hadn't heard from Anthony since their brawl three days ago and she didn't have to fight the urge to call him. There was no urge. There was no need to hear his voice to make her feel better and no need to feel his touch to make everything okay. For the first time in a year, she no longer needed the man that never needed her in the first place. Something in her head just clicked. A light switch turned on and illuminated 100 watts of common sense into her brain. The fight she had with him was the trigger that turned her self-preservation switch from "Off" to "On." There was no time to think about his ass. She was too busy living life. With dinner and shopping with Lauren, throwing herself into work, and reading a juicy new novel, there was no time for much else. Life was good.

She bounced her way across the parking lot, singing Sierra Nightly's, "The Drama is Over" softly to herself. Almost as if it was an omen, the song had played on the radio during her drive to the center, moving her to tears and energizing her at the same time. She decided that it would be her theme song from that point on.

The drama is gone
You took it when you left
Now I can move on
And start to love myself
I don't know
Where my road will lead
All I know is it's all about me
Yeaaah!

Ryan belted out that last line with the power and soul of Sierra herself. An older man, passing her in the parking lot, looked her up and down as if she was crazy. She responded with a smile and a nod. He shook his head, probably convinced that she needed to be committed and was seeing a therapist for very good reason.

She skipped a little as she reached the top step to the doorway and flung the door open like she was an A-list celebrity making her grand entrance. She halfway expected applause as she sauntered into the lobby. She was dressed to kill in a sexy new cream sweater by Dolce & Gabanna, mocha-colored Roberto Cavalli leggings, and a killer pair of Manolo Blahnik, four-inch stilettos. The overspending shop-aholic in her was very much alive and kicking. Ryan wasn't too sure if she even wanted to drop *that* bad habit. That was a whole other addiction that she chose not to focus on.

Her shiny black hair swung from side to side as she approached the receptionist's desk to sign in for her appointment. The receptionist directed her to take a seat until she called her name. Never losing the bounce in her step, she walked over to the waiting area to sit down. The waiting room was small. The chairs positioned along the sides of the wall were empty except for a few magazines other clients had left behind. Ryan examined the same room she'd been in on several occasions for the first time. She noticed the warm, spring colors painted on the walls, the heart-warming painting of a mother and her child holding each other in unconditional love, and the soft sounds of smooth jazz wafting through the air. Everything was the same but so incredibly different. It was soothing and comforting and she appreciated it all as if it was arranged for her personally.

She sat directly across from the check-in window. A table topped with *Ebony, Essence,* and Oprah's *O* magazines was positioned beside her. She noticed a copy of *Ebony* with Sierra Nightly on the cover and smiled at the uncanny coincidence. Taking it as another sign, she picked up the issue and began to flip through the pages. When she got to Sierra's interview, she situated herself to get more comfortable in preparation to read eight long pages of inspiration. She was placing her purse on the chair beside her when she noticed a notebook on the seat. She figured someone must have left it by mistake. She picked up the red and silver notebook and started to walk it over to the check-in counter for them to hold until the owner came to claim it.

She didn't make it to the counter. The name she saw etched across the front cover, in black felt marker, made her stop abruptly in her tracks.

"Did you need something, Ms. Stephenson?" The receptionist asked from behind the counter.

Ryan didn't take her eyes off of the name that jumped out at her in bold, black ink, "Umm…no. I'm ok. I think I just answered my own question. Thank you." She did an abrupt about face and headed back to her seat.

The name was not of someone that she knew, but it was one that she certainly recognized. It was the last name. The last name made her sit slowly back down in her seat. It made her turn back the cover of the notebook and read the tattered pages chronicling a young girl's shattered life. Pembroke, the name known to Detroiters as a street on the west side, was the last name that clutched tightly at Ryan's attention and wouldn't let go.

Simone Antoinette Pembroke.

11/19

Dear Journal,

I don't know if this journal stuff is going to work. I'm just doing it because Dr. Gloria told me to. I guess it's supposed to make me feel better or something, but I doubt it. Anyway, here goes my first journal entry ever.

Dr. Gloria says to write about anything that I want to. Anything that comes to mind. Lately all that's on my mind is how alone I feel. I don't have any friends. My only friend, the girl I thought was my only friend, turned out to be my enemy. I don't think she ever liked me, and deep down, I kind of knew that, but I let her be my friend anyway. I guess because I was desperate for somebody to like me. I was lonely. Pretty sad and pathetic, huh? Well I was told that this crap wouldn't work unless I was honest, so that's what I'm doing, being honest. I look at a lot of the other girls in school, walking down the halls with their cliques and laughing and playing around at the lunch table, and I just wonder what that feels like. What does it feel like to be a normal, happy teenager? I have no clue.

Everybody talks about how pretty they think I am. "You think you so pretty don't you? You think you all that?" That's what all those girls in school say. All my mother's friends and the people at Sunday school go all crazy every time they see me, like I'm some kind of freak or something. A freak of nature. That's what my father called me one time. You're so beautiful, it's almost as if it was a freak accident or something. Like that's supposed to make me feel good. I don't want to be pretty. Don't want anybody to love me or hate me because they think I'm pretty. I just want to be normal (whatever that is). I guess that's it for now. Bye!

Simone

11/20

Dear Journal,

Today was a bad day. Well, everyday is a bad day, but today was really bad. None of the girls in school will talk to me. Not even the ones that used to say hi in the halls just to be polite. Kristen told everybody in the 9th grade that I was a ho. Not sure what all she said, but it must have been bad enough to get everybody to turn against me. It's not like I had friends in the first place. I mean I never really wanted to hang around a whole bunch of people, so I didn't have a clique that I belonged to or a bunch of girls hanging around me. Girls usually took one look at me and assumed I was stuck up or thought I was too pretty or something stupid like that. But, this time it was different. It was like they were disgusted with me. Turning their heads to talk about me when I passed by. Right in front of my face! They didn't even care if I heard them calling me all kinds of nasty hos and bitches. Like they were happy they had something on me. It hurts. It hurts a lot, but I can't let them know that. I just keep walking like I don't hear them and they keep on talking. Kristen is the loudest one. And she's the one that's the real ho! Nobody is trying to hear about that though. The *boys talk to me though. All day long asking me all kind of nasty questions about the stuff they heard about me at the party. Telling me what they want to do to me. This one boy, I don't even know his name, asked me if I'd let him stick his dirty little penis in my booty! I almost threw up right there on the floor.*

I felt so bad when I came home. Really down. I couldn't wait to get to my blades. I found a new spot to cut. I started doing it on my inner thigh. It's easier to hide because nobody's gonna be looking there. It felt so good too! I cried when I did it. I always cry when I cut. It's like I'm letting everything out. From the inside out. Makes me feel alive after being dead on the inside for so long. I know that sounds crazy, but that's really how it feels. I want to do it everyday. I want to feel that feeling every single day and that scares me a little bit. I'm pretty sure I'll do it tomorrow and the next day too.

Anyway, I can't wait until I'm out of high school. Maybe I can talk to my mom and get her to transfer me out of Stonecreeke and back to the Christian academy. Yeah, right. That won't happen. Stonecreek is a status symbol and I know she won't give that up. A girl can dream though. I'm getting sleepy. Guess I'm done for now.

Simone.

11/27

Dear Journal

I cut below my belly button this morning in the shower. Eight little cuts, but it still didn't seem like enough. So, I did it on my arm too. Right above my wrist. It helped a little bit. I cried really long and hard. Must've stayed in the shower for about an hour, but nobody noticed. My mom has me on constant surveillance since she found out. Always popping up on me and checking to see if I'm ok. Making sure that I'm not cutting. So, I have to be more careful now. Most of the time I make sure nobody's home before I do it. But this morning, I couldn't wait. I woke up early. My father had already left for work, but my mom was still home, sleeping. So, I did what I had to do.

I don't understand why this is happening to me. Why God made me this way. Why He put me into this life. I think about how things used to be a lot. How everybody was so happy. At least I thought we were. I was. We used to sit at the dinner table every night and talk about our day. Used to watch TV together and go on family trips. We still do those things now, but it's different. It's so uncomfortable, like if I make the wrong move or say the wrong thing, my mom will be able to see right through the act. It feels like I'm wearing a big sign on my forehead that says "Crazy girl on the loose. Watch out!" I know I may sound a little dramatic, but it's the truth. I just want things to be back to the way they used to be when we were normal.

Sometimes I imagine that I have a time machine that can

take me back to last year or even further back than that. Maybe take me back to when I was a little girl. That would be nice. All I remember is playing with my daddy. We played all the time. He'd help me with my school work, teach me how to read and write, help me pick out my clothes in the morning and even tried to do my hair. My hair was always horrible when he'd get done with it and my mom would start fussing and have to redo it. That still makes me smile now.

Then everything changed. It's funny because there were no warning signs. No red flags waving in my face that gave me a clue as to what was about to happen. Where did it come from? When did my daddy decide that he was going to rape me? When did he decide that I was no longer his little girl? What was going through his head? What made him come back night after night, again and again, to have sex with me -- his daughter? What did I do to make this happen? What signs were there? How could I have avoided it? What could I have done? I ask myself these same questions everyday, but I'm never able to answer. I'm not sure there are any real answers. I feel like I am trapped.

Simone

11/21

Dear Journal,

May 5th. That's a date that I'll never forget. That's the date of the first night my daddy came into my room and raped me. It's crazy, because when I think of somebody being raped, I think of the girl kicking and screaming. The guy is hitting and slapping her. Sometimes he's holding a gun up to her or a knife. He's telling her all kinds of dirty mean things and threatens to kill her if she tells. My idea of rape was always so violent, but that's not how it was with us. It was nothing like that. It was slow and soft. He treated me like I was his lover. Like we were making love. He kissed me and touched me like I was his wife. Like I was my mom or something. He tells me he loves me the whole time and tells me how beautiful I am. I just lay there until it's over.

Sometimes I cry, but not every time. Sometimes I'm like a zombie, never moving or making a sound. It never seems to make a difference to him. I guess in his mind, I liked it because I wasn't fighting back. The truth is, I didn't know what to do. Didn't know what to think. I know that he loves me. I've never doubted that, so I know he didn't do it to hurt me. He tells me he does it because he can't help himself because of the way he loves me and he wishes that some day I could feel the same way. It confuses me. I don't hate him. I know that I probably should, but I don't. I feel bad for him. I want to help him. Every time I see somebody on TV that's been raped, they're always so angry. They're screaming and going crazy and they hate the guy who did it. They want him dead. So, I don't understand why I don't feel that way. It hurts so bad and I know he's the reason why I hurt myself. I know what he's doing is wrong and I'll probably be messed up for the rest of my life because of it, but I'm not angry with him. I'm mad at myself. I'm not sure if that even makes sense, but I am. I'm just as bad as he is.

Just as guilty because I don't hate him for it. I don't want anything bad to happen to him. I love my Daddy. He says that he can't help it and I believe him. So, if I didn't kick and scream and he didn't hit or slap me and if I don't hate him, does that still mean he raped me? I ask myself that question sometimes too. I never can find any answers.

Simone

"Ryan? Ryan Stephenson?"

The receptionist broke Ryan's concentration a little, but she didn't lose complete focus. The journal was the most riveting thing she'd ever read. There were only a few more pages to go, and she had to get to the end. She had to put the pieces together and solve the puzzle. She wouldn't put it down until her curiosity and suspicions were satisfied.

She answered the receptionist without looking up, "Yes?"

"I apologize, but Gloria is running a little behind with her last appointment. It will be about ten more minutes before she is ready to see you."

"Huh?"

"Ten more minutes."

"Oh….um hmm." She went back to her reading.

11/23/07

Dear Journal,

I'm so scared right now. I don't know what to do. My dad hasn't touched me since that time when I went crazy on him. I'm pretty sure he knows why I did. He knows that I liked it and I think that scared him a little bit too. I should be happy that he hasn't been in my room, but I'm not. I'm scared of what's about to happen. I don't know what he's going to do. Last night, he came into my room and started talking like he was going to kill himself. Sounding like he was going to do it that night, but he didn't. I was so relieved to see him the next morning I almost ran to him and gave him a hug. I couldn't do that though. It would be too awkward. He asked me if I'd ever thought about dying. I didn't say anything, but he knew the answer. Sometimes I think I deserve to die. When he came into my room last night, I was actually a little excited. Just a little bit. As sick as that sounds, as horrible as that is, I think I was excited. It's hard to explain and something that I couldn't control, but I almost wanted him to have sex with me. Almost. That makes me a monster just like he is. Makes me just as bad.

That's why I feel like I deserve to die sometimes. I feel so ashamed of myself and the things that I think about sometimes. I don't even know if I'm going to heaven or hell anymore. I used to think that I was a good person that bad things happened to, but I'm starting to think that bad things happen to me because I am a bad person. I mean, it only makes sense. Bad things happen to bad people, right? Everything happens for a reason. Maybe this is my punishment.

I wonder what would happen if my mother ever found out. What she would do and what she would say. She can't stand the idea of anyone hurting me. Makes her go crazy. She's so protective. I'm her perfect precious little girl and it's her job to protect me. That's what she always says. I wonder what she would say if she knew that I wasn't sure how I felt about Daddy having sex with me. There's no telling what she would say. I will never tell her that part. I could never tell anybody. No one would understand that. I don't even understand it.

I go see my therapist tomorrow and I know all she's going to do is ask me a whole bunch of questions that I don't want to answer. Questions about why I cut myself and how I feel inside. I want to just grab her and yell at her. Tell her that none of this matters. It doesn't matter how many times we talk or how many times I write in this stupid journal, nothing is going to change. I can't be saved. What's done is done and there is nothing anybody can do about it.

Simone

Ryan's heart beat faster as she turned to the last pages of the journal. There were no more heartbreaking words of a young, abused girl crying out for help and begging for some type of relief from the torturous life she was living. She let out the breath she didn't know she was holding in and tried to brace herself for what was next.

A collage of photos covered the last two pages. There were pictures of a beautiful baby, about three months old, with a head full of thick, curly, black hair, blazing green eyes, and hazelnut skin. Her chubby arms and legs were wrapped around a white woman, Ryan assumed was her mother. The date stamp in the lower left corner read 07/18/92. There were several more pictures of the same happy, smiling baby. Then there were more showing her age progression to a young toddler. Each one was labeled with a handwritten caption as a description. *Simone, 2 years old having fun at the beach. Simone, 5 years old, first day of kindergarten. Simone 8 years old, just hanging around the house.* In each picture, she was stunning. The still images glowed with radiance and popped out with life. When Ryan got to the more recent pictures, school portraits from eighth and ninth grade, she began to rack her brain as the beautiful girl's face sparked some recognition. She couldn't put her finger on it, but she knew that she'd seen her somewhere before. She had the type of face that embedded into her brain and didn't let go. It was unforgettable. But Ryan couldn't place it at the moment.

She moved on and inspected the other images. There were more photos of Simone posing with neighbors and friends. With smiles glowing and eyes filled with love and happiness, they could have been the models of a Norman Rockwell painting. She'd almost forgotten the heinous confessions she'd just read as evidence of her lack of authenticity.

The left page was reserved for pictures of Simone and her mother. They were labeled, *Simone and Jessica Pembroke, mother and daughter.* Her eyes rested on the one in the middle. It was the largest one, serving as a centerpiece to the mini Pembroke family shrine. She glanced over the girl and her long, black hair hanging well below her shoulders, almost to her waist. She sat on a wooden bench with her legs crossed and her arms in her lap. Her big, round, green eyes leaped off of the page and forced Ryan to linger on her image a little longer than she intended to. She was breathtaking.

Standing behind her and to the left was her mother, an

average looking white woman. She was a little on the short side with bushy brown hair and artificially tanned skin. Although she didn't come close in comparison to the girl's beauty, Ryan recognized the resemblance between mother and daughter. Then, she thought she recognized a little more than that. She brought the notebook closer to her face, squinting her eyes to bring the woman's small features into focus. She mentally replaced her wild, brown hair with bleached blonde strands, her thin, pink lips with large, collagen-filled puckers and her fake, Brady Bunch smile with an evil, hate-filled glare.

That's her, the woman from the mall! That's the one who damn near knocked me to the ground. She's Simone's mother! That crazy bitch is her mother.

No wonder the poor girl was so messed up in the head. Her mother had an obvious self-image problem and anyone who was stupid enough to step to Ryan had to be crazy too. But there was still no explanation for what she had done. She had never met her before that day. Ryan had never seen her face. She looked back at her daughter's familiarity, thinking that it may have something to do with her, but her search for a confirmation came up empty. She didn't know the woman.

She mumbled to herself, "Bitch."

Frowning, she turned her attention to the right page, the one reserved for images of Simone and her father. She immediately recognized the handsome forty-something man. Her breathing stopped abruptly and her heart jumped up to her throat. His closely cropped hair and neatly trimmed goatee gave her chills. His peanut butter complexion and charming smile sent shock waves through her body. His solid, athletic build draped in expensive, tailored clothes, brought tears to her eyes. With her hands shaking and nausea attacking her

TER 26

AN

auren and told her everything
nd what she was about to do,
he pick her up so she could go
auren's support. She wasn't sure
o hold it together without her.
he was doing the right thing. It
her faithful friend there to push
any things to accomplish: stop
ughter another day, avenge his
rried, let Jessica know she was
most importantly, to let Jessica
her own home right under her
a massive one. She pulled out of
rtment complex and got on the
e. The two women rode silently
and sorrow.

he silence, "I can't believe you're
e this whole thing. Who would
ny was married?"

Lauren. He's been raping his
hs."

stomach, she stared into the eyes of *her* Anthony Pembroke. That was the name she'd known--Pembroke, like the street on the Westside. That name had stopped her in her tracks and forced her to open the journal to read the repulsive account of a troubled girl's life.

There he was smiling like they were the perfect family, as if the perversion of their lives was non-existent. He sat in a chair behind the kitchen table. Simone stood behind him with her arms wrapped around his neck, cheesing from ear to ear. They were good actors.

Anthony was the father of a fourteen-year-old girl who he was raping, and the husband of a white woman. He was the pedophilic monster who had destroyed that beautiful girl's life. The caption below the picture read *Simone Pembroke and Anthony R. Pembroke, me and my Dad.* The "R" stood for Ross. Anthony Ross Pembroke, junior partner of Creswell & Lattimore Law Firm, the Renaissance man, one of Detroit's most eligible bachelor's, wasn't a bachelor at all. The smiley face placed after the caption indicated that the picture was taken during happier times, before Simone's self-mutilation and before the disgusting freak began raping his daughter.

With her mouth and eyes agape, Ryan could feel her lunch rising from her stomach and into her throat. She choked and gagged to force the regurgitation back down. The bitter taste coated her tongue and snapped her out of her trance. She looked back at the picture of his wife, Jessica, and their past encounter suddenly made sense. Jessica knew about her. She knew that Ryan had a relationship with her husband and she was out for revenge. The "accidental" bump in the mall, the grim look on her face, her sarcastic words: they were all because Ryan was sleeping with her husband. Ryan clearly remembered that day. The look on that woman's face was full of malice. It was *murder*.

Oh my God! Jessica tried to kill me! She was the driver of the Range Rover! It wasn't a prank at all. That bitch had tried to force me off the road.

Ryan's face was flushed and sweat beaded on her forehead. Everything that was so unclear before came into light. The cancelled dates, the lies, the sudden changes in his behavior were all because Anthony was married. Or maybe it wasn't that at all.

Maybe it was because he had fallen in love with his daughter and had to make a choice between the two of us.

Ryan had obviously lost.

The vomit she had managed to force down her throat moments ago slowly crept back up on her again. She jumped out of her seat, carrying the notebook with her, and rushed out of the door. She ignored the repeated calls from the receptionist as she ran into the parking lot. Before she reached her car, her body gave in to her twisting stomach and she threw up on the ground. Gripping the roof of her car for balance, she kept herself from falling over as she heaved and gagged until her insides were empty.

Something needed to be done about the horror show that had taken over all of their lives but she just wasn't sure what action to take. She thought about calling Anthony to confront his scandalous ass, but what good would that do? He'd just deny it, despite the evidence staring her in the face. There was no guarantee that he'd talk to her at all. Plus, she didn't want to put Simone in more danger than she was already in.

No, she needed to tell someone else. An authority needed to step in and save this girl from her father. She'd call the

CHₐ

R

WHEN Ryan called
she had found out
her best friend insisted that
with her. Ryan appreciated
if she was going to be able
She wasn't even certain that
was a big risk and she neede
her forward. There were so
Anthony from hurting his
ass for lying about being n
done with her husband, an
know what was going on i
nose. The task before her wa
the parking lot of Lauren's a
freeway towards the Intersta
with minds heavy with wor

Lauren eventually broke
going to do this. I can't beli
have ever thought that Anth

"Forget being married,
daughter for the last six mo

"Well yeah, that too. I didn't really want to bring that part up." She flipped through the pages of the notebook and stopped on Simone's 8th grade portrait, "Wow, she really *is* beautiful. I thought so that night we saw her before, but this picture is just--she is gorgeous. Just think, her whole life is destroyed because of that asshole. The poor girl is in so much pain."

Ryan thought she heard Lauren's voice crack with the threat of tears. She ignored it. There was no time for sentiment, "Hurry and wrap it up before we get there."

Lauren followed orders, covering the journal in red Christmas wrapping paper speckled with small white snowmen.

"You couldn't find anything better than that? Something a little less corny and conspicuous?"

"What in the hell do you expect? You asked me to get something to wrap it in, so I brought wrapping paper. Who cares anyway, it's what's inside that's important." She sealed the package shut with scotch tape on all four sides. "There! Merry Christmas."

Ryan's stomach turned with anxiety. For a moment she thought she might throw up again, but she managed to remain steady. What she was about to do would take three lives -- four counting her own -- and turn them upside down. This was a perfect time to pop a Xanax, but she thought better of it. Lauren pulled a black marker out of her purse and labeled the package. As Ryan drove up to the exit, she suddenly forgot her way.

"Oh shit, Lauren, is it left or right?"

"I think it was left. No, wait a minute, right."

"Are you sure? We are not in the area to be driving around

all aimlessly looking suspicious. I know the police are over here like crazy."

"Yeah, I'm positive. Turn right."

Ryan followed Lauren's direction and turned right onto Rochester Road. Things were starting to look familiar as she drove from her memory of the night they both took Simone home from The Blue Martini. She cringed a little as she thought back on that night.

• • •

The way the poor girl looked, sitting helplessly on the sidewalk, shivering cold with her dress and stockings soiled and ripped, was heartbreaking. Her hair and makeup was ruined. Her small body looked crumpled on the cold concrete of the sidewalk. Ryan almost tripped over the girl as she stumbled out of the nightclub. The disheveled young girl put her hand up to shield her head from Ryan's leg. She scooted out of the way just in time to miss the pointed, front tip of Ryan's red, designer pump.

"You better watch out, girl. Yo' drunk ass almost fell on yo' face." Lauren chuckled at the thought of Ryan's close call.

"What in the hell was that?" Ryan looked back as she and Lauren staggered their way to the car.

"Girl, you're just drunk, trippin over yo own feet! Come on."

"No, I think I tripped *over a girl. Look!*"

"*Yeah a* homeless girl. Come on! I'm cold. This dress is riding up my ass."

"How many homeless people do you see sitting around in downtown Birmingham, Lauren? I think it's a young girl."

"Who in the hell cares? She's probably drunk just like we are. I'm cold and I'm starting to get a headache. Those Appletini's where no joke."

Lauren's complaints were ignored because Ryan had already started walking toward the neglected girl.

"Ryan, what are you doing?" Lauren hurried behind her friend.

Ryan stood in front of the girl, and then bent down to meet her face to face. When the stranger saw the two women coming towards her, she ducked her head inside of her coat. Her long, wild hair was all that was showing, spilling from the opening in her coat like ragged streamers. Ryan touched her shoulder lightly, and the girl flinched.

"Please leave me alone."

Ryan didn't move.

"Ryan, you heard her. Let's go."

Ryan ignored Lauren and spoke to the girl in a low, soft voice, "Sweetie, are you okay?" She touched her shoulder again. Again, the stranger flinched. "We're not going to hurt you. Do you need some help?"

The girl looked up at the friendly face offering assistance. Her eyes told Ryan that she was scared and confused.

Ryan sensed that she was warming up to her, so she grabbed her left arm in an attempt to help her to her feet.

"Lauren, come over here and help me get her up."

"Are you crazy? I'm not touching her! You're the one out here acting like Mother Teresa, not me!"

"Lauren you are killing me!"

"No, that junkie on the ground is who is going to be killing you."

"She is not a junkie! Look, she has on a damn evening

gown. She can't be any older than fourteen or fifteen years old. What if she was raped or something?"

Lauren stood in place with her arms folded across her chest, unconvinced. Ryan rolled her eyes and continued to help the girl up by herself. She didn't seem to be fully conscious, and Ryan could smell the liquor and vomit on her. She turned her head a bit to keep the odor from getting in direct contact with her nose. She leaned the girl against the wall of the building for support as she was about to topple over herself.

"Hey, can you hear me? What's your name?"

The girl was frantic, but still only seemed semi-conscious. She opened her eyes, and they darted about in what seemed to be delirium.

"No! No! Leave me alone. Please! No, please don't hurt me. Please!" Tears and dried mascara streaked her face as she pleaded.

Ryan grabbed both of her shoulders and leaned in closely so she could look directly into her eyes. She momentarily lost her words at the sight of the girls striking face. It caused her to fluster a little in an attempt to conjure up some meaningful words. When she spoke, it was softly with trust and reassurance in her voice. "Sweetie, we are not going to hurt you. Whoever did this to you is gone. All we want to do is help you, okay? Will you let me help you?"

The girl responded with more tears.

"Lauren, do you have any tissue or anything in your purse?"

Lauren made an ugly face, then dug through her purse until she retrieved a wad of tissue and handed it to Ryan.

Annoyed, Ryan snatched the tissue from her friend, and

then turned her attention back to the girl. "What's your name, baby?"

The girl calmed down a bit and took the tissue from Ryan with a trembling hand. As she began to wipe her face, she managed to answer through her crying, "Simone."

"Simone, I'm Ryan and this is my friend Lauren. We're going to help you, okay?"

Simone looked back and forth between the friendly faces staring at her. Ryan saw her relax a little and sensed that she was willing to let them help.

Lauren stepped in closer to get a better look at the stranger. She whispered, "Wow." Simone lowered her head in embarrassment.

Ryan turned to Lauren, "Call the police."

Lauren pulled her cell phone out of her small handbag and flipped it open, but Simone's panicked words froze her in place.

"No!" Simone violently tried to break free from Ryan's hands and snatch the phone from Lauren. The two women took a few steps back in caution.

"Please! Don't call the police!"

Ryan twisted her face in confusion, "Simone, whoever did this to you needs to be arrested. The police are only going to help you."

Simone began to cry frantically once again. She repeated, "Don't call the police. Please! Can you just take me home? Please, no one hurt me. No one did anything to me. I Just.....I just had too many drinks, that's all. And…and my ride, they left me. I just want to go home. Please can you take me home? I'm begging you."

"You're not hurt at all? You don't need to go to the hospital?" Lauren asked.

"No! No hospital. No police. Please, if you want to help me, please just take me home. Will you do that for me?"

Ryan and Lauren looked at each other in bewilderment. Lauren shrugged her shoulders, and Ryan took that as her cue to comply with the girl's request. They carefully helped her to the car and drove her home. It was 2 o'clock in the morning.

· · ·

Now, it was 4 o'clock in the afternoon, and everything looked completely different in the daylight. They drove down the winding, maze-like streets of the upper class Rochester Hills neighborhood looking for Cherry Grove Lane. The views of the massive houses and beautifully manicured lawns were impressive.

Lauren fidgeted in her seat, shifting the Christmas-wrapped journal in her lap. "Ryan, are you sure you want to do this?"

Ryan was irritated by Lauren's uncertainty. She needed to feel secure in her decision, and Lauren was adding doubt into the mix. "What do you mean am I sure?"

"Think about it, Ryan. You said this woman tried to kill you right? Do you really want to stroll up to her door and hand her a notebook wrapped in Christmas paper? I mean, what in the hell are you going to say? What if her crazy ass attacks you or something?"

"Look, I don't know for sure that she was the one on the road that night. I can only speculate at this point. And even if it was her, she still deserves to know what the hell that disgusting bastard is doing to her daughter. You read it your-self, her mom loves her. Shit, I'd want to know so I could kill the mutha fucka."

"Yeah, I just don't want *her* to kill *you*."

"I know. I am taking a big risk. What if I just leave it in the mailbox?"

"If you leave it in the mailbox, Anthony--or 'Ross'--could get it. Then all of this would be for nothing."

"Anthony isn't at home. It's too early; he's still at the firm. I know his schedule like the back of my hand. That worka-holic asshole doesn't step foot outside of that firm any earlier than 7 p.m. Even on a Saturday."

"Yeah, you're probably right. I'll be willing to bet 'the little woman' has never had a job in her whole over-privileged life, so more than likely she'll be there to get the mail."

"Right."

"Okay, that makes me feel a little better."

"Then that's what we'll do. That way, she still finds out, but she doesn't have to know that she found out from me."

"Look, there's the house." Lauren pointed to the brown and blonde, brick home on the corner to the right.

Ryan stopped her car at the end of the circular driveway in front of the house. Her heart stopped as she looked up at the huge mansionette that stared back at them. This was Anthony's home that she never knew anything about. This was the home that housed countless secrets, deception and lies. It was Simone's prison -- the house of pain. It was beau-tiful, standing tall and proud. But from the things Ryan knew that went on behind those doors, it might as well have been the torture chamber in Dracula's Transylvania castle, complete with dark clouds, lightning bolts, smoke and bats.

The love she had for Anthony was completely dissolved, replaced by abhorrence, anger, and pity. She didn't know him. She had no clue who he was. She never knew. The man who she thought she knew and loved was only a character created by a skilled actor. She didn't miss him and knew that she never would. She couldn't miss what she never had.

Once again, she second-guessed her decision. Lauren placed her hand on top of Ryan's as it rested on the gearshift. She squeezed it a little as they looked at each other. "This is it," she said, "Let's go."

CHAPTER 27

JESSICA

JESSICA cut the radio off almost as soon as she had turned it on. For some reason, the sound of Lorraine Dubois' voice annoyed her and she was certain it would bring on a headache.

She rode in silence with the 9mm resting in her lap, feeling the cold of the steel through her pants. She gripped the handle and held onto it to calm her shaking hands, only letting it go for a moment to wipe the sweat dripping from her forehead. The skin of her lower lip broke under the pressure of her teeth and started to bleed, but she didn't notice as she drove through the winding roads away from her home.

She was on her way to the home of her husband's mistress to end her life. She hadn't done much planning. Her actions were fueled purely from the emotions of a woman scorned, and a wife's and mother's instinct to protect her family.

If we are going to survive as a family, that bitch has to die.

That's what she told herself as she dressed that morning. She reassured herself again as she picked Simone up from therapy. And as she walked out of the house, gun in hand, towards her car, she told herself that same thing once again.

She vowed to do whatever it took to protect what was hers

-- her husband, her daughter and her life. But now, she was starting to feel differently. As she sat in her car, stopped at a traffic light, she realized that she was no longer so convinced.

I could never leave my baby.

Simone's beautiful face flashed before her eyes. A single tear escaped as she realized that she was jeopardizing her beloved child's well being by risking her freedom for revenge.

Her baby needed her now more than ever. She was cutting herself and the root of her pain was still unknown to Jessica. What would it do to her if her mother went to jail for the rest of her life because of a jealous rage. It would destroy her and Simone would have no one to blame but her mother. Jessica couldn't accept that. She couldn't leave her baby. It was almost funny how none of that crossed her mind as she bought the gun or when she first decided that she would kill Ryan. The thought of getting caught and going to prison never even occurred to her. But now, as she was actually on the way to carry out her plan, the only thing on her mind was the safety of her child. She'd vowed long before Simone's conception was even a thought, that she would never neglect her child as Wanda had to done her. She would never expose her child to the same pain and isolation she'd experienced. She had a lot to prove to herself. She would be the perfect mother and raise the perfect child. Anything else would mean failure.

Jessica made up her mind.

I'm gonna let that bitch live. This isn't her fault. It's not her doing alone.

Ross was the responsible party in this. He was the one who held an obligation to her and their family, not Ryan. And Ryan wasn't worth all the pain and destruction it would cause her family if Jessica was convicted of her murder. She would talk to Ross, wife to husband, and all three of them could get counseling. It could work. Families have suffered through infidelities before and survived. They could do it too.

She opened the glove compartment and placed the gun inside. She then, turned the car around and headed towards home. But when she arrived she was astounded by what she saw. It was almost like her worst nightmare. Jessica had to close her eyes and reopen them slowly to make sure that her mind wasn't playing tricks on her. With her mouth agape in disbelief she watched as Ryan sashayed her fat ass up her driveway, holding what looked to be a Christmas present in her hand.

The nerve that bitch has to set foot on my property. To disrespect me and my family by even daring to come to my home!

Every shred of common sense Jessica had used to convince herself not to blow that whore's head off her shoulders flew out of the window as she yanked the glove compartment open and snatched the gun out. Gone was the calm, sensible and high minded Jessica Pembroke. Jessie Wolinsky jumped out of the car.

"What the hell do you think you're doing, bitch?" she yelled across the lawn to the other side of the driveway where Ryan was now standing.

Ryan looked nervously at the gun swinging in Jessica's right hand by her side, "Jessica….I umm."

"Jessica? Oh, you think you know me, huh? It's 'Mrs. Pembroke' to you, bitch." Jessica moved closer to her, taking slow steps until she was within two yards. Ryan remained frozen, obviously terrified of the petite, armed woman before her.

Jessica sensed her fear and used it to fuel her anger. "You

must be outta yo mutha fuckin mind coming over here to my house like you belong here, after you've been fucking my husband! You just begging for me to stick my foot up yo fat ass! Don't you know people get shot for stealing and trespassing?" She raised the gun and aimed it square and steady at Ryan's heart.

Ryan was shaking now. She dropped the package on the ground and raised her hands in surrender, "Please Jess...I mean Mrs. Pembroke. I didn't come here for any trouble. I'm not seeing Anthony anymore. I didn't know he was married."

"Shut the fuck up!"

Both women jumped at the sound of the car door slamming as Lauren slowly and carefully got out of the car to stand by Ryan's side. She spoke calmly, "Please put the gun down before someone gets hurt. You don't want to a make a mistake that you'll regret for the rest of your life."

Jessica went back and forth pointing the gun at both Ryan and Lauren. She tightened her grip on the handle. "I said shut the fuck up! You think this is a game? You think I'm playing with you? Bitch I will fuck you up."

Neither woman responded. Their eyes widened as tears suddenly formed and began to roll down Jessica's cheeks.

"I've worked hard all my damn life. I worked my ass off to get here. I did everything I could to have the perfect life and the perfect family and you think you're going to take that from me? You think I'm going back to that fucking trailer park? To the titty bar? Huh? I'm not going back! I did everything he wanted me to do. Everything he told me to do. I was the perfect wife. The perfect mother. Do you hear me? You think you can just walk into our lives and take everything I've worked so hard for? Well guess again. I'll kill you first. I'll kill both of you before I'll ever let you take what's mine."

Ryan spoke slowly, "Please, I swear, I don't want to bother your family. Your husband and I are over. I promise. Maybe I shouldn't have come here. Maybe it was a bad idea, but there is something that you need to know. There is something important that I came to tell you. That's the only reason that I'm here."

"You ain't got nothin to say that I want to hear."

"Then just take this package. Please. There is something inside that you need to see." Ryan kicked the package towards her. Jessica only took her eyes off her targets for a moment to glance at the package through the corners of her eyes. Immediately, she regained focus on the two women in front of her.

"What is it?"

"It's about your daughter. It's about Simone."

The mention of Simone's name disarmed Jessica enough to cause her to lower her aim by a few inches, but the gun remained pointed at Ryan and Lauren and they stayed in place. "What are you talking about? You don't know anything about my daughter. You can't tell me shit about Simone."

Lauren said, "Your daughter is in trouble, Jessica. This is more important than who's sleeping with your husband. We know that you love her. We know that you wouldn't want anything to happen to her. She needs you. We know that she's been cutting herself. You know that too. It's all in here. Everything you need to know. Now please, put the gun down."

Jessica's voice softened, Lauren's words were sinking in. "Then, what are you going to do?"

Ryan reassured her, "We're not going to call the police. Right, Lauren?" Lauren nodded in agreement.

Jessica stooped to retrieve the package. It was labeled in black felt marker: "To: JESSICA PEMBROKE. URGENT OPEN IMMEDIATELY." She looked back up at her captives, "Don't move."

They followed orders, remaining still. She uncovered the notebook with her daughter's name written on the cover. She recognized it as the journal Simone had taken to therapy with her earlier that day. "Where did you get this?"

Ryan seemed to relax a little as Jessica calmed down. She lowered her hands and Lauren did the same. "She left it at Frontier Counseling. I go to the same place for therapy. I opened it because I recognized her last name. You really need to read what's inside."

Jessica stared hard into her eyes, evaluating the honesty of her words. Whatever it was inside the notebook was important enough for Ryan to risk her life. Whatever it was, involved the safety of Simone. She decided to trust her enemy for the sake of her child.

She turned on her heel and didn't say another word as she walked into her house with the gun in her right hand and the notebook in her left. She left Ryan and Lauren standing in the middle of the driveway, speechless and confused. It wasn't until she was inside her home with the door closed did she hear the car start up outside as they drove away.

Jessica went into the kitchen and sat down at the table in the breakfast nook. She placed the gun on the table beside her. It was a Saturday, so Delores was out doing the grocery shopping. Simone went with her to help. Ross had decided to work from home so he was in the office researching a case.

When she was satisfied that she was alone and would not be interrupted, she opened the notebook and began to read its contents. She turned the pages slowly, reviewing each line with the scrupulous eye of a forensic examiner. She didn't want to miss a word, not a punctuation mark or a symbol. Her face remained expressionless and her breathing was steady as she flipped through the journal, allowing each word of her daughter's pain to burn into her brain.

When she completed her reading she closed the journal slowly and picked up the 9mm. She left the kitchen and made her way towards the spiral staircase – a showcase feature of their showcase home. Her face held no expression. Ross' words echoed through her head.

"You don't know how to act."

"You don't know your place, how to play your role."

"Your actions today were inappropriate and you've proved that you are nothing more than trash."

He scolded and reprimanded her for her outrageous actions, yet *he* was the one who didn't know how to play his role. *He* was the one who didn't know how to act. It is inappropriate – beyond all comprehension -- to rape his 14-year-old daughter. It was inexcusable to abuse their child. *Ross* didn't know how to act. *Ross* didn't know *his* place. *Ross* didn't know how to play *his* role. *His* actions were abominable and he proved that *he* was nothing more than trash.

It's not me, it's him.

Her autopilot lead her to the door of his home office. She paused for just a few seconds before turning the knob to open the door. When she did, she found Ross inside, sitting on the edge of the desk. His head was in his heads, but he looked up to meet Jessica in the eye when he heard her enter. She saw that he had been crying. A salty trail of dried tears streaked his face. He eyed the gun in her hand, and then looked back up to her face. Jessica didn't move. Her eyes were dead. Her face was stony.

Ross slowly stood to his feet. She read in his eyes that he knew why she was there. He knew what she was there to do and he was ready. Their eyes locked as she lifted the gun and aimed it at his upper torso.

She thought she saw him nod as she pulled the trigger, but she wasn't sure. Everything seemed to happen in slow motion, from the bullet flying through the air to the smoke rising from the barrel of the gun. Within seconds, his body jerked into the air as the hollow point bullet struck his chest. He landed face-up on the desk, spread eagle. Bright, red blood splattered on the desk, the drapes, the walls, and the floor. She could hear him choking and gurgling blood as she stood on the opposite side of the room.

She paused for a moment to let him fully realize his pain. She wanted to ensure that he suffered for a few minutes before he met his ultimate fate. She then walked around the desk to get within a closer range to him. Standing on his left side, she reached over and pushed the open end of the barrel into his forehead. He closed his eyes in preparation as she pulled the trigger once more. His gurgling stopped, as did the strained rise and fall of his chest. He was dead. She remained silent as she walked out of the bedroom and back down the steps.

Calmly, she returned to the kitchen. She pulled the cordless phone off the wall and sat at the breakfast nook table. Her purse was sitting on the chair beside her. She reached in and pulled out a dime-sized bag of weed and some ZigZags. After a few hits, her buzz began to kick in from the drug coursing through her bloodstream. Her eyelids were getting lower and her body was more relaxed. She slouched and finished half the joint before making her next move. She picked up the phone and called 911.

"911 emergency."

"Please send someone to 27565 Cherry Grove Lane."

"What is your emergency?"

"My husband was fucking my daughter so I killed his black ass." She took a long slow drag of her joint, "Oh yeah, I'm smokin' weed too."

CHAPTER 28

SIMONE

DELORES parked the car on the street in front of the house. She couldn't fit it in the driveway, as it was crowded with police cars, an ambulance, and other vehicles. Simone had a sick feeling in the pit of her stomach, as she stared at the flashing lights and the crowd of people standing around the house.

"Oh my God, what is going on?"

Simone's body trembled as she evaluated the scene. She could feel it in her blood. It was her father. Something happened to her father.

He's done it. He finally killed himself.

"It's Daddy!" She shrieked as she jumped out of the car. Delores tried to hold her back, but her attempt was in vane, as Simone broke loose and raced wildly towards the front door of her home. Before she could make it across the lawn, two police officers halted her. They held her down as she fought and clawed in a desperate attempt to break free, but it was to no avail, they had her pinned. She didn't have the strength to fight them off.

"Let me go! Let me go! Where is he? What happened? Is

he dead?" Her screams were muffled by the officer's chest as he held her close.

There were people everywhere. Police officials were crawling all over the property, in and out of the house. Yellow tape surrounded the perimeter. The reflection of red and blue lights bounced off of the glass of the large picture window in the front of the house. Detectives in suits and forensic examiners, wearing rubber gloves, scoped the premises. It was like a scene right out of a movie. It didn't feel or look real, but the bright lights didn't fade to a commercial, and the people wouldn't go away. Her breathing was unsteady and her heart was beating out of control.

"Oh my God! Oh my God! Where is my mom? Mommy!" She screamed and cried, struggling to break the cop's hold on her tiny wrists. But there were no answers to her pleas. She looked up as the front door of the house opened and two men walked out, ushering a gurney. On top was a black body bag, the silhouette of her father's corpse lay inside.

A myriad of emotions flooded her mind. She didn't know which one of them she should allow to control her thinking and take over her actions. There was too much going on inside of her, too many feelings to feel. There was fear of what was to come of her life now that her father was gone and the fear of what happened and why. She was afraid that her ugly truth would be exposed and that everyone would know her secret--his secret.

But there was relief that he was gone and no longer able to hurt her. She no longer had to sit up late at night, praying to God that he didn't come into her room, then condemning the Lord when he did. She no longer had to face her shameful sexual desires and hate herself for becoming the monster that he was.

Simone felt pain for all that she had been through, and she also hurt for her father knowing he'd felt that pain too. She was angry that God allowed this to happen to her and her family, but grateful that He finally answered her prayers. Simone was lost inside the whirlwind of her conflicting emotions. Not knowing how to react or what to say, she allowed her body to go limp and her tears to fall silently to the ground.

She watched as the two men rolled the gurney into the back of an ambulance. She dropped to her knees like a rag doll; still the policemen wouldn't release her. The front door of the house opened again. This time her mother was being escorted out by two police officers. Her hands were handcuffed behind her back and she held her head high, almost proudly. The policeman on the right of her held a clear plastic Ziplock bag containing Simone's journal. She yelled across the lawn to her mother, "Mommy, what happened? Are you all right? Please tell me what's going on!"

Her mother turned slowly towards her. Her face brightened at the sight of her beautiful, only child. It looked as if she was about to smile, but she didn't. "It's okay, baby. He's gone. He can't hurt you anymore."

"What did you do? What did you do to Daddy? He needed help. He just needed help." Simone's sobs were becoming uncontrollable and her words were barely audible.

Her mother spoke in a soothing tone, like the way a mother talks to her child when she's sick or just had her heart broken for the first time. "There was no helping him, baby. This was the only way. This was it. He wanted it this way."

Simone let her mother's words sink in. She knew they

made sense. She knew her mother did the only thing that could have been done. She was right, there was no other way. She remained silent as the two policemen ducked her mother's head into the patrol car. Mother and daughter stared at each other balefully through the glass of the back window until the car eventually disappeared.

God did answer prayers. He answered her father's prayer. He took his life just like he wanted. He took his pain away and left Simone to heal. This was the only way. She dug deep inside of her heart, past the hurt, grief and confusion, and thanked the Lord for another chance at life.

CHAPTER 29

RYAN

"I still can't believe it. This is crazy, Ryan." Lauren walked out of the small kitchen in Ryan's condo and popped a cheese puff in her mouth before plopping down on the couch next to her best friend.

"I know. It's all been like the worst nightmare."

They sat for the next fifteen minutes watching the ten o' clock news in silence. Tears ran down Ryan's face as she listened to the anchorwoman reveal the details of Anthony Pembroke's murder. The only man she'd ever loved was dead at the hands of his wife.

She cried for so many different reasons. She cried because she felt responsible for his death. If she hadn't gotten involved and kept her mouth shut, none of this would have happened. She cried because the relationship she thought she had was nothing more than a lie. She never had anything at all. It was nothing more than the lies and deception of a married man who was also raping his 14-year-old daughter. She cried for Simone. She felt sorry for the girl as her life was ruined. She'd lost her innocence, her mother and her father, and any chance of ever having a normal, happy life in the millisecond of a gunshot. It was heartbreaking.

Lauren wrapped her arms around Ryan's shoulders, "It's going to be alright. Everything is going to work out for the best. God wouldn't place any burden on you that you can't handle."

"Don't get all religious on me, Lauren."

"I'm not. But it's the truth. Always remember that. You *will* make it through this."

"What am I going to do?"

"You're going to pick your life back up and move on. You're already doing so well. You have everything going for you; you just have to know what to do with it. And when you can't quite figure it out, you've got me and your mom and everyone else who loves and supports you to help you through. Trust me, everything will be okay."

"Why didn't I see it? Why didn't I see the signs?"

"You were so in love with being in love that you couldn't see what was happening to you. You were blind, but everything in the dark comes to light eventually. No matter how painful it might be."

"I wonder what is going to happen to Simone."

"I don't know. I can't say that I wouldn't do the same thing if I was her mother, but where does that leave her in the end? That girl will probably be messed up for the rest of her life."

"Don't say that. People can heal. I'm working to heal."

"Yeah, they can heal with a genuine desire and with a lot of help from trained professionals. With all that money the Pembroke's had, I know that won't be a problem."

"I love you, Lauren. I don't know what I would do without you. Through everything we've been through, you've always been a true friend and I want you to know that I thank you for that."

"Aww Girl, I love you too. And you're going to find a good man to love one day. Real love, not the kind of love that don't love you back." Lauren held her best friend in a tight embrace, "Ryan, there is nothing more important in this world than loving yourself."

"I think I've finally figured that out and I'm willing to give it a try."

"And I'll be right there in your corner, cheering you on."

Ryan's heart filled with gratitude as she looked into the eyes of her only friend of 20 years and said, "Thank you."

JESSICA

JESSICA sat on top of a thin, soiled mattress inside of a cold jail cell. She wrapped herself in a scratchy blanket, stamped with the words "Oakland County Jail", to keep herself from shivering. The cell reeked of the tasteless jail food she had vomited in the stainless steel toilet. The puke green paint on the walls and floor, gave her a headache. She was the only one in lockup; the others had come and gone as she waited a month for her trial date. She was alone, but she didn't cry. There were no more tears left inside of her. There was no room for tears. Her mind was consumed with thoughts of Simone and what this all meant for her. What would happen to her baby? Where would she end up? Would she continue to cut herself -- or worse? Would Simone hate her for doing what she had to do to protect her? The thought of her only child alone, with no one to care for her, crying out to her mother for comfort, made the bile rise back to Jessica's throat. She leaned over the side of the bed and vomited once more, never bothering to flush the toilet.

The charge was first-degree murder. She was facing a life sentence and Jessica didn't have the money or the energy to beat it. Ross' bank accounts were frozen and he didn't leave her a dime, as per their signed agreement. There was no way out of this abyss, and this reality drained the life out of her as each hour passed.

He had to die. *Anyone* could understand that. Any mother would have done the same, but no one wanted to admit that. No one wanted to acknowledge the ugliness of her desperation. Jessica stared at the puke green wall and emptied her mind. It was best to keep a clear head. There was no sense of thinking about anything she couldn't change. Everything was just happening to her and she had no control. Her entire life had been that way. She tried so hard to escape her mother and her past. She did everything she could to redesign herself to fit into the role of the perfect wife and mother, living the upper class life. She tried so hard, and in the end it meant nothing. She gave up who she was because she thought she had to, but it was all in vain. She never wanted this for herself or her child. She would trade it all back if she had the chance. She was and always would be Jessie Wolinsky. It was time to finally accept that.

"Pembroke." The light brown-skinned corrections officer, standing tall and thin at about 6'4" approached the cell. He announced her name as if it was a nasty taste in his mouth. Jessica watched with a blank face, as he unlocked and entered the cell.

"Stand up and turn around, hands behind your back."

The orange jumpsuit she wore made a swishing sound as she did as she was told. She felt the cold metal of the handcuffs as the officer put them on a little too tight.

"Turn around."

She did. He escorted her out of the cell and into a slightly bigger room, just as bare and cold. He guided her to the table in the middle of the room and told her to sit in one of the three chairs. After she was seated, the officer removed the handcuffs and left the room, locking the door behind him. Jessica waited, what she guessed to be ten minutes or so before the door reopened and two men walked inside.

They were dressed in expensive suits, Brooks Brothers was her guess. Their briefcases, made of fine leather, swung by their sides as they made their way to the chairs on the opposite side of the table. Jessica recognized one of the men as Conner J. Daniels, senior partner of Creswell & Lattimore, Ross' law firm. A white man in his mid to late forties, with a pinched nose and radish colored cheeks, he'd frequented her home for dinner parties and drinks in the past. He looked at Jessica with what seemed to be contrived sincerity. He was the first to speak.

"Hello, Jessica."

"Conner."

"It is a shame we have to meet under such unfortunate circumstances. How are you holding up?"

"Why do you care?"

He laughed a practiced chuckle and adjusted his tie, "We care about all of our clients. Isn't that right, Terrence?" He looked to the caramel-colored black man by his side for confirmation. Terrence too adjusted his tie before answering.

"Yes, of course. You are our number one priority, Mrs. Pembroke. Your well being is what drives our visit today."

Jessica frowned, "You're representing me? Why?"

Conner took over, "Jessica, we know what Ross did to your daughter. We've been studying the facts of your case for the past three weeks, and quite frankly, we can't afford to let your husband's actions ruin the firm's reputation. We stand to lose a lot if this information is made public in a lengthy, ugly and sensational trial." Conner paused and Terrence picked up where he left off.

"We've pulled a lot of strings and are using a lot of resources to keep this out of the media and the details of this case under wraps. That includes, providing you with the best legal defense possible."

Jessica hunched her shoulders, unconvinced, "And what defense is that? I killed him. Case closed."

Conner jumped in, "Yes, you killed him, but we are more interested in the reason why. With the evidence we have of his relationship with Simone, we are prepared to argue extreme emotional distress. Under the circumstances, no jury will convict you, not with our team representing you. Being the largest and most powerful law firm in the state has its advantages."

"So where does that leave me? I get off then what? I have no money. I have nothing and how do you know I won't go to the press after the trial ends?"

Terrence said, "We thought of your financial situation and the possibility of you going to the media. We are prepared to offer you a settlement to keep things…" he cleared his throat, "quiet."

"Hush money?" Jessica raised an eyebrow.

"Call it what you will, but more than just your freedom is at stake here and we are willing to do whatever it takes to protect the reputation of our firm." He slid a folded piece of paper over to Jessica, "I think you'll find the terms of the settlement offer to be very fair."

Jessica opened the paper. As the bold, black numbers jumped out at her, she allowed herself to smile inside. Five million dollars was enough money to move out of state, obtain the help and support Simone needed, and live the rest of their lives in comfort. She would finally be able to live on her own and stand on her own two feet. Jessica looked up at the attorneys with eyes shiny with hope. "Gentleman, let's discuss the details of my case."

SIMONE

SIMONE lay in bed surrounded by darkness. She was as still as the night as she stared at the ceiling as if it would produce an image. Her heart beat at a steady pace and her breathing was smooth and easy. Her blanket lay loosely over her body and her feet peeked through from the bottom. She held her journal close to her chest as the words of her last entry swam around in her thoughts.

I am at peace and I trust in the Lord that everything will be okay.

She smiled to herself as she realized that she meant those words. She was at peace. He was gone. Her father had left long ago, leaving a monster in his place. Now, it was gone too. Her mother loved her enough to protect her from that monster and she was grateful for that. For the first time in months, Simone was able to lie in her bed at night, free of the fear and anticipation of her father's visit.

Because there was no immediate family to care for her, she was transported to a group home for girls. Even there, surrounded by other troubled teens and a jaded staff, she felt good. Every girl there had a story. Everyone had a past and Simone was no exception. She opened up to them about her cutting and was relieved to find that she was not alone. Friendship was something new to Simone, and she wasn't sure if she could ever trust anyone enough to give them that title, but she found her housemates easy to talk to. They talked and cried together and Simone looked forward to their company. Through prayer and counseling, she found that her desire to self-mutilate was diminishing.

It was far from the life she had lived with the big house and the private school, the expensive clothes, and fancy cars, but she was okay with that. Simone knew that things weren't always as they seemed. Those people who envied her for the things they thought she had, had no idea of what she'd been going through. All of the material things in life meant nothing. Happiness was everything.

Before closing her eyes to go to sleep, she prayed to the God she thought no longer existed. She thanked Him for answering her prayers and delivering her from the life she had begged every night to leave. Then, she talked to her father, the father she remembered before the pain.

"Daddy, I know you love me and I love you too. I will never forget you. All the things we did together, and the times we shared. They meant the world to me, Daddy. I'm so sorry we ended up this way, but you knew what had to be done. I know you knew because you told me. I just want you to know that I'm okay now. I'm okay and eventually, I will be happy. Good night."

She didn't know what was going to happen to her mother or where she would end up. All she knew, as she closed her eyes, was that she was going to be okay. That was enough to keep her going another day.

Breinigsville, PA USA
26 October 2010
248143BV00001B/9/P

9 780578 023489